Parental Sins

Miguel Antonio Ortiz

Hamilton Stone Editions

Maplewood, New Jersey

Cover design by Adalberto Ortiz

Library of Congress Cataloging-in-Publication Data

Ortiz, Miguel Antonio.
  Parental sins / by Miguel Antonio Ortiz.
    pages cm
    ISBN 978-0-9836668-3-7 (alk. paper)
  1. Puerto Rican families--Fiction. 2. Country life--
Fiction. 3. City and town life--Fiction. 4. Puerto Ricans-
-New York (State)--New York--Fiction. 5. Immigrants--
New York (State)--New York--Fiction. I. Title.

  PS3615.R825P37 2014
  813'.6--dc23
                          2013021734

Julia and Federico

Chapter 1

JULIA EXPECTED TO conceive soon after her marriage to Arturo Ortega, but a year went by and there were no signs of pregnancy. Desperately in need to discuss the problem, she was more than glad to see her sister, Ervina, who had hiked up the trail from town. As they sat in the kitchen drinking coffee, they gazed beyond the mango tree on one side of the yard, an expanse of red clay that separated the house from the mountain trail that led up from Naranjito.

"It's not always so quick," Ervina said. "Don't be concerned."

"I'm not worried," Julia responded. "I just want to be sure that I'm doing everything right."

"Nature takes care of itself," Ervina assured her. "I didn't know anything more than you."

"Still, maybe I should see Dr. Aufemio and find out whether there's anything wrong with me."

"That will be a waste of time," Ervina said. "You'd be better off seeing Doña Urbana. She'll tell you what herbs to take."

To avoid revealing to Arturo any negative outcome of the visit, Julia decided to hike into town to see Doña Urbana without telling her husband. She chose a day when, to add some hard currency to the household income, he went off to day-work at one of the neighboring plantations.

Descending on the mountain road, she stopped to gaze at the landscape that suddenly overwhelmed her. Subdued by some process of nature bent on being quiet and calming to any casual observer, the subtlety of the colors fascinated her. A red hue underneath the general view emphasized the clay base on which tropical plants of several varieties of green struggled with each other with a politeness usually thought absent in a setting so exposed to sunlight and the discharge of the clouds that now regally proceeded over the scene announcing their status as rulers while simultaneously pretending an indifference to human judgment.

The sudden awareness of the landscape transfixed her and dissolved the boundary between herself and what unfolded before her. Her feet would have transformed into clay, and she would have been absorbed into the ground, but that on hearing a *reinita,* she looked up into the mango tree where the bird, its beak turned toward the sky, sang as if the clouds had ears to appreciate the song. "You silly bird," Julia called out, and imagined the bird's response, when it turned its head to look at her: "No worse than you, you silly woman." Looking down at her own feet, Julia confirmed that she had avoided transforming into clay and disappearing into the landscape.

Descending the slope, she arrived at an opening in the trail that revealed an overall view of the town. On sunny days, the bell tower of the church had the appearance of a pin on a map indicating an important spot. Although the natives of the place soon relegated it to the list of the common, the view proved of startling interest to those who had not yet grown accustomed to it. An observer might focus his attention on the small size of the town, a minor point to those who lived there, most of whom had never been to a more populous place. Naranjito's one street ran through the center of town—progressing by the square, with the church on one side and the town hall on the other—and exiting on the other side toward some other insignificant destination.

As long as in town, Julia decided she might as well drop by Dr. Aufemio's, though that would add to her expense, his fee being more than Doña Urbana's, to whom clients paid whatever they thought proper. Many people met their obligation by giving her produce from their gardens. Dr. Aufemio had also resorted to that method, though at first he had expected his patients to cover his fee with actual currency, but he eventually converted to the country customs that skipped a step in the process of turning the goods into coins and then again exchanging the coins for goods. Of course, society had already grown too complex for that to be entirely convenient, and barred from using the same method in dealing with those from whom he bought medical supplies and equipment, he preferred to be paid in cash.

The mountain trail led to a wooden bridge at the edge of town. She crossed the stream, and found herself immediately on the main street, also the road that led out of town. She scarcely ever traveled more than a few miles on it to visit relatives that lived farther down the slope. She walked by the general store, the tavern and the town hall before she arrived at the square dominated by the church. Entering to pray occurred to her, but she discarded the idea, seeing no reason why the heaven connected to the church would have any reason to listen to her without exacting an exorbitant price.

She made Dr. Aufemio's office her first stop.

"I haven't seen you in ages," Dr. Aufemio said, then waited for her to announce the ailment that had brought her to see him. Dr. Aufemio, a man of medium height, barely taller than Julia, wore glasses. The roundness of his belly pointed to eating as one of his indulgences. He looked directly into her eyes and waited for her response, but he finally concluded that it would emerge only after further inquiry.

Forced to formulate a question, he proceeded. "So what ails you at the moment?" he asked, certain that his directness would have the appropriate result, but the lack of response from Julia pushed him to the edge of discomfort. So he further conscribed the question. "I mean, of course, medically," he added. Clear enough, sure as he spoke, but getting no immediate response, uncertainty reemerged.

Julia had failed to anticipate the conflict in which she found herself. For now, in front of Dr. Aufemio, his being a man dimmed his being a doctor. She had assumed he had enough knowledge to clarify her problem, but she now wondered why she had counted on medical information. How would he know whether she was indeed barren? Was there something written on her face that only a doctor could decipher? What if the problem resulted from a quirk in her build, requiring exact instructions on how to perform the act? Was she ready to acquire that information from a man other than her husband? Would not the doctor have to examine her to arrive at such a conclusion? What would he have to examine? Suddenly amazed that these questions had waited until the present moment to arrive, she realized why Ervina had recommended a talk with Doña Urbana rather than a visit to Dr. Aufemio. Julia wished that Ervina had expressed herself more clearly.

"I haven't been able to conceive," Julia finally said, and fell silent again without further explanation.

"For some people it takes time," Dr. Aufemio said.

"I've been told that already," she replied. "I'm concerned whether I'm to blame or whether…" She let her words fade away, being reluctant to utter what she knew her husband would consider an insult.

"Blame is of no use in this matter," the doctor continued. "What difference would it make to determine who is unable to produce what is necessary? The end result is the same."

"Perhaps not," she answered, "if he can have a child with another woman, he must go out and do it."

Dr. Aufemio kept quiet while he pondered the matter. That view from a married woman, the last thing he expected, added another dimension to the situation. Trying to decide the appropriateness of expressing it, he pondered the next question. He had no choice, he concluded, since the patient had come to see him in an attempt to deal with the problem. "What if the obstacle is not within you?"

"Ah, what then?" she exclaimed. She had pondered that question a great deal, but an answer had refused to emerge.

"You see what I mean?" the doctor continued. "Your way of thinking leads to more complications. In any case, you're trying to deal with a problem that may not exist. You must give it more time to work itself out."

Yes, she saw what he meant. She saw more, though perhaps *seeing* fell short of an exact description. Perhaps she *felt* the existence of the problem to be dealt with at the moment, instead of waiting for it to prove false, as logic predicted most likely.

"Then I must wait to see what happens," she said.

"Yes, of course, that's the best thing to do," Dr. Aufemio concluded.

Julia waited for him to urge her to make another visit should she fail to arrive at a viable solution, but he said goodbye without suggesting that he might at a later time have something else to say.

Out on the street again, Julia proceeded across town, a short walk, the whole town being but two streets. She followed the lesser one, and was soon ascending a slope. The street quickly reduced to a path that curved around the dwellings, shacks the farther she got from the town square.

Doña Urbana's house, however, scarcely in the category of a shack, stood out from the rest. Indeed, the house, small but clearly well built and maintained, resembled the ones of the more prosperous inhabitants who lived closer to the town square. Julia walked up the front porch to look through the open front door, which gave her a clear view to the other end of the house and to the back door. In the backyard, Doña Urbana, against her waist, held a straw basket full of dry corn to feed the chickens.

For a moment, Julia stood at the door observing the old woman and trying to decide whether to proceed through the house to the backyard, or respecting the privacy of the interior, take the roundabout route. The door being open, as customary, did not indicate permission to cross the threshold without a clear invitation from the dweller. Julia was just about to retreat from the porch to circumvent the open corridor, when Doña Urbana, looking up from her task and back toward the front porch, caught sight of her and waved to her to come in.

Doña Urbana limped as she walked, the result of having fallen, when young, down the side of a ravine after having stumbled on a loose stone. The fall caused injury to a bone in her right leg, which repaired itself without proper attention, resulting in an uneven growth. At the time of the accident no one asked why she had been walking off the regular path on the hillside, presuming that the fall had been from the top, but on hearing someone mention the luck involved in surviving such a long fall, she inadvertently responded that the distance was a great deal less than that. Only her mother absorbed that piece of information, and only after the permanent consequence of the injury became apparent did the mother decide to inquire why Urbana had been in that unusual place. "I don't know," Urbana had responded, and the mother looking straight into her eyes saw that she lied and told the truth at the same time. How she could do both simultaneously remained a puzzle to both the mother and the daughter, though Urbana had merely a vague sense of being enveloped in a contradiction.

Julia walked through the house to reach the kitchen where the door opened to the backyard. She was about to descend the two steps into the yard, when Doña Urbana looking up said, "Sit down, sit down, I'm coming right in." Julia smiled and retreated to the bench by the kitchen table, and she sat down to watch Doña Urbana proceed with her task.

"Well, well, here you are," said Doña Urbana, as she entered the kitchen and placed her basket on the floor by the door. "Have a cup of coffee. I just brewed it but a little while ago."

Julia took that as a sign that Doña Urbana had been expecting someone to drop by, but the identity of the expected visitor remained unstated. The old woman poured two cups of coffee, brought them to the table and sat down with her guest on one of the long benches. "It's a funny thing to see you today," Doña Urbana said. "Only last night I dreamt about you."

"Did you?" Julia said, as if astonished but accepting the anticipation of her visit as natural. She waited, merely sipping the coffee, for the appropriate indications of what had to be said or done to fulfill the need of the moment.

"I dreamt you had five children, but you had no husband or lover, so I was confused as how you managed the feat."

"And did you ever find out?"

"I asked you for an answer, but you only smiled and kept silent."

"Ah, then in your dream I was a virgin mother."

"It was a very realistic dream; that possibility was not considered."

Doña Urbana's dream having answered the question Julia had come to ask, she maintained a satisfied demeanor as she continued to drink her coffee. She seemed oblivious of the unanswered question within the dream, and Doña Urbana, observing her visitor's mood also continued to drink without making any reference to the question, as if the answer, being obvious, needed no further attention.

"I like your coffee," Julia said. "When you come by to see me, I will brew you a cup from the coffee Arturo grows himself. You will like that, too."

"No doubt," Doña Urbana responded without revealing her surprise at Julia's lack of interest in the perplexity of the dream.

A festive mood invaded Julia as she ascended the trail on her way home. Thoughts about the future and her ability to fulfill the task she had been anticipating overwhelmed her. She decided to make the evening meal a celebration. Arturo deserved to be treated well. She needed to reassure him that everything would work out. He had not yet expressed any anxiety, but she suspected that he questioned her ability to conceive. She could now reassure him that everything would turn out well.

When he entered the house, by the back door into the kitchen, as he usually did when returning from toil in the fields, the stew was bubbling and filling the room with a delicious odor.

"Well, did I forget today was a special day?" he asked as soon as he saw Julia, who had, in addition to the cooking, combed her hair in a manner she usually reserved for festive occasions.

"No," Julia said, "it's just an ordinary day."

"Ah," he said, "then it must be part of what I've been feeling lately."

"And what is that?" she asked with a smile, having deduced that he must be extremely happy if he often experienced the feeling of good fortune.

"Sometimes I look at ordinary things and I'm moved by them, as if I had never seen them before."

On some other day Julia would have been startled by that revelation, but at the moment, immersed in her own feeling of relief, she neglected to dwell on what he said. The dissipation of her personal concern allowed everything else to seem ordinary. "Well, one's bound to notice something new every day," she said, her mind more on her visit to town than on Arturo's words.

"That's for certain," he replied. "There's a new *capataz* at the Ardiente place, quite a fellow, Federico Atorey."

"I thought he worked at the Renez plantation," she casually said.

"He did, but that place is half way around the mountain, and his wife wouldn't give up their house here, so now he's back."

"If he were my husband, I wouldn't mind his being away most of the time."

"Most women wouldn't say that," Arturo said. "He's quite a fellow."

"I suppose he is," she said. She recalled having encountered him at the Christmas festivities three years before, just after he had been married, and his wife, Pepina, had already conceived. At the dance in the town square, Pepina became dizzy, no doubt, brought on by her pregnancy, but that evening her husband made no out-of-the-way allowances. He drank as much as anyone else, and when his wife, exhausted and experiencing some lightheadedness, stopped dancing, he chased after other women. Julia, at the time still single but already promised to Arturo, rejected Federico when he accosted her.

"Don't tell me," he said, "you do not dance with married men."

"I do," she answered, "but only with those who limit the dance to the dance floor."

"You will change your mind sooner or later," he retorted. "In the meantime, I will dance with someone else."

She fumed as she watched him dance, and she imagined him missing a step and spraining an ankle.

Chapter 2

FROM THE BEGINNING, Pepina's pregnancy was uncomfortable. In the morning she felt nauseous. Anything she had eaten for supper wanted to make a backward trip. The traditional remedies for the ailment had little effect on her. For a while, Doña Urbana saw her every day and formulated various concoctions trying to find the one that would work, but her efforts proved useless.

"This will pass," Doña Urbana assured her, "and in the end, you'll have a reward."

Pepina gazed back in consternation, wishing that Doña Urbana's prediction would materialize but having little faith that it would.

On her engagement to Federico Atorey, she had become the envy of many of her unmarried acquaintances and even some of the married ones. Some warned her that she was taking on more than she could handle. She interpreted those warnings as jealousy disguised as advice. "I got what everyone else wanted," had often been her retort.

Going down to the creek to do her wash, she had stumbled upon friends discussing her engagement. Some believed that Federico needed a different kind of wife—someone who would curb his drives sufficiently to make him a bearable husband. Very few believed that Pepina had the ability to subdue him.

"Maybe that's why he picked her," Peregrina Guzman said. "So he'd have someone to do the cooking for him without his having to change his ways."

"Maybe he's in love with her, no rhyme or reason," a more charitable acquaintance suggested.

When Pepina appeared, everyone fell silent. Embarrassed by the little she had heard, and sensing that her engagement was considered more a dangerous gamble than good fortune, she pretended not to have heard anything. She put down the bundle of clothes and in silence received a few smiles of embarrassment from the other women. Trying to get rid of her discomfort, she convinced herself of their jealousy.

When Federico Atorey had first approached her, she had taken his attention as mere flirtation, but he continued until she took him seriously. At first flattered, she soon became proud, as if she had always believed herself irresistible and now Federico Atorey just another victim to her natural charm.

"Well, you've caught yourself a man," said her father, Enrique Iglesia, a shy, disconsolate person just as amazed and elated by the development. Like many other men in Naranjito, he envied Federico Atorey's easy manner. Don Enrique had accepted in himself the lack of those qualities of manhood he idealized in Federico, a man who even when he drank heavily remained lucid, who without fear of rejection approached and charmed women, and who took any negative development as humorous. In the opinion of many, Federico kept cool regardless of circumstances. Others saw Federico as a competitor and readily pointed out his faults whenever they found a receptive ear. Of course, most of those men talked only with the assurance that what they said would reach Federico's ears anonymously, retaliating with ease being part of Federico's reputation.

Ivan Jimenez, mayor of the town and Enrique Iglesia's friend, numbered among the few who had no compunction in expressing his negative view of a competitor, Federico being the only one of any note. A generation older than Federico, Ivan for that reason alone expected more respect, but Federico affected an indifference to age, his own and that of any man with whom he dealt. "Children speak when the chickens pee" was the old saying, and Federico applied it also to any man who considered himself old. Until the day he died, Federico remained oblivious of age, the decrepitude of his body construed as an attempt by nature to prey upon his soul, an entity unaffected by time.

"Your daughter deserves a better man," Don Ivan said to Don Enrique. "I tell you this: he'll make her suffer."

"She wants him, and there's nothing I can do," Don Enrique retorted. "Maybe long ago, when we were still Spanish, fathers picked husbands for their daughters, but I don't remember those times."

"And what are we now?"

"Heaven knows, the Americans are here, but we're not Americans. In any case, they don't pick husbands for their daughters."

"Is that what they say?"

"I have no idea what they say. I've never seen an American. Now that they don't have the Spanish army to chase, they don't come this far into the mountains. It took them only a few days to sweep from one side of the island to the other, and now they stay in San Juan."

"It'll be a hundred years before they move back up the *cordillera*."

"Perhaps in a hundred years we will have invaded them. Just wait and see."

"That's a long wait. You and I will be long gone by then, but right now you owe your daughter some advice. She can do better than Federico."

"There's nothing I can do," said Don Enrique, to avoid admitting that he favored the union. His daughter being picked up by someone like Federico was more than he had expected. He would have thought the same even had he disagreed with her about the extent of Federico's love for her. "Sometimes we just have to accept whatever comes along," Don Enrique continued, trying to stay in the good graces of his longtime friend.

Nothing would convince Don Ivan that Federico had a positive side, but being only the godfather, that title being at this point in Pepina's life only symbolic, he kept his mouth shut, letting his friend interpret disapproval only from the sternness of his look. Doña Tristana, Pepina's mother, who had caught some of the conversation, turned away to hide her doubts, while under her breath letting out the words, "I wonder who's been caught?"

Chapter 3

FOR THE FIRST six months of the marriage, Federico acted like the ideal husband, as if Pepina were the only woman in the world visible to him. His behavior having drastically changed, everyone began to suspect an error in having judged Pepina incapable of subduing him. Washing clothes down by the river, the women talked about the transformation.

"So you think he's not the man he used to be," Enrica Guzman said with a smirk. "Give him time, and you'll see that a leopard never changes his spots."

"Well, that may be true about leopards, but he's a man."

"That's true. Love may have changed his ways. I've heard stories of that happening. Not all our husbands are unfaithful."

"I'm not talking about everyone," Enrica said, "though that's another matter that can be argued. I'm saying Federico is who he is, and only a heavenly miracle will change him."

"And are you saying that divine intervention is gone?"

"To that, I'm not saying yes or no," she retorted. "I'm just saying, let's not jump to conclusions."

"Well, everyone says he goes straight home from work without even stopping for a drink as he used to."

"He's not yet thirsty enough."

"He gets enough to drink at home."

"Men soon lose the taste for home water, that's for sure."

"Well, we'll know soon enough."

"Otherwise we can announce a miracle, at least on our side of the mountain."

They all laughed, each relieved that she and her husband had escaped being the subject of the conversation and hoping that Pepina's good fortune indicated that luck sometimes made an appearance. Enrica's doubt persisted, although every day, like an animal in a drought waiting for the rain, it became weaker. Some part of her wished to be proven wrong, but more time had to elapse to remove Federico's reformation from her list of the unlikely. She did not hire a rainmaker, but the rain came before her field of doubts had withered. Pepina had been pregnant but six months when Federico returned to his old habits. Pepina's acquaintances had been keeping an eye on the matter, some hoping for a miracle, and others just waiting to see Federico relapse.

Down by the stream on wash-day, Enrica Guzman prided herself in having recognized the man's inability to discard his vices.

"Was I right?" she rhetorically asked as soon as the subject came up.

"They say he's taken up with Lydia Rodriguez."

"That's only talk. Who's to say that it's true?"

Indeed, determining the truth of anything was difficult, and for Federico Atorey just as much of a predicament as for anyone else, except that for him no problem lingered. Anything that failed to be quickly explainable he sentenced to exile in that part of his mind characterized by darkness, like throwing an object into quagmire that made its retrieval impossible.

Riding home from work one evening, he experienced the mystic revelation that he had no true reason for loving the woman he had married. He suddenly saw her in the same light that everyone else did, a weak ordinary person who would be more of a burden to him than a source of ease or satisfaction. The question of why he had married her loomed before him, but he found no answer supported by reason.

Being attracted to a woman, of course, never required a logical explanation, but marriage fell into a different category. His choice perplexed him, but instead of becoming frantic or depressed at having committed an error, Federico Atorey burst into laughter at having been used by fate to illustrate a quality of nature.

From that day on, other women returned to his life, or rather, he returned to theirs, though he found it more difficult to be accepted. Having been caught and branded removed him from the list of being someone for that purpose, but for him that failed to be an insurmountable obstacle, and indeed in some cases it became an advantage.

Federico's eyes returned to roaming for women. The pregnancy so absorbed Pepina that she scarcely noted the change. In those days, women little expected their travail to be understood by men, and so dependence on their husband's involvement in dealing with pregnancy remained minimal. Pepina depended on her own mother and on Doña Urbana, who arrived every day to concoct herbal drinks and dispense advice. Although Doña Urbana had little direct contact with Federico, she adeptly analyzed what she heard and linked it to past observations.

"Even when you're pregnant," she said to Pepina, "you have to keep your husband in mind. An unleashed horse will easily leap the fence."

"Ah," Pepina responded, "no one wants to forget his past. He's different from what he used to be. I didn't trick him into marriage."

The nine months passed and the child arrived. The process absorbed all of Pepina's attention. She had stopped breast-feeding the newborn before she noticed a difference in Federico's behavior. At first she attempted to look the other way, trying to convince herself of the inaccuracy of her observations. On waking, some dreams are completely forgotten, but the memory of others persist without respite; she now realized that what she had taken as Federico's reformation had been an illusion created by her own weakness and desire.

She engaged in a vain attempt to reawaken his feelings for her. "I'm the mother of your child," she said to him.

"Of course you are," he responded. "Who says otherwise?"

"Why do you torture me?"

"What the devil are you talking about? Am I different from any other man?"

Having taken the question seriously, bewilderment transformed her face as she absorbed his failure to deny his transgression. She realized that he expected from her unflinching acceptance. She had thought of herself as nothing until Federico's attention had convinced her otherwise, and now she saw that she had reverted to insignificance.

"He's your husband. Fight for him," Doña Urbana urged her on one of her visits.

"Can I give him something to drink to bring him back?"

"Only coffee," Doña Urbana said. "Maybe that will wake him up."

"I feel like not getting up in the morning," Pepina confessed.

"A cup of coffee for you too," Doña Urbana continued. "You have to get up and fight for your life. Otherwise you'll just wither like a plant without water."

Whether Doña Urbana predicted the future when she mentioned the word "wither" was difficult to determine under the circumstances. She might have just been alluding to an obvious possibility. Surely, Pepina did not randomly pick up the word as a suggestion for a course of action, though some may claim that the choice was unconscious. Still, Doña Urbana was considered a powerful influence whether or not she intended to be.

Down by the river on wash-day the women failed to arrive at any more definite conclusion.

"Well, I'd be sick too if he was my husband," Rita Gonzales said. She was the youngest one there that day and soon to be married.

"As I remember, you thought he was a good catch. Weren't you upset that he never paid attention to you?"

"Perhaps what you remember are your own feelings," she retorted.

"I'm certainly not ill right now."

"The question is whether Pepina is ill."

"She spends a lot of time in bed. Can't get up in the morning."

"I pity her child."

"Well, I'm sure she feels better after Federico leaves in the morning."

"Her mother goes over to take care of her and the baby."

"How long will that last?"

"When you make your bed you have to lie in it."

"I think he lays on other beds."

"Are you someone who knows that for sure?"

"I'm as sure as you are."

"We all hear the same rumors."

"They say he often rides by the Ortega place."

"He's Arturo's friend."

"And Julia's?"

"Julia's a righteous woman. She's no different from any of us."

"Well, then, need I say more?"

"Is there something you're telling us about yourself?"

They all laughed, maintaining the illusion that little of what each said was taken seriously by the others.

Chapter 4

NOT LONG AFTER Federico Atorey had become *capataz* at the Ardiente plantation, he began to stop by the Ortegas' after Arturo had left for the day.

At first, Julia assumed that he had some task related to his job that brought him by her place, and that he merely stopped to have a word with Arturo assuming that he might still be at that time of day in one of the fields close to the house, but after his visit coincided several times with Arturo's leaving early to reach work places farther away, she realized that Federico stopped by to see her rather than Arturo.

Although at first amused to be found attractive enough to draw a man out of his way, she was soon annoyed by his presumption that he might score an eventual victory.

"You do assume a great deal," she said to him on his next visit.

He remained mounted on his horse and gazed down at her.

Becoming aware of what he might be observing from his vantage point, she automatically brought her right hand to the collar of her dress to make sure that nothing unbuttoned was enticing him to stare.

That gesture, accompanied by the discomfort on her face, elicited from him a smile that annoyed her.

"I assume nothing," he said. "I'm only an observer."

"I hope, then, that you're noticing my displeasure," she said, and retreated into the house from where she heard his laughter before he rode away.

That afternoon, she had just fetched water from the

spring well and was about to get wood from the shed into the kitchen before deciding what to cook for the evening meal when she heard voices out front.

"It'll be much easier to go in through the back door," a man said.

On hearing them, Julia left the kitchen to look through the front door, but when she got there whoever had been talking was already out of sight by the side of the house, so she walked back to the kitchen to see four men entering, carrying the body of a fifth.

It took her a few seconds to decipher the unusual scene and realize that Arturo was the one being transported.

"This way. This way," she said, leading the group to the bedroom where they placed the sick man on the bed. "What's wrong?" she managed to utter in confusion.

Looking for a wound or some other obvious injury that would have caused him to collapse, she sat on the bed next to the ailing Arturo.

"He passed out," one of the bearers said, "for no reason."

She ignored the absurdity of those words as she heard others coming from Arturo's mouth, more confusing than those of his bearers.

"What is he saying?" she asked turning to them, though she knew the question was useless.

"Makes no sense," one of them said, his eyes moving from face to face looking for support of his observation.

"He must have been hit on the head," Julia said.

"No, he just fell down suddenly."

The others nodded in agreement.

"Someone go fetch Dr. Aufemio," Julia said.

By the time Dr. Aufemio arrived, Arturo had emerged from his state of confusion having no recollection of what had happened and surprised to see Dr. Aufemio in the house.

"Do you remember when you got home from the field and how you got home?" Dr. Aufemio asked.

"Presumably I walked home the way I always do," he answered, "though I don't exactly remember."

"You must come to my office tomorrow, and we'll see what we can find out," the doctor said. "For the time being, stay in bed even if you feel well."

Julia walked Dr. Aufemio out to where his horse was tethered under the shade of the mango tree.

"Is he all right?" she asked knowing that the answer would have little meaning.

Dr. Aufemio always refrained from conveying bad news until the matter became so clear, and the conclusion so obvious, that he had no choice.

"It may be nothing," the doctor said. "Sometimes peculiar things happen, then go away with no explanation. I'll have to examine him more closely before I can tell, but I wouldn't worry, if I were you."

As she watched him ride to the edge of the *batey* and disappear into the foliage surrounding the trail, Julia realized that the answer to her question was clear enough.

Arturo ignored the incident, forgot that it had occurred, until a month later when it happened again, this time preceded by a headache that persisted for several days.

Dr. Aufemio prescribed medication to alleviate the pain, but there was nothing else he could do.

"Nothing?" Julia asked in dismay.

Were not these modern times? Already automobiles made travel from one end of the island to the other possible in just a few hours. Electricity would soon be brought to everyone who lived in the mountains!

"Experiments are being done with brain surgery in the United States," he said, "but you would have to go there for very unpredictable results. Surgery might extend his life a little or end it right away. Even if he were still alive after the surgery, he would not be the same person."

"And the pain?"

"For a while yet, it will only be occasional."

A serenity inexplicable to Julia descended on Arturo. Most of the time he felt no discomfort, but the way he looked at everything around him changed.

Whereas anxiety became the usual state for her, he retreated to a place devoid of problems. He seemed to have only one regret. "I will have no heir to carry on my name," he said.

Those words perturbed Julia. Arturo would leave with that one regret, believing that she had failed him. She was certain the fault was not hers. Confusion compounded her grief. Ready to have a child, she wondered what delayed Doña Urbana's prediction.

"You're not gone yet," Julia said to her husband. She saw in his face the effort to contain himself from expressing blame and regret for a failure he attributed to her.

"That's true," he replied.

She hung on the word "true," and saw more to it than the obvious. The truth had to be created rather than accepted. She had accepted him as her man, accepted her marriage as the path to the fulfillment of her life as well as his. But he wanted assurance that his name and his blood would continue. That was all. About to die without having achieved the little he had set as his goal, the preservation of his name, Arturo Ortega would leave this world believing that she had failed him. On his deathbed he would be gazing at her as the culprit—the one person who had prevented the fulfillment of the little he had wanted out of life. That thought mortified Julia. He would be leaving this world without the truth.

Destined to bear children, she could prevent that—she was certain. But how could that truth be of any use to him, if the conclusion had to be that none of them would carry his blood or bear his name? She had to solve the dilemma; the problem of fulfilling a responsibility forced her to convince herself.

"Arturo," she said, "you'll get what you want."

He tried to determine the validity of her words, and he saw a fervency he had scarcely noticed before. He wondered whether the approaching event transformed her, or whether his own senses, sharpened by the proximity of their end, created the perception. For a moment the thought transfixed him, but it quickly left, like a bird making a casual stop and moving on without regret.

Chapter 5

JULIA MADE HER decision, an abstract occurrence with no visible danger, like imagining, absent from the scene, a dive from a cliff into waters below. At the spot, however, contemplating from the heights all the possible mishaps of the execution, it becomes a different matter. On seeing Federico Atorey turning his horse into the *batey* one morning, dread of having adopted an insane plan overcame her. What if Arturo's illness turned out to be an illusion, a diagnostic error on Dr. Aufemio's part? Even if Dr. Aufemio was correct, wasn't the possibility of miracles an accepted fact? On a miraculous recovery, she would have committed a grievous sin without an acceptable excuse.

The fulfillment of her husband's emotional need to have an heir the only thing she sought, she would sacrifice her body to attain only what he wanted. She could wait until after he died to have a child for her own satisfaction, but why let him move on to the next world feeling that he had failed? She feared that his survival would become her punishment. But how could she consider that a punishment, when the result would have been to save Arturo's life? Indeed, she might be forced to suffer in secret guilt, especially if the miracle were extended to allow Arturo to propagate a child of his own after she had provided him with one engendered by someone else.

These possibilities of what might happen instead of what she had originally imagined now made her look at Federico's approach with more dread than she had anticipated. As he rode up to the back door whistling his usual tune and expecting the customary greeting, what he would have gotten from any housewife in any dwelling on the mountain, she refrained from moving to the door. "Let him go," she said to herself, "What am I doing? Have I lost my mind?"

He was about to turn the horse back to the road when she appeared. "You're late today," she said.

"So, you've been timing me," he said and grinned. "That's a good sign."

"Is it?"

"That tells me you've been thinking about me."

"And you assume that thoughts are always complimentary."

"Well, I didn't say that," he answered, "but no thought at all is worse."

"I hear that you mistreat your wife."

"She has a roof over her head, and she's well fed, and a real man never beats his wife, so whoever talks ill of me is a liar through and through."

"So you say."

"Just try me out and you'll see for yourself what kind of man I am."

"Restrain your hopes," she said. "You'll be happier that way."

For the first time she sent him away without anger, and he took that as an indication that he had won her over. Only time had now to elapse, as a matter of course, before she gave herself to him. He had been nearly at the point of considering his approach futile, but now her sudden change elated him. He seldom examined the complexities of life preferring to simplify everything, especially the explanation of unexpected results.

"There is something you must know," she said to him the next time he rode by, "I do love my husband."

"Indeed you do," he said, "just as I love my wife."

Piqued, she retorted, "No, not like that at all."

"What does it matter how you love your husband as long as you love me as well?"

"Who said that I love you?"

"Indeed, no one."

"You must assure me," she said, "that anything that happens between us is kept secret."

"The assurance of a secret is beyond my power," he said, his words more truthful than the moment required. His usual response would have been to assure her without reservation, but perhaps noting her decision to be beyond reversal, and anything he said at the moment irrelevant, moved him to be truthful. Had he sought an explanation for his honesty, he would have been reluctant to accept that one, but he had no other. Any question without an obvious answer, he soon discarded. "The only thing I can promise is that the revelation will never come from me," he assured her. At the moment, that was enough.

Two days later, returning from the well with fingers of each hand through the ear of a gallon jug of water, raising her eyes and seeing Federico's horse standing in the shade just outside the kitchen door startled her. Indeed, they had not discussed when or where they would meet for their first encounter. She had stopped thinking about the matter once she had conveyed her willingness to engage in the affair, as if just her assent, without further attention, sufficed to engender a child. Federico emerged from the shadow quickly advancing to relieve her of the jugs of water.

"Put them by the door," she said, "but don't go in."

Placing the jars by the door, he turned with a quizzical look that annoyed her.

"In my own house I only do it with my husband," she said.

"Well then, the storm shelter is good enough for me," he said, looking toward the nearby structure built into the side of the slope.

"Not there either," she said. "All of this belongs to Arturo."

"If we persist with that rule, we'll have to make love without touching each other. No doubt you have figured out how to do that, but I'm confused as to what we'll get out of it."

"You'll get what you want," she said.

"This sounds like a business deal," he said. "Am I missing something?"

"You won't miss a thing," she said.

"I thought you loved me. That's why I'm here."

"Is that why? I presume you're going to say that you love me."

"Why else would I be here?"

"Yes," she answered, "why else?"

"Perhaps I've made a mistake," he said. "I'm not exactly asking for a favor. Is this going to be worth all the trouble that I'm taking?"

"You can decide that afterward," she said, "but I promise you'll get exactly what you want. Wait here a moment."

She disappeared through the kitchen door, and returned shortly with a folded blanket, and without a word she proceeded across her backyard and up the trail along the sloping grass field where a cow grazed bound with a long rope to a stake in the ground. She headed farther up in the direction of a copse, which obstructed the view of a ravine down into which she led him. A stream flowed along the bottom. They walked a short distance against the current until they arrived at the waterfall.

"Well, now we take a shower," he said, but she ignored the comment and continued on, finding another path that unexpectedly placed them behind the cascading water that hid a cavernous space. "So you have a place of your own," he said.

"I came here often when I was a child. It was popular then."

"And now?"

"A story grew that it was haunted, and so we stopped coming here to play."

"And now you want to take a chance."

"On the contrary," she said.

Beyond the rock surface near the water extended a large patch of moss over which she spread the blanket. The circumstances more unusual than he had expected, Federico hovered on the verge of confusion. Indeed, he had been somewhat amazed when Julia had suddenly become more pliant to his advances, and though he had soon proceeded as usual, as he now watched her, the questions resurfaced.

She seemed overly comfortable with the process, when all along he had assumed this to be her first time with someone other than her husband. What else didn't he know? This time, getting what he wanted deviated from what he had imagined. Julia's seeming to be the one in complete control made him uncomfortable. Yet, the only remedy at the moment would be to walk away abandoning what he had worked to attain.

In silence, Julia pulled her dress over her head, and in derision stared at him for a minute as if he, instead of she, were doing something shameful. She proceeded to push each strap of her undergarment off her shoulders causing it to fall to the ground. He remained immobile, paralyzed by the unexpected ease with which she executed each movement as if alone under the waterfall. She did nothing overtly to offend him. Opening for him a door always shut to all but one, and yet, he remained bereft of any feeling of conquest, she domineering the moment. He had been taken in, seduced, when all along he had believed himself in control. Not yet completely undressed, she raised her hands to undo the binding of her hair, letting it cascade over her shoulders and for the first time at the waterfall her lips parted into a smile.

"Well, now," she said, "I'm all yours."

Within, he questioned that remark, but he kept quiet. Approaching close enough to touch her, as if blind, he proceeded to verify with his hands the form he had imagined. His hands drawn to her face, gently his fingers examined her features, moving from under her eyes along her nose and down over her lips to her chin, executing a physical absorption of her image. His blood rising to the surface of his body, his hands kept descending, now caressing her breasts. His hands descended first over her back, his right hand then moving to part the hair below in search of the moisture that reassured him.

She had closed her eyes as she descended to the blanket, and laying there as limp as possible under the circumstances, she waited for the inevitable. She attempted to imagine, as she listened to the sound of his buckle being undone and its falling with his garment to the ground, that Arturo rather than Federico stood over her. The sound of the cascading water reminded her, as she waited, of a dirge, while she told herself to prepare for an opposite event. She closed her hands into fists as she felt his body descend over her; automatically she brought her arms up to embrace him, but forced herself to maintain her hands clutched. As she listened to his panting, warm tears descended from the corners of her eyes.

When he had finished, he rolled to one side assuming without inquiry that she had gotten everything she wanted. Indeed, in this case she had no way at the moment of verifying whether she had obtained what she sought. She had done all that she could, and with that consolation she attempted to dissolve the lump in her throat. Conscious that her emotions remained invisible to him, as she brought the palm of her hands up to wipe traces of her tears, she wondered whether he had noticed them at all or whether his silence merely revealed the assumption that they were her normal reaction. She arrived finally at that conclusion, relegating him with some ambivalence to the realm of ordinary men. Later, when again submerged in the memory of the event, her feelings of regret at his lack of compassion overwhelmed her.

The encounter, more stressful than she had anticipated, elicited disturbing feelings, and she began to wonder how much else would deviate from the expected. Fear of continuing action over which she lacked reasonable control now plagued her. Her aim may have been achieved that first time, but she could not be certain until her monthly rhythm provided some evidence. For that she had to wait. But to see him only once a month until she got what she wanted seemed absurd. She had launched on a project, and she had to continue until its completion or until some supernatural power stopped her. On a rainy day, when lightning streaked across the sky, she thought of herself as a likely target, and her heartbeat increased each time she saw the flash of light followed by the roll of thunder; the closer one followed the other the more uneasy she became, but once the storm proceeded over the mountain, making way for domineering sunlight, she took it as a sign of approval.

The need for secrecy complicated matters. The urge to visit Doña Urbana to discuss the problem required suppression each time it emerged, increasing the stress she had to bear. Other women kneeled in church before the Virgin for succor in bearing the strain of everyday life, but what relief would the Virgin offer to one whose sin was more than the opposite of virginity? "But how am I different from her?" Julia asked herself. "Her child was engendered by someone other than her husband." Still, Federico Atorey was a far cry from a Holy Spirit, the similarity absurd. "I'm doing it for the good of my husband. I must remember that or I will go mad."

No doubt Doña Urbana would keep the secret, but the risk of confiding in her was too great. After all, she was not protecting herself or Federico, who needed none and would be more than glad to boast of another conquest, but Arturo who awaited death with more immediacy than most. She was doing the very opposite, retaliating against that specter, assuring the predominance of a human will. Yes, what she was doing was necessary. The next time she met Federico at the waterfall, she refrained from clenching her fists.

For a month she met Federico by the waterfall every Wednesday afternoon, yet the blood still came. Surely if she saw him more than once a week her aim would be achieved. She suggested that they meet more often, and he took the suggestion as a compliment. Still, the blood came again the second month. Either Arturo was right about her inability to conceive or some unseen power thwarted her plan as a punishment for her sin.

"You talk much less than usual these days," Arturo said to her one night.

"What need I say?" she asked, fearing he had discovered that she had something to confess.

"My illness is making you worry," he said. "You will not be alone after I leave. Someone will marry you for the land. It is not barren even if you are."

Her face became distorted in an effort to keep from expressing the anger sparked by his words. Attempting to keep him from noticing her reaction, she turned away, but she need not have bothered; the room contained insufficient light to illuminate her face, where her feelings clearly flickered obvious to anyone interested in them. Her anger, suppressed for the moment, transformed into a passion the next time she met Federico.

"You can no longer deny that you love me," he said after he had dressed and was ready to emerge from behind the cascading water.

After having combed her hair and rewound it into a bun, she placed the last hairpin to secure her work. Trying to determine the depth of his ignorance, she glared at the man and wondered whether he would ever look at her with sufficient insight to see her clearly. Were all men equally blind to the essence of the women from whom they derived pleasure? Did he see anything beyond her legs wrapped around him as she sighed and finally screamed to convey ecstasy to him? Nothing to be done, he would continue to live in ignorance as profound as her husband's. Why she bothered with either one of them became the question without a reasonable answer.

"You think that it matters whether or not I love you?" she asked, getting up to fold the blanket on which she had been sitting while rearranging her hair.

Her having given herself to him with more intensity than he had anticipated removed any need to further convince her, yet he persisted. "It matters to me," he said emphatically, the words absurd and false and at the same time more startling to him than they were to her.

"You made me pregnant today," she said.

"You can tell the very same day?"

"I know it," she said, "and when I verify it, I will stop seeing you."

"Then I hope you're barren forever," he said.

"So you and Arturo have opposite aims when you make love to me," she said, aware of the absurdity of the situation.

"Then that clearly proves who loves you for yourself rather than as a means of getting something else."

"That may be," she said, "but you will see me no more when I'm with child."

Imagining her bloated body aroused him again, and he grabbed hold of her.

"No more," she said, stepping back. "I have to leave now."

Confused, he let go of her. Emerging from behind the falling water, they climbed the path up the side of the ravine to where his horse stood in the shade, its tail swinging from side to side trying to keep bugs from his rump. Federico swung into the saddle and bent over to pick her up.

"No," she said. "Why take a chance now on being seen together? I'll walk home."

She followed the path on foot, and once he had progressed out of sight, the words "Goodbye" fell from her lips as she tried to raise her hand in a futile attempt to wave, her arm restricted by an invisible weight.

Chapter 6

A RTURO ORTEGA'S FUNERAL was a major event in Naranjito. Julia had expected many people to attend, but on the day of the burial the number astonished her. The church became replete, and people stood in the side aisles and all the way to the back. A stranger stopping by on that day would have found nothing unusual about so small a church being full, but any resident of the town and adjoining countryside knew better. Even the well-to-do of the town seldom managed to fill the church for a funeral. Usually, to those grieving, the number of people at a funeral mattered little, and only later, when thinking about the event in an attempt to absorb it, did the turnout become something to consider. On the day of her husband's funeral, Julia experienced the opposite; she focused on the social minutiae.

Everyone interpreted her look as deep grief, a look of concern and worry interpretable as pain caused by the loss of her husband. No one looked beneath the surface to see what she felt, and had she been sure of that, she would have been less anxious. Her insecurity proved to be an advantage, producing an effect easily misinterpreted in her favor, since she most feared the detection of her lack of grief at her husband's death, which caused no pain whatsoever. On the contrary, she felt relieved, though she could not say why, being certain that her secret would never be revealed. She had been convinced that had Federico betrayed her, Arturo would never have believed him.

She had been surprised by the success of her scheme and by her husband's lack of suspicion. She had continued to doubt the success of her endeavor and his acceptance of the child as his own. She had feared that once her belly swelled his eyes would immediately open, and he would react the way most men did to such an occurrence. Considering the reservation of her body as the essence of his manhood, he would fail to appreciate the sacrifice she had undertaken for his sake. But he saw nothing of the sort; rather, he transformed her back into the object of his love. But his admiration of her came too late; she was more affected by his ignorance than by his gratitude.

At Arturo's death, her look fooled Federico as much as it did everyone else. He had more reason than most to be deceived. She had kept to her word and had refused to meet him again after she conceived. He reasoned that she would grieve at her husband's funeral, but in mourning she would be in a state of emotional need, and that might provide him a chance to ingratiate himself, something he needed to cope with the unexpected emotional happenstance in which he found himself.

His relationship with Julia had been different from any other he had ever had with a woman. She had decided when to begin it, and more importantly when to end it. With any other woman that behavior would have merely convinced him of her worthlessness, but with Julia, the opposite happened. He desired her now more than ever. An outsider might assume that Federico's motives stemmed from anger, but he felt no anger toward Julia, a reaction as puzzling to him as to anyone else, had anyone else been aware of it. On being rejected, an emotion that had always been alien invaded him, and his sudden melancholia puzzled anyone who noticed it.

Julia gave birth to a son, but Federico remained indifferent to being the biological father. In truth, there might be other unknown offspring of his about town, and seeing that Julia, rather than afraid of being discovered, relished her new state, he moved the event into the category of inconsequence. Arturo's departure raised Federico's estimation of being the actual father of Julia's child, something to use in his attempt to win her back. He could never bring himself to accept the absence of love in her relating to him. He had considered her attitude a façade used to hide the anguish of a married woman in love with someone other than her husband.

Pepina accompanied Federico to the church service that preceded the funeral procession to the cemetery. Her decision to attend had been independent of his, but she had been happy enough to discover that he also would attend, and the two of them would be seen together in public as an affirmation of her hold on him.

"Everyone has come out to his funeral," Federico said, arriving at the church even before it was completely full. "I never knew he was this popular."

"Everyone isn't here for him," Pepina said. "He's dead and doesn't know whether we're here or not."

"Who then?"

"Why are you here?"

Yes, of course the answer was clear, but all these people could hardly be Julia's lovers, even if she were promiscuous, all her lovers, along with their wives, could not be this many. He tried to reverse the situation, imagining himself in the coffin. Would the church then be empty because Pepina was a faithful wife? If he wanted a large turnout at his own funeral he had to encourage Pepina to acquire as many lovers as possible. The idea made him chuckle, attracting the attention of some who added a veneer of disdain to their sorrowful look. Little did he care what most people thought, but if disparaging remarks reached Julia's ears, they might create another obstacle to his next attempt to win her over. The other possibility then invaded his imagination. If Pepina were in the coffin, then every woman with whom he had ever flirted would arrive, pulling her husband along, to comfort Federico in his anguish over the loss of a wife. He had never before been aware of this advantage to his flirtatious nature. He suspected, however, that Pepina would not appreciate this particular remedy to his possible sorrow over her own demise. Pepina, at the moment annoyed by his amused look, squeezed his arm to communicate her displeasure.

"Well, you brought it up," he said. "I thought everyone came here for him rather than for her."

"The same way you did?"

"Of course. I always appreciated the man."

There was a great deal of truth to that statement, although the public would be divided on the judgment of its veracity, many having difficulty in understanding the betrayer's high opinion of the one betrayed.

"I will volunteer to be a pallbearer," Federico said to himself, but his having made the remark aloud made Pepina believe that he was addressing her.

"Pallbearers have already been chosen, I'm sure," she answered.

"I will trade places with someone," he said, moving up through those standing before him.

The previously assigned pallbearers had already stood up to approach the coffin when Federico reached the front of the main aisle where the coffin lay. "Please let me take your place," he said to Mencio Granudo, someone with whom he often associated and who owed him a few drinks. Don Granudo had no personal reason to reject the request and saw an opportunity to clear his account and perhaps shift to a positive balance.

But the matter was more complicated. The widow had assigned him the task, and to relinquish it without her approval might be mistaken for a rejection of the honor—a loss hardly equal to the price of a few drinks. Luckily for both men, Julia's attention haphazardly drifted toward them and by eye contact the request transmitted to her. She approved by a nod of her head that went unnoticed by most other people in the church, except the few in the habit of staying alert to the nuances of social interaction, a practice that provided them with inspiration to gossip.

After having obtained his first goal of becoming one of the bearers, Federico proceeded to position himself at the front end of the casket, providing himself for the march to the cemetery, a close view of Julia immediately ahead of the coffin. At the cemetery, after having placed the coffin over the grave for the final prayers, the bearers remained in place. The grave diggers would lower the casket, but while the ceremony progressed, Federico remained in direct view of Julia who pretended to be indifferent to his proximity.

Pepina had yet to discover why Federico made such an effort to be noticed at the funeral. His lack of concern for the widow annoyed her more than his assault on the social hierarchy of the town, which she assumed was the aim of his scheming. Only Julia clearly saw what lurked within him as well as within herself, but whereas Federico knew exactly what he wanted and how much he would do to attain it, confusion plagued Julia. Her attempt to fulfill the emotional needs of her husband in the final days of his life had given rise to something else. She had succeeded in what she had started out to do, but an unforeseen problem had emerged. She had depended on the objectionable points in Federico's character to keep her safe from an emotional attachment. Indeed, what she perceived as antagonism toward him served as the reason, besides his availability, for choosing him rather than someone else. So now that she stood by her husband's grave, about to see the coffin descend into the ground where it would decay, letting the worms invade the flesh which she had once loved, the look of consternation on her face was mistakenly attributed to a recognition of mortality, rather than the reality of having Federico's presence remind her of the predicament she had created for herself.

She took full responsibility for the problem. Neither the actions nor desires of either of the men mitigated her sense of guilt at having created the dilemma that she had now to resolve. Nothing that came to mind seemed a possible escape from a life of pain. Her use of Federico had transformed itself into an unquenchable desire; she named it that, afraid to call it something more dangerous. Desire, attributable only to the body, a secondary entity, could be controlled. If she mistook it for love, then it would be transferred to her soul, which had a life of its own beyond reason. If she loved him, then nothing could extricate her from the damning situation.

The coffin down in the grave and the earth being shoveled over it, she looked up to see Federico, and seeing him revived her consternation. Some people had begun to suspect a liaison between the two, although Federico had maintained his word of secrecy, but truth, sooner or later, mysteriously seeps through any attempt to restrain it. At the moment, however, everyone without exception attributed Julia's look of distress to her husband's departure rather than to Federico's presence. Even Federico subscribed to the general interpretation, distasteful to him, since it indicated that his goal would be difficult to attain.

Chapter 7

A FEW DAYS LATER, Doña Urbana unexpectedly greeted Federico as he rode by her house on his way home from work.

"So, what have you seen in the crystal ball?" Federico inquired still in the saddle, uncertain whether Doña Urbana expected him to dismount.

"I think you would be more interested in what someone else has seen," she answered.

In general, Federico paid little attention to any position acquired through the practice of religious customs or traditions. Often, the mention of a priest elicited only derisions from him. He saw them as drinkers of wine as opposed to a man's true drink, rum. But more importantly, if they maintained their vow of celibacy, he considered them less than men; if they did not, merely liars deceiving the public for bread and wine. Doña Urbana, of course, was not a priest. Though she engaged in a practice akin to theirs, doing so with less fanfare and pompousness rendered her less objectionable. Besides, attuned to the needs of everyday life along with a sense of humor, she put the most bizarre situations into perspective.

He had difficulty determining her mood by the look on her face. Had she something serious to tell him or was she merely taking advantage of his presence to relieve the boredom of the day? "I suppose you have an apprentice," he said, deciding on the lighter tone. "Is she good enough to deal with my problems?"

"Are you admitting that you have problems?"

"In that respect I'm no different from any other man. Life is only the journey from one place to another with slight respites in between. The trick is to maintain the appearance of having a good time."

"Is that all life is?"

"You tell me."

"I saw you at Don Arturo's funeral. How does it feel to lose a friend?"

"Well, I'll tell you," he said taking a deep breath, "better to be a pallbearer than a cadaver."

"Hasn't the cadaver achieved the solution to life's problems?"

"That may be," Federico said, "but that's one of the mysteries of life. Better to face the problems we know than the ones that may turn up beyond the grave."

"Perhaps you're right," she said. "Dismount and have a cup of coffee with me."

"Gladly," he said descending from his horse.

He had taken only a few steps onto the porch when, looking through the open door, he caught sight of a figure enveloped in the late day shadows. The recognition of the shape and the realization that the darkness of the figure stemmed more from the color of her dress than from the lack of light in the house paralyzed him. He stood by the door watching her, and she likewise held her stand in the darkness, as if a decision had to be made, and the burden was on him to make it.

For the first time in his life his own action confounded him, or rather, the lack of it, if indeed the paralysis of the body can be called a lack of action or whether the lack of movement is itself an action as implied by physical law. Acted upon by an external force, the scientific explanation; still, the question remained of what in this case constituted the external force. Up to a few minutes ago he had been in motion; of that, he was certain. He now wondered whether anyone else on the scene noticed his condition. Only in dreams had he ever experienced the inability to move. That, of course, brought up another problem; he did not want the figure in the darkness to disappear, and that would certainly happen if he woke up. He would gladly prolong the dream if only his paralysis ceased.

"I'm here," she said.

She had chosen to awaken him, or so he believed for an instant. His power of movement restored, he walked toward her without consciousness of the wooden floor underneath his boots, and having reached and embraced her, joining his lips to hers, he was again unable to determine whether he was in a trance. She gently pushed him away.

"Now you know," she said.

He kept silent, rejecting the notion that he had known all along that this moment would arrive. He had known something, but he could not say exactly what. The absence of knowledge failed to startle him, but his awareness of it, and his need to support his actions with honesty, for the moment puzzled him. He concluded that the strangeness of the situation, something different from his usual expression of desire, had only one explanation, that he loved her.

"So you have lost your tongue," she said.

"What can I say?" he retorted. "You know that I love you."

"Then you must always say it, or your silence will frighten me."

"Is that all that frightens you?"

"No," she answered, "but it's all that I can ask."

"You can ask me for anything."

"Except for the ultimate."

"My life?"

"It belongs to someone else."

"You're mistaken."

"Am I?"

"Tonight I will pack up my things, and tomorrow I will move in with you."

She laughed, perhaps to hide that his words frightened her as much as they reassured her of his feelings. But there was more to life than emotion, more than fantasies of desire. What about the reality of everyday life? At the moment, she had no control over her actions, the pretense remained essential for her self-possession, and reality had to be abandoned in order to avoid the unbearable.

"I will move in with you tomorrow," he repeated.

"No," she said, "we must wait a year while I mourn my husband. That will give you a chance to arrange for Pepina's life."

That was the first of many pretenses she was forced to assume in dealing with a part of her life over which she had lost control. She tried to abate the guilt she felt for taking something away from another woman. She instructed him on what to do before she would allow him to dwell under her roof. But even this attempt to exhibit some compassion for Pepina was short lived. At first Julia forced Federico to go home every night after his visit, but as the weeks went by his departure grew later and later until one day, three months later, she found him still in her bed at sunrise. She served his breakfast at the kitchen table without saying a word about the change. When he returned that evening, he brought a package of personal belongings.

Chapter 8

UNWILLING TO ACCEPT her fate, Pepina took a while to recognize her husband's gradual detachment as permanent. He was just a man, and men are what they are. The ideal goal of making them completely faithful is rarely achieved and sometimes, when attained, of doubtful value, since the husband's manhood then became questionable in the eyes of his neighbors. Even her father when young had been unfaithful, though now he had changed and expected every man to do the same.

On noticing Federico's behavior, Don Iglesia reacted angrily, except that the object of his anger remained unclear to Pepina. Was her father angry with her or with her husband? At first she defended Federico, pointing out that he behaved like every other man, and in any case, he came home every night. When that stopped, she pretended to be ignorant of where he had gone, while everyone else in town gossiped about his having replaced Arturo in Julia's life.

Don Iglesia made an about-face. Whereas at the beginning he had congratulated his daughter on her conquest, he now acted as if all along he had opposed the union and had warned her of the danger of attaching herself to such a man.

"He'll be back," she said to her father, "when he tires of her."

"Then what? You'll act as if nothing happened?"

Seeing no alternative, she kept silent for a moment. "Mother waited for you," she then said, causing his face to distort in dismay and change color, she uncertain whether to interpret that as anger or embarrassment. "He'll be back," Pepina added. "I'm the mother of his son."

"And are you the only one who can make such a claim?" he rhetorically asked, knowing full well that she must already have heard the town gossip that Don Arturo had indeed gone to his grave without engendering a son.

She raised her hands to cover her ears, pain distorting her face. "I'll wait for him," she said looking at the floor.

He stifled a grunt that instead emerged as a heavy breath along with the twisting of his mouth.

"What other choice do I have?" she asked rhetorically as she turned, retreating farther into the house she would eventually occupy alone until the end of her life.

Chapter 9

JULIA CONCEIVED A SECOND child eighteen months after the birth of the first.

"There's another child on the way," she said to Federico one evening at suppertime.

"Is there?" he asked, unemotionally. He had sat down at the table as she was about to bring the food from the kitchen.

Having expected more of a response, she remained silent for a minute confused by his seeming indifference. "This one will carry your name," she said.

"True enough," he said.

"You don't care?" she asked, annoyed and perplexed by his indifference.

"What's the difference?" he said. "There's no doubt about this one being mine."

"And have you doubt about the other?"

"No, as long as you don't."

"Only your name he lacks," she said trying to suppress her annoyance. "Everything else is yours."

"Then there's nothing else to be said," he concluded.

Discomfited by his attitude and uncertain that her life had ever been typical, she longed for a normal life that at the moment seemed impossible. An attempt to escape from the arrangement she had created presented the likelihood of painful consequences. Federico's expression, as he looked up from his plate, startled her. The indifference on his face alerted her to her ignorance. She had the urge to ask him for an explanation, and trying to subdue it, she pretended to have no reason for it. She sat down opposite him at the table believing that if she kept still the prowling beast might go by without noticing her. The sudden notice of uncertainty gave shape to the monster; her guilt, taking on a shape, plagued her and demanded a higher price than she had expected. Convinced that all that she had done had been beyond her power to prevent, she faced a conundrum: the feeling of guilt, along with the certainty that the path had been unavoidable.

Chapter 10

DON IVAN JIMENEZ, a close friend of Pepina's father, and for all practical purposes Pepina's godfather, as mayor, carried out government functions in Naranjito. Anyone arriving in town had no problem finding the mayor's office, but whether the mayor was there or not was never predictable; he kept erratic hours, the running of the general store being his primary business and the job of mayor a secondary function.

He always expressed his point of view on any matter, a quality in most cases greatly admired but in Don Ivan considered somewhat odd. He often veered into subjects of little interest to anyone else, his audience wondering why he had brought up the matter. That habit elicited various interpretations. Some gave him the benefit of the doubt, ascribing to him a spiritual awareness that made him sensitive to matters imperceptible to everyone else, while others concluded that he was so self-absorbed that he cared little for what everyone else thought, and he dealt with matters relevant only to him. A third group thought him emotionally disturbed, that is, insane, obviously in a minority, since they failed to keep him from the office of mayor, assuming that most people who consider a candidate insane generally vote for the opponent. Of course, this conclusion is difficult to support given a general analysis of election results anywhere in the world.

Federico's abandonment of Pepina persisted as the expressed reason for Don Ivan's enmity toward him. Although the church intended godfathers to be a safeguard for the faith, insurance for the religious training of a child in the event of parental absence, the role had deteriorated into a means of attaining social connections, totally abandoning its religious purpose. In most cases, the responsibility of a godfather became a mere formality. The fact that Pepina was no longer a child further obfuscated Don Ivan's pretense that his enmity toward Federico stemmed from his position as her godfather, Federico's abandonment of her having no effect on her religious feelings. Failing to discuss the matter with anyone, even his wife, Don Ivan's antagonism towards Federico increased, and he kept attributing the hostility to Federico's abandonment of Pepina.

There was no rational justification for Federico's treatment of his wife, yet not even her father resented him as much as Don Ivan. Even among those who, for whatever reason, were closely involved with the church, the view of Federico as a man among men had altered little, and perhaps had been enhanced due to his ability to do whatever he pleased without being constrained by fear. Some envied him and were less than amicable, but even they, aware of the basis for their spite, willingly looked the other way in the matter of his relationship to Julia, whom no man in town found reason to disparage. A beautiful and charming woman, only age would take away her beauty, though her charm would be soon enough hidden by resentment stirred by the man she loved.

The mayor maintained close ties with Father Hormiguero, the parish priest, with whom he readily discussed his enmity toward Federico, although doing so forced him to present it as a shortcoming. At least once a year, Father Hormiguero used his favorite passage in the New Testament, the gospel of the lost sheep, as the basis of a sermon. On Don Ivan's bringing up Federico's transgression against Pepina, the priest automatically referred to lost sheep. To Don Ivan, of course, Federico brought up the image of the predator rather than of the sheep.

"You must have patience," Father Hormiguero said.

"There must be something the church can do to right this wrong. Excommunicate him."

Father Hormiguero considered the suggestion excessive. Some of his colleagues would have thought expulsion reasonable enough, but if excommunicating men for their sins became a practice, the number of men in the church would become negligible. Already on Sundays when from the pulpit he examined the faces of the attending parishioners, men were a worrisome minority.

"That's somewhat excessive," Father Hormiguero said before he realized that his words might be wrongly interpreted to mean that he looked on Federico's behavior as a minor transgression and that he little cared about Pepina's suffering. "Either in this life or the next he will have to pay for his transgression," Father Hormiguero added to clarify his meaning. "Besides, Pepina's suffering will not be ignored on Judgment Day." But even after having delivered that statement, he felt uncomfortable seeing the possibility that he had failed to convey what he really meant.

The fear that his words fell short of conveying what he intended became one of his main worries, not only in personal conversations, as in the present case, but more so when delivering a sermon from the pulpit, an activity promoted to major importance in his vocation. Seeking relief, he had, on one occasion, consulted a colleague who assured him that preaching was a minor concern. Practical, but far from essential in the everyday requirements of the church, the preaching could be left to the missionaries. Father Hormigero, for a while, accepted that rationale, but he was soon forced to abandon it, and coping with what to him seemed a weakness became a necessary path to self-fulfillment.

"I would like to see him punished long before then," retorted Don Ivan.

Father Hormiguero, sure that Federico had already accumulated enough faults to render his life troublesome, saw little need to get involved in providing more, which in any case would little help Pepina, an aim he saw as more practical. Once Federico had taken on the burden of two households, life became more difficult for him and reduced his ability to carry out his responsibilities. "There is a practical side to this matter that has to be kept in mind," Father Hormiguero said.

Listening to the priest, from whom he had expected a sanguine condemnation of Federico, Don Ivan approached the limit of his patience. Of course, all men were sinners, but there had to be a limit. Although Don Ivan failed to say so to the priest, he objected not to the infidelity that his goddaughter had to suffer but Federico's brazenness in proclaiming it. His misbehaving out in the open, rather than in secret, insulted the mayor, who resented being judged, in comparison, a lesser man.

"Something has to be done," Don Ivan insisted.

"Indeed," retorted the priest, "God will send us a sign."

Don Ivan, on the verge of losing his temper, perceived Father Hormiguero's penchant for tolerance as a lack of judgment. Indeed, it could be considered exactly that, since Father Hormiguero would rather put off any final conclusion until the unavoidable day when executing the penalty would fall on Saint Michael.

"Well, as soon as you get it, you let me know what it is," Don Ivan said.

Getting up in fear of transgressing, he walked out of the rectory restraining himself from slamming the door and reducing his status to that of a recalcitrant child. Instead, he walked brusquely down the street until he reached the tavern where he sat at the bar to calm himself with a glass of rum. Manuel Rodriguez, the tavern keeper, having no other customers to attend to at the moment, stayed close enough to the mayor not only to notice that his lips were moving but also to hear some of the emerging expletives. For a moment, as he formulated the curses, Don Ivan had the image of Father Hormiguero in mind, but that image was soon replaced by Federico's. Manuel Rodriguez assumed Federico was totally responsible for the mayor's discomfiture.

"Some people say he went for the land," Manuel said, "but I don't think so."

Don Ivan looked up at Manuel befuddled by his words. "You have reason to support him, I suppose," said Don Ivan. "He's your biggest customer."

"I'm not sure of that," Manuel said trying to avoid being placed on one side or the other. "And I heard he's to become a father again, so the matter is not so simple anymore."

For Don Ivan, the bartender's mind became a clear example of simplicity. Or perhaps everyone in town had a simple mind, since no one, not even the priest, condemned Federico's evident transgression against Pepina. He suddenly realized the possibility of having failed to see something, and reexamining the words he had just heard, the obvious struck him: everyone defended Julia rather than her lover, who by chance benefited. For a woman, Julia had the unusual ability to shed blame without a residual trace. He imagined that she felt no guilt about having gotten herself into the position of husband stealer, being no more than a loose woman, though in this case the man, rather than the woman, received payment. On hearing that Julia was to have another child, the idea came to Don Ivan of how he might get even with her as well as with Federico.

Chapter 11

WITH THE BABY asleep in a straw basket, Julia trekked down the mountain to register him at the town hall. She heard the gurgling water of the stream as she crossed the bridge into town for the first time with the newborn, the first of her children to claim the name Atorey. Halfway to her destination, she felt the glare of eyes on her back, though she failed to catch anyone gazing at her.

She wondered whether only her imagination created the feeling of scrutiny. Perhaps no one noticed her at all. The townspeople had lives of their own with enough travails to absorb their attention, her own predicament only a slight distraction easily discounted and forgotten. At first, she kept her eyes down as she made her way down the street, but halfway to her destination she could no longer bare that pose. She raised her head and carried herself proudly, and on reaching the town hall, she was ready.

Don Ivan refused to register the child under the name Atorey and suggested to Julia that she use her dead husband's name, the legal thing to do.

"But Federico is this boy's father. The name is Atorey."

"I've heard that Federico was your older son's father also, and you made no fuss about naming him Ortega."

"As far as the world is concerned," retorted Julia, "the first one is Arturo's son, and now is Federico's turn."

"I can only do what's legal," Don Ivan insisted.

"Then you will have to deal with my husband," she said, forgetting for a moment that Federico was married to Pepina.

"I believe your husband is dead," said Don Ivan.

"I will register this child somewhere else," she said.

"You can try," said Don Ivan, "but legal registration has to be at the place of birth."

"We shall see," Julia said.

The unpleasant encounter with Ivan Jimenez at first made her distraught, but by the time she got home she had worked up considerable anger, which she expected Federico to share, so that his indifference at first stunned her but then proceeded to increase her fury. "You must go down and insist that he do the right thing."

"And if he refuses?"

"Whatever you have to do. You're a man."

"Eventually I will make him pay," Federico said, "but that won't affect the name."

"We'll go down the mountain to Bayamon," she said.

"It's useless," Federico insisted. "There's nothing to be done right now."

"How can the child go without your name? This is improper," she said to Federico.

"What does it matter?" he answered.

"It is your right to make the claim," she said.

"Whether he has my name or not, he will still be mine," Federico said.

"A child must have his father's name, otherwise he will be publicly abused."

"I do not reject him, so he will be accepted, and everyone knows the reason for the wrong name and will understand."

"Everyone here," Julia said, "but everywhere else the name will be a problem."

"What does it matter?" he asked. "Haven't I already a son who lacks my name?"

"I had a reason to do that," she said, but emotion suddenly paralyzed her throat and prevented any more words from emerging.

Normally a profusion of tears would have followed, but she refused to let that happen, the beginning of a process that she tried to avoid but which slowly grew inward; so that in time, displaying any emotion became a burden. The shutdown was gradual and transparent to Federico, but even had it been immediate he would have ignored it. Julia failed to admit his faults, and her ears closed to the criticism that others voiced against him. Her love was unconditional. She had no idea how it had emerged from blankness and enveloped her without her conscious desire. She saw no evil in him, but rather the qualities of a man whom women naturally admired. She would raise her children to look up to him as a model, and they had no way to decide whether they were headed in the right direction. Only later in their lives, too late to avoid disasters, did they realize that they had been led astray.

That first time, however, Julia retreated into the bedroom with the newborn, leaving Emiliano in Federico's hands. She failed to come out for supper, and at bedtime the door was still closed. The next morning she emerged to prepare breakfast as if nothing unusual had happened the day before. The subject never discussed again, all of her subsequent offspring bore the name Ortega.

Chapter 12

WHETHER DON IVAN expected Federico to ignore the slight meted out to Julia is an interesting question. Although most people misguidedly believe that they use reason to arrive at everyday decisions, that process is actually rare. At the core of Don Ivan's emotions thrived a need for self-indulgence. It manifested itself in the belief that everything he did had an obvious rationality beyond explanation to anyone including himself. Consistency not one of his habits, on political issues he sometimes made complete turns, a normal occurrence in politics, except that his change of opinion, or rather of feeling, exceeded practical needs.

For instance, his feelings about Americans had now reverted to what they had been just prior to the invasion, when everyone in town tolerated his insistence that, although he had been born on the island, he was indeed a Spaniard, since, according to him, inherited blood rather than place of birth determined nationality. Most people in Naranjito thought that a humorous idea and considered Don Ivan's view another of his idiosyncrasies, which they were willing to tolerate as interesting, even if absurd. The question of whether he had a blood transfusion as the Americans invaded arose when everyone noticed his willingness to display the Stars and Stripes as soon as the Spanish garrison retreated.

Indeed, flying the American flag became at the moment common enough among those who, like Don Ivan, belonged to a particular class that cultivated practicality in everyday economic matters. They willingly accepted an idealized image of Americans as a people who believed in democratizing the world, just at the moment when those democratizers had nearly completed their expansion across the west and were ready to move into the Caribbean to ensure influence over the southern continent. Far from being a scholar, the desire to scrutinize American history evaded Don Ivan, and of course that was perfectly understandable. Yet, those who might be considered more informed and who at the time had been struggling to obtain from Spain some degree of autonomy for the island had similar expectations. The fact that the United States was created through the conquest of the native people was ignored, since that too was a part of the history of Puerto Rico, whose native population had been exterminated by the Spaniards. In the north, after the Native Americans had been removed as an obstacle, expansion continued, California and the Southwest wrested from the Mexicans. The belief that American armed forces moved into the Caribbean to spread independence was, from the beginning, an illusion without historical support.

Don Ivan had the propensity to create fantasies of minimum relevance, but in the American case, contrary to the usual, his imagination had been captivated by a popular expectation and subsequently disappointed by its failure to materialize, so that more than ten years after he had been happy to wave the American flag, he had reverted to an anti-American stance, except that now he could not even think of himself as a Spaniard. Legally in fact, he, along with every other native of the island, had no citizenship. Spain gone from the scene and the status of the island undefined, Puerto Ricans, not being citizens of any independent country, had no way of acquiring a passport. "The man without a country" had been multiplied so that now the phrase applied to the whole population of an island, except that in this case the stigma was not retribution for a crime but rather the sign of one being perpetrated.

The language of the people different from that of the conquerors provided a source of immediate conflict.

"English!" Don Ivan exclaimed. "All the lessons are to be in English?"

"It's not a bad thing to learn English," Father Hormiguero assured his parishioner. Not himself comfortable with the idea, but with so many things in the world making him uncomfortable, the priest had developed a habit of looking at the positive side of whatever came up and thereby removing as much discomfort as possible. "It's a good thing to learn another language," he reaffirmed.

Don Ivan looked straight into the eyes of the priest trying to discern whether the clergyman was indeed serious, or whether he was engaging in some prank against him, an increasingly popular pastime among his fellow townsmen. Rarely did Don Ivan have a conversation with his confessor without losing his temper and eventually walking away convinced of the priest's idiocy. Luckily, performing religious rituals necessary for the balance of everyday life required little intelligence. Don Ivan saw no conflict between the obtuseness he saw in the priest and the public performance required of the clergyman. However, over time the priest and the mayor had developed a relationship that surpassed their evaluation of each other's foibles. Don Ivan often asked himself why he bothered to talk to the priest outside the confessional, always a rhetorical question with no answer from anyone, perhaps because the answer was too obvious to require expression.

"Yes, it's a good thing to learn another language," Don Ivan agreed. "The question is whether it's a good thing to erase one."

Father Hormiguero's mind drifted into imagining how an eraser might be applied to the mind as if it were a blackboard on which the language existed. No, there was no way to erase the language once it was placed there early in life, long before one went to school. He tried to explain that to Don Ivan.

"Not right away," Don Ivan answered, "but if you're illiterate in one language more and more you'll only use the one in which you're literate, and eventually the unused one disappears."

For a minute, Father Hormiguero silently tried to find a rebuttal to Don Ivan's argument, not because he had any personal need to see Don Ivan in the wrong, but because Don Ivan's point of view, contrary to Father Hormiguero's natural inclination, pointed to a conflict that had no obvious resolution. "Perhaps you're right," the priest finally said hoping that the absence of rebuttal might prompt Don Ivan to arrive at a conclusion on his own.

"Of course I'm right," said Don Ivan, at last happy to have convinced the priest of something. "The question is: what can we do about it?"

Father Hormiguero had no answer. As far as he was concerned the church was apolitical, a point he was reluctant to stir up at the moment, fearing to push Don Ivan down a more troublesome path.

"We can boycott the schools," said Don Ivan. The words came out of his mouth but approached his ears as if uttered by someone else, and he was hearing them for the first time. Yes, he analyzed his own words, turning them over in his mind as if the priest had uttered them. "Yes, of course it's a wonderful idea," he said turning again toward Father Hormiguero after having been gazing at the rectory garden from the open window, through which the morning sunlight flooded the room. "In the Sunday sermon you can ask the parishioners to keep their children home from the public school as long as instruction is only in English."

"I can't do that," Father Hormiguero protested. "Religion is beyond language. One can be a Catholic in English just as well as in Spanish." The statement emerged with less vigor than it required. He tried to be reasonable, but being aware of facts unknown to Don Ivan, at the moment perhaps unwise to reveal to him, disturbed Father Hormiguero's spiritual equilibrium. The Vatican was having American priests fill vacancies on the island. Father Hormiguero did not know whether the Americans had requested that policy just as he did not know why the Vatican would agree to comply. One fact, however, hovered in Father Hormiguero's mind: a small percentage of Americans were Catholics, but that minor number provided a disproportional amount of funds for the church. Father Hormiguero was reluctant to admit that the national origin might dominate the political leanings of a priest, and yet the idea aroused in him discomfort.

Don Ivan, ignorant of what bothered Father Hormiguero, remained obsessed with the usual dilemma. Was Father Hormiguero a complete idiot or did he have some other reason for behaving obtusely? How could he express such a view about language when every day he reverted to one that for centuries had been dead? "You'll say the mass in English rather than Latin?" Don Ivan asked, and seeing consternation momentarily contort the priest's countenance, he was again pleased to have found a weakness in his friend's usual conformity.

"That's a totally different matter," Father Hormiguero said instinctively, not having yet figured the difference. "Religion is something else altogether," he said trying to arrive at a reasonable argument.

"You think Latin is God's native language?" Don Ivan persisted knowing he had an unusual advantage. "Did Adam and Eve speak Latin?"

The questions startled Father Hormiguero. The absence of something so obvious from his intellectual ruminations made him wonder what else escaped his notice, but the philosophical odds and ends of life were not what he needed to deal with at the moment, but rather, the practicality of taking action against the government—the opposite of what had become traditional. "Well, precisely," he said, at last having thought of something logical. "To God language is irrelevant. Whatever he communicates is understood regardless of the language of the listener. That's in the gospel."

"Just what I'm saying," gloated Don Ivan. "If we don't have to change our language for God, why should we change it for anyone else? This hasn't just been a matter of language," Don Ivan continued, trying to get to a point that the priest would embrace. "Through the schools they are trying to get to our religious customs."

"But Don Ivan, you know religious freedom is a big thing with Americans," Father Hormiguero said continuing his attempt to convince himself that the church had nothing to worry about under American rule.

"But it's a nation of Protestants," Don Ivan insisted. "Have they ever had a Catholic president? Of course not, and they never will. But that's no concern of mine. What bothers me is their dictating on which religious holidays we can close the schools."

"Schools are closed on Christmas and Good Friday. When else do you want them closed?" Father Hormiguero honestly inquired. Yet September, the Feast of the Epiphany did not immediately come to mind.

Don Ivan made an effort to stay calm enough to make his point. "Have you forgotten your childhood? Did a Santa Claus bring you your presents or did the Magi?"

"Ah," Father Hormiguero exclaimed somewhat embarrassed by his forgetfulness. Indeed, by January 6 Christmas was long gone for the Americans even though they had a song called "The Twelve Days of Christmas." Puerto Rican children got their presents on that day, and yet the Americans insisted on keeping the schools open.

"We have to know when to put our foot down," Don Ivan concluded. "If we give away our culture, what have we got left? Who are we?"

"Some people have no objection to becoming Americans," the priest said. "Do I remember you waving the American flag some years ago?"

"We're all sinners at some point or another," Don Ivan heard himself say, and he wondered whether a transformation had taken place, and he had become the man with the white collar and black smock.

Father Hormiguero, in turn, considered washing his hands of the matter, but he restrained himself, imagining whose company he might have to keep should such words escape his lips. Nevertheless, he wondered whether silence sufficiently exculpated him.

"If you won't help me," said Don Ivan, "I'll have to go out and do it without you, but let me give you some advice: If you want more men active in the church, then you have to act more like a man, and I don't mean that the way Federico Atorey would mean it."

At that point, Father Hormiguero expected Don Ivan to storm out of the room as he often did whenever he lost his temper as a result of a disagreement, but this time Don Ivan restrained himself, as if he suddenly remembered something that required that he remain calm. The priest waited to hear what else his visitor had to say. Listening to his parishioners, after all, was required of him; so he tried to bury the resentment aroused by the mayor's words. Don Ivan acted uncharacteristically, unable to arrange the words to express his thoughts, his tongue paralyzed. For a moment, Father Hormiguero considered that the mayor's mind had momentarily blanked.

In fact, Don Ivan had confused himself, astounded by having uttered the name Atorey when the discussion had absolutely no connection to the man. He feared being driven to confess a sin he had committed, but he controlled his dread that already the priest might be aware of what had happened. Julia or Federico having consulted Father Hormiguero about the naming of their children was quite unlikely, but certainly the children had been baptized, so that Father Hormiguero knew about the naming, and of course he had to go along, since the church would not recognize the union of Federico and Julia unless Pepina exited this world, an unlikely occurrence anytime soon.

"This time Don Atorey is on your side," Father Hormiguero said recognizing a sore spot in Don Ivan. "He already keeps his children out of school."

Indeed, no Ortega attended public school in Naranjito until Federico heard about the boycott being organized by Don Ivan.

"It's about time these boys learned more than to just read and write their names," Federico said to Julia one evening after having heard Don Ivan's plan. "They should go to school from now on."

"Suddenly you want them in school rather than out in the fields?" Julia inquired. "Has it got anything to do with where Ivan Jimenez wants them to be?"

Federico smiled at Julia without answering her questions, but she kept her gaze on him insisting on an answer. The transparency of his intention obvious, he saw no reason to be forthcoming even with the mother of his sons. "Have you any objection to their going to school?" he finally asked. "I thought that might please you."

"Ah, something to please me!" she exclaimed. "What I always wanted, sons who can speak English."

"Come now," he said, "some things are determined by fate. The best way to deal with life is to adjust to the inevitable."

"And you always recognize the inevitable."

"Of course I do. It's my most useful talent."

Julia saw no reason to continue the conversation, but the question of how to recognize the inevitable persisted.

Toño Rivera ran the only public school in the district, and to Don Ivan's displeasure, he felt compelled to enforce the dictates of the government in San Juan.

"The classes have to be in English, Don Ivan, and there's nothing I can do about it," he explained to the mayor.

"When you have no students at all you'll lose your job."

"If I don't carry out my instructions from the Education Department I'll have no job."

"I guess there's something else you don't have," Don Ivan concluded and proceeded to make his exit in the flamboyantly angry style he had perfected.

The next day half the students stayed away, their families having been persuaded either by Don Ivan's rhetoric or their own anxiety over being forced to speak English. The other half were content to learn English as a necessity for the future or were completely indifferent as to what they learned in school, the alternative to being out tilling the fields under the hot sun. The Ortega boys fit into the latter category, though Juan immediately fell in love with books.

Toño Rivera did not particularly desire to have English as the language of instruction; on the other hand, he saw no moral perversity in using it. The advantage of being bilingual was clear to him. He saw the learning of English not as giving up his native language but as adding one to cope with the circumstances. He presented the learning of a new language as a means of being practical. For centuries, Puerto Ricans had conformed to historical necessity; both, political repression by Spain and the disasters of tropical weather, were taken in stride. Now they faced the new problem of getting used to the rule of a nation with a different character. In order to explain the predicament they were putting him in, he went out to see those who kept their children home that day. He had received instructions from San Juan to expel all the students who participated in the boycott.

"If your children get expelled they won't be able to return whether we go back to teaching in Spanish or not," he repeated wherever he went.

Only half the people he spoke to saw the practicality of sending their children back to school, and the next day he was forced to expel everyone who failed to answer the roll call. Although the majority of children in the mountainous districts avoided school under normal circumstances, the parents of those expelled soon realized that they had put themselves in an uncomfortable position; and shortly, it became convenient to blame Don Ivan for the predicament.

"Well, what can I say?" Federico gloated as he sat under the mango tree next to the cantina to share the usual drink with his friends. "I think my boys have learned enough English, but they haven't been expelled, and they can go back to school anytime they choose. I'll drink to the mayor's health, though it may not last long with so much resentment going his way."

The Dance

Chapter 13

IN TIME, HIS dispute with the mayor made Federico a pariah in places that had previously welcomed him. His status greatly diminished at the Ardiente plantation, he decided to leave Naranjito, abandoning his quarrel with Don Ivan as well as any responsibility he still felt for his wife, Pepina. Federico moved his family to Vista Alegre, a *barrio* of San Geronimo.

The overtones of the name Vista Alegre are too great to ignore, and yet to determine how the place acquired the name is difficult. Where would such information be found? In the Hall of Records? Probably not. Even if the name were officially used by the post office, that source might only reveal the irrelevant detail of when it was first recognized. The origin of the name has been swallowed by time. In all probability, it arose by consensus; the question is really what possessed the inhabitants of the place to consider it a Happy View. Imagine the mass of citizenry simultaneously possessed by a fit of mockery. Of course, place names are not always produced instantaneously. An old philosopher with a bent for the ironic may have begun to call the place Vista Alegre, and slowly other inhabitants of the place, seeing the humor in that name, adopted it, and the rest through usage followed, some with a conscious sense of the irony and others in total innocence, oblivious of any connection between names and the places they denote.

Possibly, Vista Alegre did not always present the aspect that it did at the time of our story. To say that the most prosperous people of the town lived somewhere else would be to understate the case, though certainly the inhabitants of Vista Alegre did not consider themselves the worst off. That distinction belonged to those who lived in *El Fangito*, a place whose purely descriptive name possessed no irony whatsoever, The Muddy Place. These events did not happen there, so we will forget about *El Fangito* and stay in Vista Alegre, which might have been at some point in the distant past a place that corresponded to its name. It had become, by the time of our story, a neighborhood of poor dwellings remotely deserving of the name Alegre.

The inhabitants of Vista Alegre, like poor people everywhere, knew how to enjoy the occasional good time. It may be fair to say that the poor when they give themselves to revelry are more inclined to exuberance than folk of ample means, whose wealth has allowed them more leisure to develop arbitrary rules of propriety. These rules, created to distinguish their adherents from the ordinary run of humanity, end up being constraints, and the fence set up to keep out the rabble ends up being a prison for its creators. The simple folk of Vista Alegre had their share of misery, but they had not been oppressed enough to lose their joy of life.

Although her mother had died when Ramona was only fourteen years old, leaving her with the responsibility of taking care of the family, and though obliged to put in long hours at the cigar factory to help support her siblings, Ramona was known throughout Vista Alegre as someone with a cheerful disposition, and no one thought that strange or out of place. A beautiful young woman with a long life to look forward to was expected to be cheerful.

In Vista Alegre, the Ortegas became acquainted with the Sotos. How the Ortegas had acquired their name was for Ramona an interesting but insignificant fact, something that had occurred long before her birth, something of little importance in everyday life. Similarly, although she carried the name Soto, the blood of the Rincons flowed within her. Both names had Spanish origin, but from where in Spain and when they had arrived on the island had been forgotten. No one thought that of any significance. The Ortegas, more prone to attach themselves to a place of origin, connected to the mountain town of Naranjito. For some obscure reason they considered that something to brag about, and in general thought themselves superior to the Sotos as well as to most other people. The reason for such an attitude had also been forgotten, but the stance persisted like a trait biologically inherited.

By the time the Ortegas and the Sotos met in San Geronimo, Ramona's mother, Juana Rincon, had died, and occasionally the memory of her mother overcame Ramona. The year of the illness had been a long one, but it had not been nearly long enough for Ramona to learn all the things she needed to become the woman of the house. She would always remember her mother in the bed by the wall, the print of the Sacred Heart right above the wrought- iron headboard. At first, she thought her mother's illness was a bad dream from which she would awake with a sigh of relief, but there was no waking from that nightmare.

Ramona felt as if the grief would never leave her. The thought that she would have to live the rest of her life in pain panicked her. But she did not have to think about the rest of her life, only about the present. She had to manage each moment on its own, a lesson her mother had tried to teach her as soon as the disease became apparent. Ramona remembered the day clearly, and she would remember it for the rest of her life, the day that Juana Rincon Soto had come home from the health station and had separated the dishes, had set her utensils apart from those to be used by the rest of the family—the first step in a process that would culminate in the ultimate separation.

Ramona prayed that year more than she had ever prayed before. Prayer became a habit that would last for the rest of her life, though what she prayed for was not granted. She prayed for her mother's recovery, a selfish prayer brought on by self-concern. How would she manage without her mother? At fourteen, she considered only her own frailty, her possible inability to take on the task her mother would leave to her even though she was not the oldest daughter. Ramona knew even then, just as her mother knew, that her older sister would not be up to the task, but Ramona was not as certain as her mother of her own fitness. Or Juana may not have been certain at all, but what other choice had she?

As Ramona knelt by her mother's bed, Juana instructed her. "Listen to me, Ramona, this is what I want you to do. It's up to you to take care of the little ones unless your father remarries or brings a woman into the house. In that case, I want you to give them out to whichever of their uncles or aunts are able and willing to take them. You'll be separated, but that's better than growing up with a stepmother, someone who's not your own blood. You understand me, Ramona?"

"Yes, Mama," she said. She tried to hold back the tears, but she failed once again, as she would many more times before the year was out.

After her mother's death, Ramona donned a black dress at first merely out of custom. No one expected her to wear it for very long, but it became a habit she could not abandon. She believed that her mother watched her, and in turn, she had to let her know, by wearing the dress, that she still felt the sorrow of having lost her, that she missed her, that she loved her. But the black dress became a reminder to everyone else of a sorrow they wished to forget.

"You need not wear that dress anymore," her father said, as kindly as he could. He would himself be in mourning for the rest of his life, not solely because Juana had died, but because she had died before he felt absolved of his guilt for having betrayed her. Looking into the past, he contemplated the unexplainable, but the puzzle persisted. He had to assume the responsibility for having acted. He could not get out of having made a choice, and yet he did not recall having considered options. He had proceeded without questions. That too puzzled him. He gazed at the glass of water resting on the kitchen table. Did he have a choice in extending his hand to pick it up and bring it to his lips? How thirsty did he have to be before the question of choice became irrelevant? There had to be a point where reason ceased to function, and some other force dominated.

He was now paying for the sin which he did not recall having had the choice to avoid. Of course, that idea sounded ridiculous, the same as saying that placing one foot in front of the other as he walked was automatic, devoid of decision. Obviously a decision had to be made on exiting through the front door, which way to turn once on the sidewalk, up the street or down, north or south, to the grocery store or to the barbershop. He had to go a step further, had to discover his desire. There lay the problem. To discover is not the same as to decide. Becoming conscious of action does not provide control.

Perhaps he sought an excuse to placate his conscience. He had succumbed to temptation. That was common enough, a convenient truism. Sin impossible to avoid, all that was required was resistance. He remembered no struggle at all, led on by his desire, the need to fulfill a natural inclination, nothing else. He had not intended to hurt Juana. He loved her. His actions had nothing to do with how he felt about her; on the surface that seemed a contradiction. He could not blame Evita, mentally only a child. That left only him to assume responsibility. Perhaps there is some other entity invisibly arranging incidents for humans. In the past, that used to be taken for granted. Angels walked the earth disguised as humans. Surely they made things happen. And so when Evita strolled through the tobacco fields to the annoyance of some of the workers was that really Evita or some supernatural being disguised as Evita for the purpose of enticing him? He would never know.

She had walked by the tobacco fields as the workers toiled under the hot sun.

"*Capataz*," one them said to Pedro, "some of the men are annoyed that you let her walk about the field distracting them."

"She's the *patron's* daughter. What can I do?"

"Out here you're *capataz*."

"So it looks to you," Pedro said as he walked away.

He now wondered whether he should have kept walking, fled from the Rincon plantation as far as he could go. He might have avoided succumbing, losing his reason. But how was he to know that such possibility lurked about waiting to pounce on him? How was he to know that at the end of the day he would find her in the barn where the tobacco leaves hung to dry? There she stood smiling in the semidarkness. He had only to walk away to save himself, and her too, from the force that always pulls on the chain of propriety until it snaps.

Desire overwhelms reason, a dilemma of everyday life. There she stood. He gazed at her, and she reciprocated with a smile that assured him. He no longer recalled whether something within him argued restraint, or whether reason had already been drowned by desire. Regardless, he was responsible for the consequences.

When her belly grew, he was dumbfounded, as if that possibility had not occurred to him. "We must leave," Juana said, "before my father recants his promise to spare your life." He had been spared immediate execution, but he had not been spared punishment. Every day he still wondered whether Eduardo Rincon had known exactly what he was doing. From that day on, Pedro longed to be put out of his misery, but his wish was denied until long after Juana was gone.

Urging his daughter to end her mourning seemed useless, so he retreated. The dead can only leave this world by the consent of the living, and as Ramona would not release her, Juana instructed her daughter to let go.

"You must give up the black dress," Juana said to her.

"I cannot give up my love for you," Ramona responded.

"Then you must do what I ask," Juana insisted. "Your happiness is what I need."

"What will the world think of me if I forget you?"

"Is a black dress what reminds you of me? Your laughter and happiness is what will keep me from suffering."

That night, with tears in her eyes, Ramona took off the dress and stored it, never to wear it again. In the morning, she prepared breakfast and served the rest of the family; no one said a word about her return to regular garments.

Chapter 14

RAMONA WOULD BREAK into song as she worked around the house, or even in the street where she would forget herself and hum tunes as she walked in her unmistakable gait. On Sundays, she sang in the church choir at High Mass, the most enjoyable service of the day. Her voice so unique among the parishioners of Santa Isabela Church that the Reverend Friar Alfonso, the choirmaster, created solos for her where none had existed before.

Those who wanted aesthetic appreciation served along with their spirituality, as well as those who opted for distraction rather than brevity to get through the necessary ritual, appreciated the service and made it popular. As word of mouth spread Ramona's renown to other parishes, some traveled the extra distance to hear Ramona sing, on occasion creating standing room only at Santa Isabela. Fr. Alfonso took it as a sign of God's special favor that Ramona had been placed in his congregation. In street processions, he noticed that those near Ramona sang the most fervently.

Music permeated her body, and she didn't let her religious devotion interfere with dancing. A growing number considered that activity an invention of the devil, always ready to lead young people into sin, but Ramona needed no argument to justify her inclinations. When pressed, she explained that anything that bestowed such happiness through grace and beauty could only come from God. Whatever urges and impulses Ramona may have had beyond the aesthetic, she kept within the bounds of the dance. Human nature being what it is, not all those who danced with her, or who merely watched, enjoyed the dance merely as art. Some hoped to lure her into activities frowned upon by the high-minded and condemned by the righteous. Those young men soon found their efforts thwarted. Some bore their disappointment with good cheer. Having considered their chances no better than a baseball player's up at bat against a star pitcher, they remained content enough when they realized that she would only dance. Those who felt offended flaked away and avoided her, and that suited her fine. Those more serious, intending to propose marriage if she gave them the slightest opportunity, met the same fate as the others. She was not to be had at any price.

At the cigar factory where they both worked, Ramona and Maria Ortega sat at a long table with other women, the tobacco leaves stacked in front of them in neat piles. They removed the hard center stem of the leaf, the part that could not be rolled into a cigar. Carefully they cut on either side of the stem with a small knife and discard the stem in a straw basket behind them. Every two workers shared a basket. Always Ramona and Maria sat next to each other and used the same basket for their stems. Both dexterous with the knife, their basket filled quicker than that of any other two workers. When the basket overflowed one of them got up from the table and emptied it into a large barrel at the end of the row. The stems along with discarded leaves, those deemed unsuitable for cigars were to be shredded and used for cigarettes. That was done somewhere else. The barrels would be sealed, loaded into a truck and driven to the cigarette factory.

Enrique, the foreman, saw to it that everyone was supplied with leaves. He fetched them from the bales stacked in the next room, and he collected the leaves that had been trimmed and passed them on to be inspected for color and texture. They would be graded for different quality cigars, and the ones totally unsuitable would end up with the stems.

When Enrique got to Ramona's and Maria's end of the table he lingered making small talk to them about how fast they maneuvered the knife and how there wouldn't be enough tobacco to keep them busy if they kept working at such a furious pace.

"He likes you," Maria said to Ramona.

"No, it's you he hangs around for," Ramona responded.

"Not me," said Maria. "He knows I'm taken."

"That doesn't make any difference to him," Ramona said.

She didn't mind the attention, but Enrique was not for her. Though flattered, she looked for something more than charm. She affected indifference, having nothing to gain by allying herself with a man. She had enough men in her life. Since her mother's death four years before, Ramona had been obliged to care for her father and brothers as well as two younger sisters. She had stayed home and managed the household until her sister, Lola, was old enough to keep house with some semblance of order; then Ramona went to the tobacco factory to make sure that her two sisters had shoes to wear to school and that she herself had something decent to wear when she went to church on Sunday. She noticed that men seemed to be ignorant of those necessities. Money that would otherwise be spent on food and clothes they spent on drink. Ramona had stopped going to school before the fifth grade because she had no shoes to wear, and she would not go to school barefoot as some of the other girls did. She wanted to spare her sisters that dilemma.

"You've got to have fun some time," Maria said.

"I can have fun without men," Ramona retorted.

"What about your natural urges?"

"They're quite under control," Ramona said. She kept her comments on the subject under control too, because she did not want to seem judgmental of Maria whose natural urges were quite out of control with a married man.

"He can't marry you!" Ramona had exclaimed when Maria told her about Tomas.

"That doesn't matter," Maria said.

"How can it not matter?"

"I love him."

"He has children."

"That's why he has to stay with his wife, but he loves me."

"He can never marry you."

"That's all right, Ramona. That's all right."

Ramona did not see how that was all right, but it was not her place to judge. The Ortegas were a strange family, and perhaps that accounted for Maria's view of marriage. She carried the name Ortega although her father's name was Atorey.

"You know," Ramona said. "I don't understand these things."

"What's there to understand?" Maria rhetorically asked. "It's just love. I fell in love with Tomas and he with me. Why is that so difficult to understand?"

"There are plenty of other men," Ramona continued, "so why him?"

"Sometimes these things just happen," Maria said. "Some things are beyond our power to decide. That's all. We just have to adjust to what comes along."

"And no one objects?"

"Well, his wife is not as agreeable as I am. I'm completely willing to share, but she's very unhappy about the arrangement, or so I'm told."

"And is he the one who tells you her objections?"

"Whose side are you on? Would you rather that I be the one who suffers, give up the man I love?"

"I'm just trying to understand your ease with this setup."

The arrangement was common enough. Maria had merely

to consider the difference between her father's surname and her own. But the similarity between her relationship and that of her parents did not immediately strike her. She viewed her life as a unique expression of herself, and she saw nothing wrong with her love for Tomas.

"His sister, Inez, is on my side," Maria said. "As a matter of fact, she introduced us. So it's not as if the rest of his family is against me."

"I'm not against you either," Ramona assured her.

"Yes, I know," Maria conceded. "You're just trying to understand. Sometimes I wish I understood why I do what I do, and I don't, but I have to go with my feelings. Sometimes I dream that I'm on a horse that doesn't respond to my signals. I have no control over him. He decides where to turn and when to stop, but I'm always pleased at the end of the ride. So that's the way life is, I suppose. We're just along for the ride, and hopefully we'll be happy."

"I suppose you're right," Ramona said, although not quite convinced. Many things in the world were unexplainable, and so was Maria's relationship with Tomas.

Unlike Maria's other brothers, Juan was shy. He suffered from severe acne, which caused him to feel disfigured and consequently extremely self-conscious. Thinking himself ugly impaired his confidence and made his lack of social savvy more obvious. The ability to make small talk eluded him. He had installed in his mind a censor that scrutinized each thought and rejected all those that seemed banal, or useless, or self-evident. The conscientious censor greatly constricted his realm of possible expression. Trying to find an answer to the problem by observing others always at ease in conversation, he realized that the trick was to utter the most trivial thoughts with the same conviction as when saying something important. Knowing the cure and putting it into practice, however, were two different matters. Once in place, the censor was almost impossible to remove. Lulled to sleep in friendly company, it awoke to be an exemplary sentinel at the most inopportune moments.

Moreover, Juan did not dance. To him, it seemed that others acquired the skill without much effort, but to him it was an unsolvable mystery. He heard the music and it enlivened his spirit, but instead of freeing his body to move with the rhythm, it paralyzed him. His limbs became heavy and sluggish. The different parts of his body seemed disconnected. This ailment had spared his brothers, so he considered himself singularly unlucky. He despaired of ever getting a woman to give him a second look. They would all naturally want to be with someone who, even if not good looking, would at least sweet-talk them or sweep them off their feet on the dance floor.

On first seeing Ramona, her looks transfixed him. Maria had failed to prepare him beyond the most cursory admonition that Ramona's interest in men did not continue off the dance floor. When he thought rationally, attracting her seemed impossible, but his passion emboldened him.

"I can introduce you," Maria said, "but then you have to talk to her and not just stand there like a ninny."

"Sometimes words come and sometimes they don't," Juan said. "I can't predict when I'll be talkative."

Maria loved her brother, but she did not understand him, she never at a loss for words. "You mean your words are like the weather? You can't tell when it will rain? Sometimes you talk such nonsense."

"I have to try," Juan said. "I'll try my best."

"Even that may not be good enough," Maria said, "She's sworn off men. She's never been involved with anyone."

Juan met them the next day as they left the factory in the evening, and to Maria's surprise, he talked incessantly. When they got to the corner of Alegria Street, where Maria and Ramona usually parted, Juan continued on with Ramona, and Maria proceeded home by herself.

The next day Ramona said to Maria, "Your brother is very entertaining."

"He can be that," Maria cautiously said. She knew of the likelihood that the very next time Ramona encountered Juan his social disability would reemerge.

"Is he a good dancer?"

"He doesn't dance at all," Maria said, at a lost to say something in her brother's favor and deciding to be honest, since soon enough Ramona would discover Juan's idiosyncrasies.

"That's too bad," Ramona said, "but dancing isn't everything."

"I suppose not," Maria said, assuming that Ramona, given her general lack of concern for the feelings of her suitors, was only being polite.

Chapter 15

RAMONA AND MARIA often attended the Saturday
night dances at the Christopher Columbus Society, one
of several social clubs in San Geronimo. Soon after having
met Ramona, Juan informed his sister that he too would
attend the dance that Saturday night.

"You're becoming a dancer?" she asked.

"I certainly am," he said.

Maria noted that Ramona found him amusing. Perhaps
with her he would dance as much as he had talked. Possibly,
Ramona had the power to cure all of Juan's social ills. Had
not Maria heard him talk to Ramona as if that were the most
natural thing in the world for him? What if on the dance
floor he kicked up his heels as if he had been born to it? That
would be no greater miracle than his talking non-stop to a
woman he had just met.

"Juan is going to the dance," Maria informed her friend.

"I'll be pleased to see him there," Ramona earnestly said.
"Everyone will be there."

"He's going there to see you."

"Everyone will see me," she said. "I'll be in plain sight."

"Ramona, you must promise me you won't be mean to
him."

"Why would I be mean to him?"

"He will try to dance with you, and he'll make a fool of
himself. You mustn't laugh at him."

"I'm sure you exaggerate, and anyway he seemed
perfectly normal when he spoke to me the other day, except
for his face. It's too bad it's covered with scars the way it is.

He would be nice looking otherwise. I can't believe he's as terrible a dancer as you say. You worry too much about him. He's a man, he can take care of himself."

On Saturday night, revelers overflowed the Christopher Columbus Society hall. The band hired for the occasion was a particularly popular one, El Conjunto Orongoso. It had just returned from a tour of Cuba where they had picked up some innovative rhythms, soon to sweep the Caribbean before moving up to New York. Word of the new sound had preceded the arrival of Orongoso in San Geronimo, and the young people of the town eagerly awaited hearing it and seeing what could be done with it on the dance floor. The audience, however, was not limited to the young. The old folk enjoyed the music, though their old bones could not move with the vigor of the beat. Such a mixture of generations produced a considerable variation of opinion as to the relative merit of the new sound.

Although a preponderance of older folk considered *la dansa* the paramount achievement of popular music, they did not all hold that belief, some as ready to dance to a new beat as when they had first put on a pair of long pants, or rouged their faces. Likewise, some of the young championed *la dansa* as if they had been born before its inception. Not yet a society cleft by generational differences, at least, not in music, the boogie-woogie of the Americans had yet to catch on.

On that Saturday night, no one at the Christopher Columbus Hall in San Geronimo thought of the looming presence of the Americans, nor of the conflagration erupting in Europe. Juan had not yet figured out how to keep from making a complete fool of himself at the dance. He could go there and only observe, but then what would be the point of going? He would just torture himself watching Ramona dance with others. Still, that would be better than staying away.

"Juan, I'm going down to the dance now," Maria called out to him. "Are you going to walk with me?"

"No," he answered, "I'm not going until later."

In fact he would leave shortly after her, but he did not want to walk with her, because he knew that on the way she would meet up with Tomas de Arroyo, then he would have to walk with him also. He would be obliged to make conversation with Tomas, but he would be unable to think up anything polite to say, because all that would be on his mind would be the fact that Tomas was married and had no business meeting up with Maria. Juan, always uncomfortable in the presence of Tomas, wasn't sure whether he should befriend Tomas for the sake of Maria, or whether he should be protecting her from an unscrupulous seducer. A brother, supposedly, had to protect his sisters from unlawful advances, but in this case, Maria seemed to be the one in control and inviting the attention.

Tomas, a mild mannered person more shy than debonair, did not fit the description of the predatory womanizer against whom young women had to be protected. Juan, as he did in many other instances, looked to his older brothers for clues as to how he should behave in this case. They seemed to be ignoring the matter. They themselves had no clear guidance, Maria's position not too different from that of their parents. Their father, Federico, had abandoned his wife, Pepina. He had other children with whom he occasionally had contact, and he still cavorted with other women besides Julia.

The Ortega brothers, aware of their family history, didn't have a visceral aversion to transgressing the rules of monogamy. Juan's confusion arose from a strong desire to do the right thing for his sister. Overt hostility toward Tomas would only antagonize Maria, the sister who loved him the most and who strove to look after him, an effort he appreciated. On the other hand, befriending Tomas meant being an accomplice in an uncomfortable intrigue.

He chose the third and simplest alternative; he followed his brothers and ignored Tomas as much as possible without being offensively impolite. Tomas's equanimity simplified the matter. Pugnacity absent from his character, he refused to take offense. He understood the precariousness of his position.

For those reasons, Juan preferred to walk by himself to the Christopher Columbus Hall on the night when he would first dance with Ramona. Besides avoiding the conflict that the proximity of Tomas inevitably created, the solitary walk allowed him to consider aspects of the night that might have escaped him had he been forced to engage in conversation with Tomas. His mind lingered on how he might approach Ramona at the dance without embarrassing her or himself. He felt the cool night, that is, as cool as the tropics allowed, but as Juan had only experienced tropical nights, he had only other tropical nights to compare, and by that standard it was cool.

Other features of the night, besides the apparent mildness, seemed remarkable. Clarity in the air sharpened the outline of objects visible in the semidarkness of the moonlit sky. Those of an empiricist frame of mind will undoubtedly ascribe this quality, if they admit to it at all, to the effect of the full moon on the tropical atmosphere. Indeed, the fact cannot be denied that a splendid moon hung in the northern sky over San Geronimo. Down Alegría Street toward the center of San Geronimo, the town square graced at one end by the church of Santa Isabela, its bell tower, the highest structure in the town, could be seen clearly illuminated by the celestial sphere suspended right above it. The sight convinced Juan that he had never before experienced such a night, although a full moon appeared over San Geronimo as often as over anywhere else. He assumed the moon to be a good omen; so having the forces of nature on his side, if he failed, he could only blame himself.

This added pressure contributed to the outcome of the evening, which, sad to say, was not quite what Juan had expected. Perhaps he should have amended his original assessment when, emerging from Alegria Street to cross the plaza, a black cat ran across his path. He discounted the incident, reasoning that at night all cats appear black and that, the full moon notwithstanding, this cat may not have been black at all but only appeared so in the darkness. Moreover, Juan in general discarded that kind of superstition. He hardly noticed the cat, and the consideration of its color was but a fleeting thought occasioned by the popularity of that belief and not by a strongly held conviction. This is mentioned only to dispel any impression that Juan was superstitious, a reasonable possibility given all that he had noted about the propitious aspect of the night. The overwrought state of mind, due to his feelings about Ramona, made him prone to excesses otherwise foreign to his character. He did not believe his life to be at the mercy of unknown forces. Though aware of the occasional appearance of Luck and Fate in everyday affairs, he seldom considered them.

When he arrived at the Christopher Columbus Hall, the second story of a building on Avenida Humacao near the town square, everything looked as expected. On entering, the cheerfulness of the place overwhelmed him, the result, in no small part, of the bright yellow color of the walls, muted only by the blue trim woodwork around the doors and windows. A glass chandelier of respectable size hung from the middle of the ceiling adding to the festive appearance of the room. The décor, an attempt at elegance in imitation of the more opulent classes, executed with the verve of the less pretentious, achieved something unique.

Although the members and friends of the Christopher Columbus Society appreciated the place, to them its luster had been dulled by familiarity. The decor of a room had its limitations in creating the atmosphere of the festivity. The company assembled there would have been just as festive in a simpler place. Most of them had come for the music, though Juan had come for Ramona, but the music infected him too. It excited him, but it failed to make his limbs light, as it did others, indeed as it affected Ramona, already on the dance floor when he arrived.

To say that Ramona danced gracefully would be to misrepresent the totality of the effect she created. She moved gracefully, but one might be graceful and yet not be a dancer. When she danced she included more than her body. She defined not only the space she occupied but also the space for a considerable radius. Let us not misunderstand. She respected everyone else on the floor. She created no anxiety in anyone around her, since no one doubted her mastery of herself and of the space. Her form lingered in the mind of the observer longer than usual, as if space retained an impression of her image after she had ceased to occupy it. If a philosopher were to describe her, he might say that the dance found its ideal form in her and that, naturally, the mind is drawn to recognize the ideal and is reluctant to relinquish the pleasurable image. Whatever pleasure Juan found in Ramona's form he attributed to mundane causes rather than philosophical ones. Being in love sufficiently accounted for his sanguine behavior. He had made up his mind to forge ahead, to plunge in head first without hesitation, because delay would surely paralyze him, and he would end up gawking at her all night without saying a word. She would then think him a fool, and better to be thought a fool for some action than for the lack of it.

He had a plan, but circumstances conspired against him. He got there while she danced with Alberto Montoya, one of her rejected suitors who had opted to remain a friend if only to have a worthy dance partner, for he considered himself a virtuoso. Prudence kept Juan from cutting in on

Alberto, inviting ridicule by possibly striking a contrast in performance. Even if he were a passable dancer, the difference between the two would have been too great to go unnoticed. To be foolhardy was one thing and another to be foolish. He chose to wait, but he would have to wait for a long time. Alberto's reluctance to relinquish her persisted. No one made him look as good as she did, and though he could dance well with any number of others, he achieved brilliance most readily with Ramona. She, however, would not dance with him all night. The technical proficiency of his style bored her. She would rather dance with someone who was less accomplished but more intuitive, someone who might surprise her with emotion rather than entertain her with predictable glitter.

She got rid of Alberto, who quickly regrouping his forces sought out Inez, a partner who gladly took him on, surprised at his availability so early in the evening. Usually, she would have had to wait until Ramona became exhausted and Alberto willingly sought other partners.

"So, you tired her quickly enough tonight," Inez said to Alberto as he led her to the floor. She had made her availability obvious as soon as she realized that Ramona had declined to dance with him. "I'm all yours," she said.

"Are you?" he asked smiling as she fell into step.

A discussion about the upcoming elections for governor distracted Juan as he waited for a chance to approach Ramona. Most residents of Vista Alegre adhered to El Partido Popular's slogan "Bread and Land," two items difficult to do without, though unclear what exactly El Partido Popular would do about bread and land. Certainly not about to open a chain of discount bakeries, and as to land, the only way to ensure enough to go around would be either to enlarge the island or to strongly encourage birth control, the stranglehold of the Church making the former more feasible than the latter. The other party, the National Socialist, had a more difficult to understand philosophy, though just as easily stated: The Americans were to blame for everything. This idea would have been attractive enough had there been any visible Americans in Vista Alegre, but there were none. One would have to travel all the way to San Juan to see Americans sunning themselves on the beach, and that seemed a harmless enough pastime.

The ordinary people of Vista Alegre remained unaware of American companies that owned the pineapple and the sugar plantations that gobbled up the land. The few of them who had gone there for jobs did not see Americans. They saw other people like themselves who had jobs with pay, no one to fault there. The socialists talked about national pride, about independence, but if the island became independent, they would not be able to freely travel to New York, where one might get rich and from where relatives sent packages full of good things. The socialists did not think straight. Full of *disparates*—best to ignore them, except that they made a lot of noise, more noise than their numbers warranted. The one socialist at the Christopher Columbus Society dance that night had managed to distract Juan from his purpose just long enough to miss the moment when Ramona disengaged from Alberto Montoya. By the time Juan found her again, she was in the arms of old Vincente Avila.

If you ever had a problem, you could saunter over to the mango tree on the corner of Alegria and Comerio streets where every day, Vincente, known as everyone's grandfather, took possession of the wooden bench attached to the tree. He sat there for hours talking to anyone who came by, and dispensing advice on any subject likely to be of interest to a resident of Vista Alegre. He lived near that corner with his daughter, Isadora, the housekeeper at the rectory of Santa Isabela. He had been in his youth a great dancer, and still remained better than most, though age now restricted the scope of his movements. When he danced with Ramona one saw the remnants of the dancer he once had been. But his renown in Vista Alegre did not come from his dancing but from his having acquired the leisure to sit under the mango tree to dispense advice.

Pension plans unknown in Vista Alegre, you worked until you died or until you became so incapacitated that your relatives would take care of you. An anomaly at the time, Vincente Avila received a government pension. None of his neighbors knew what he had done to earn it, the one fact about his life that he would not disclose. When he had first retired and had begun to make his daily appearance under the mango tree, speculation had been rife about the possible source of his windfall. Obviously he, or someone close to him, must have been in some government service, but he had not been a postal worker, and no one remembered him ever being in the military or seeing him in any kind of uniform. What possible government service could he have qualified for without any formal education? As a matter of fact, he could barely write his own name, and when he needed a letter to be written, he would go down to the public notary, the town scribe.

Others speculated that his son, Ernesto Avila, had been in some government job and had passed away, leaving his father as the beneficiary of the pension. This theory, however, persisted as unverifiable, since no public record of the death of Ernesto Avila existed, if indeed he had died. His disappearance from San Geronimo was the only certifiable fact. Teofolo Perez, the notary, who had written the letters that Vincente had addressed to his son when Ernesto had first gone away, swore that he lacked any knowledge that would shed light on the matter. The letters had first been addressed to New York, then to Texas and lastly to Alaska. Thereafter, Vincente abruptly stopped writing to his son.

That's all the information that Teofolo claimed to

have, but no one knew whether he was holding back. As an unwritten principle of his profession, all the information that came to him by way of his work was confidential. One had but to glance at Teofolo to know that he took his responsibilities seriously. The most earnest-looking person imaginable, both tall and thin, his moustache drooped over the sides of his mouth creating a perpetually sad expression not dispelled by the erudite cast of the eyes that lurked behind wire-rimmed spectacles. Ironically, although words provided his livelihood, Teofolo had a laconic disposition. Always forthright but with as few words as possible, he often left the impression that he had not expressed everything on his mind. He exercised his profession in marked contrast expressing the thoughts of others in a voluble style, his letters known for their ornate wordiness, a style much admired at the time. Some cynics attributed the style to cupidity rather than aesthetics. They noted that Don Teofolo charged by the page, and that the simplest of communications might, under Don Teofolo's hand, stretch out for several pages.

Some of the blame for the prevalence of that style may be laid at the feet of teachers of literature and writing, who often, when they give a writing assignment, stipulate that the result must be a certain length. Impressionable students quite naturally conclude that the length of a piece of writing is an arbitrary quality dictated by something other than the requirement of the subject or scope of the author's intent. So if the student is required to write a ten-page essay but has only five pages of relevant information, he or she is compelled to fill the other five pages with extraneous material and as a byproduct may come to the conclusion that all essays must be at least ten pages long.

Don Teofolo in his youth, as a student, may have been subjected to such writing instruction, and having concluded that a respectable letter must be a certain length, he applied that principle ever since without regard to the pecuniary effect on himself or his clients. Some of the most illustrious authors of the past were paid by the word, and to say that so mundane a consideration shaped the principles of literary creation would be preposterous. The tendency to pad books with unnecessary details, or to stretch out descriptions beyond common decency, may have existed among lesser practitioners for the sole purpose of producing a volume that takes up more room on the shelf making it more noticeable to the casual browser in the bookstore. But Teofolo was not a writer of books, so he labored under no pressure to produce thick volumes for any purpose other than to satisfy the needs of his clients.

In deference to Vincente's age, Juan refrained from cutting in on him. He waited patiently for the dance to finish, then he made a dash for Ramona fearing that some other suitor would claim her before the band resumed playing. The only thing to do was to take her hand as if to dance with her, which was not what he had intended. He wasn't at all sure of what he intended, but before he could withdraw his hand from hers the music returned, and she was in dance position. He might have yet led her away to some quiet corner had he had the presence of mind to foretell what would happen next, which would have been clear to anyone who knew him and normally to him also. Perhaps the long wait to approach her had discomfited him; or perhaps, his unexpected success at conversing with her on their first walk led him to expect another miracle. If he could talk, why wouldn't he be able to dance? That was a perfectly natural expectation. Though the likelihood of lightning striking more than once in the same place is far greater than stated in the popular saying, the falsity of the statement did not in this case prove itself.

Had Juan been a religious young man he might have attributed the loosening of his tongue to the intervention of the Holy Ghost, a realm in which that divine entity is believed to be active and to whom Juan might have appealed to repeat a favor. There is nothing, however, in the scriptures that points to divine intervention in dancing, though it seems not too much of a stretch to suppose that a spirit able to animate the tongue might have a similar effect on other parts of the body. However, the events following Juan's seizing of Ramona's hand at the Christopher Columbus Hall pointed to a strict interpretation of biblical text.

Juan's limbs remained as leaden and uncoordinated as they had ever been. Lacking confidence in his ability to dance kept him from doing so at the moment when dancing would have done him the most good. He did not have to do a great deal. Ramona would have improvised to whatever he presented. All eyes would have been on her, and he might have gone unnoticed. To act on that reasoning required a more composed state of mind, or alternatively, a totally reckless one, such as had brought him to the execution of so desperate a plan in the first place. The follow-through faded, as if he had underestimated the amount of bravura that the whole enterprise required, and he had spent his total quota before reaching the critical moment. Whatever the reason, he faltered, and he was unable to recover with any grace.

Let us not make him out to be more of a sad sack than he really was. He did make an attempt. He took a few steps, but no sooner had he done so that the music became inaudible to him, and when he concentrated on the music, he completely forgot what to do with the rest of his body. Going through a whole dance in that manner was impossible, and so rather than embarrass Ramona any further, he scurried from the dance floor. In mid-step, the young lady was left in want of a partner, a problem that she had never before encountered. Juan had the impression, as he fled, that everyone in the room witnessed his humiliation, but in fact very few people saw his predicament. Most people didn't care whether or not he was a dancer. If they noticed, they soon forgot. Each person, including Juan, at the center of his own life, has difficulty believing that the public is unaware of all his triumphs and defeats. True that his behavior perplexed Ramona, and that Alberto Montoya had derisively remarked, as Juan brushed against him in haste to get away, "She's too much woman for you, isn't she?" The mighty, or those who think themselves so, are the most likely candidates for gossip and calumny, because there is, for good or for evil, a social tendency toward the leveling of those who give themselves airs, the bestowing of honors perceived as a prerogative of the community not to be usurped by individuals. For that reason alone, Juan would have been safe, but he failed to immediately see that.

Ramona had a different perspective. At first she thought she might have done something wrong, and she wanted to avoid blame for Juan's discomfiture, especially since she had promised Maria to be kind to him. Of course, that only meant that she would be as attentive to him as to everyone else. She had resolved to do that despite his supposed social gracelessness, which she had on good report from Maria, but which she had doubted, convinced that her friend exaggerated her brother's faults, though at a loss to know why. Ramona did not always bother with reasons nor needed to have every detail in place before being convinced of any truth. The matter fitting into her conception of the world sufficed. The reverse was also true, the problem in this case. She had failed to visualize anyone as socially inept as the Juan described by Maria. Besides, she had evidence to the contrary. She had spoken to Juan, and he had proven to be more amusing than most people she knew. Clearly, Maria had been wrong about his inability to hold up his end of a conversation.

Ramona followed the evidence of her own senses. She

might have been the child who saw that the emperor had no clothes. On the other hand, the world is not always as it seems, and one must make an imaginative leap to see what is behind the appearance. The sun, after all does not move across the sky, but rather the other way around. Where there is light there are bound to be shadows, and where something becomes clear something else may be obscured. In some ways the moon is kinder than the sun, for in the moonlight we are less likely to succumb to the temptation of believing that everything is clearly visible.

The full moon held its post over the bell tower of the church of Santa Isabela, and the glow of its light still diffused over the town square where Juan had fled to escape the supposed censure of his friends and neighbors and to where Ramona followed him without thinking of the impropriety of her action.

"Juan!" she called out.

He stopped, reluctant to turn around for fear of discovering that he had imagined the sound of her voice. He had mounted a campaign to win her over completely. He wanted to marry her. Regardless of what heights he might subsequently attain, getting her to agree would be the greatest achievement of his life. But at the moment, her following him into the plaza surprised him.

"Don't run away," she said.

"I can't go back."

"You must," she said, taking his arm. Her own action confounded her, but having made the first move bound her to continue the rescue. That action later became a bone of contention between them, because he identified that as the moment that assured success, but she always insisted on a more limited interpretation. She would contend until the end of her life that she had no design beyond that night and, even for that duration, a limited scope. She intended only to salvage his feelings and nothing else. From her point of view, whatever encouragement he took was wholly unjustified. As a Good Samaritan, her responsibility would end as soon as she delivered the ailing victim to a safe place. In this case, that proved problematic since safety largely depended on her presence. Nevertheless, she had difficulty seeing it that way though impossible for him to see it in any other.

He would always point to the ultimate outcome as validation of his belief, and she could justifiably say that no one could know her intention better than she did herself. She pointed to the subsequent five years as proof that her actions in the square had not the meaning he ascribed to them. He had not yet read psychology books, though he would later on his way to becoming an intellectual, an avocation that totally suited him. Even as a dishwasher in a New York cafeteria his intellectualism survived, though when young, in San Geronimo, it remained unnoticed until much later when his library became a source of notoriety due to Father Alfonso's unrelenting vigilance in his campaign against works on the Index of Forbidden Books. Knowledge of the unconscious did not lead Juan to discount what Ramona plainly told him, though he could have pointed out that her running after him that night revealed desires beyond those she admitted.

Chapter 16

FOUR YEARS ELAPSED after Fate, at the Christopher Columbus Society dance, assured him that he would marry Ramona Soto, but Fate failed to inform Ramona of that decision, and she refused to take Juan's word that the matter had been determined by a higher power. Believing that as long as he remained faithful to his belief everything would turn out as Fate intended, Juan took her recalcitrance as a test. He persisted in his argument and she in her refusal to see it his way.

"Juan, why do you make your life miserable. I am telling you I'm not for you," she repeatedly said to him.

"Why not?" he asked. "Who will love you more than I do?"

She had no answers to those questions. She had no one else in mind, though many approached her. More men paid attention to her than necessary for her to feel popular. Some frivolously sought to pass the time away; those she tolerated, but others more serious wanted her also to be serious; those made her life difficult, but none outdid Juan's persistence. How could she bring herself to tell him the truth? That he lacked good looks, that his dancing embarrassed her. How could she marry a man afraid to be social, except with her?

"Look for someone else before you get old," she said to him.

"We'll grow old together," he responded.

From the beginning, she felt a need to protect him as she had done at the Christopher Columbus Hall, but she had meant that as charity, something she would have offered anybody who needed help, even a stranger on the street.

Ramona complained to Maria, "Your brother doesn't take no for an answer."

Though her impish disposition thrived on situations stressful to others, Maria found herself in an awkward position between the two. Her gray eyes playful, she pretended to be concerned about Ramona's predicament. "You shouldn't flirt with him if you really don't want him to pant after you like a puppy," she said.

"Ay!" Ramona exclaimed, "That's not true, that I flirt with him. I don't treat him differently from anyone else."

She tried to remember whether she had given him any undue encouragement. Nothing could be further from her wishes than to entice Juan Ortega. In the first place, he was less than handsome. True, he was more educated than anyone else she knew. He read books. He told her beautiful stories he had read. The one about the man falsely accused and imprisoned wrenched her heart, such a beautiful story. Juan Ortega had told it with so much feeling as if he had lived it himself. She had listened attentively, enthralled by the tale. The stories, rather than Juan, interested her. How could he mean anything more to her than anyone else? He was so strange. He didn't dance, and he couldn't carry a tune even if his life depended on it.

The rest of the Ortegas were quite different, always the life of the party, always happy and ready to have a good time, maybe a little too much. Emiliano, the eldest Ortega brother, wavy blond hair and the blue eyes, a strange bunch, the Ortegas, even in their coloring, he behaved the wildest—Emiliano, an Ortega through and through, the one most like the old man, Federico that is, if not in his looks, in his attitude and in his way with women. Emiliano had no compunction against cutting in on his younger brother, and Ramona could feel the heat of his gaze, a look with an unmistakable meaning. A girl could have a good time with Emiliano Ortega, and why not just for a lark, but that's all it could be with Emiliano, because for anything else he would be unreliable. "That one is just like his father," everyone said, and Ramona had no doubt of that. Not the kind of man she wanted, her mother had warned her about such men.

At first, her brothers seemed on her side on her refusal of Juan. "When you marry, marry a real man," they said to her. But she saw through them also; they feared her leaving them, before they had women of their own to keep house.

"We'll take care of him for you," the eldest of her three brothers said.

"You stay away from him," she responded.

"As long as he stays away from you," he countered.

"This is not your concern."

"You're my sister," he insisted claiming duty above everything else.

Juan tried to see Ramona every Saturday night, and over time his attempts became more successful. One night, her brothers arranged to ambush him before he reached the house in his usual attempt to see her. Now, though she did not admit it, she expected and looked forward to his arrival and casual conversation disguised her real feelings. She kept an eye on her brothers, and on the night of their plan, though they attempted to keep it from her, she sensed that they were up to something. Their movements beyond her control, she resolved to warn Juan if she could find him before her brothers did.

"I'm going out," she said to her father, Pedro Soto, sitting on the porch, as he did every night, a cigarette between his lips, and his eyes fixed on a point of interest to no one else.

He looked at her but remained silent as if uninterested in her movements. That mood had overcome him slowly after Juana had died, and nothing Ramona did in her attempt to rescue him had succeeded. Occasionally, she managed to divert him from his dark memories. She urged him to attend church to listen to her sing in the choir. For a long time he refused, but unexpectedly he turned up one Sunday and remained in a cheerful mood for the rest of the day, but sunset revived his dark mood.

She descended the front steps of the house ignoring the figure sitting in the porch. Once in the street, she let her feet decide which direction to take. As when she danced, they knew what to do without conscious guidance. She might have tried to find her brothers and shame them into retreating from their selfish intent, but she chose instead to try to warn Juan before he ventured out. She took shortcuts from one street to another traversing the backyards of the neighborhood without stopping to chat with those who stepped out to greet her. They wondered why she hurried, but knowing her good nature, no one questioned her, responding only with a wave. She reached the Ortega house to be greeted by a surprised but happy Maria who thought Ramona's appearance a joke on Juan who had just left to see her.

"I must warn Juan," Ramona said trying to catch her breath while explaining her unexpected visit.

"So you came to tell him you wouldn't be there to greet him, since you'd be here to warn him of your absence," Maria said, now intrigued.

"No, that my brothers are waiting for him."

"Men have a great deal of fun together," Maria said, who, being entranced by the expectation of humor, failed to note the panic in Ramona's voice.

"Oh, he's gone," Ramona lamented. Again, she let her body rather than her mind decide what path to follow in pursuit of him. At the moment, she would have been unable to explain her choice of streets and alleys, never having discussed with Juan the usual route he took to her house, nor it being the most popular way from the one place to the other. Her instinct on this occasion became another matter about which they would never agree. "You knew where I always got the flowers I brought to you," he would argue. But she had no recollection of the flowers as her feet chose what route to follow. Although a person for whom logic had minimal value, this time the flaw in his explanation surfaced like a cork in water. "Flowers are available in many places," she responded.

By Angela Rivera's garden, she saw him as the old woman handed him the flowers. "Juan," she exclaimed.

He turned surprised to see the woman he loved in a place he did not expect, but something else astounded him. For the first time he saw her face devoid of any resistance to his wish for a life together.

"I found you," she said.

"A long time ago," he responded still ignorant of what she meant.

Chapter 17

IN JOINING THE ARMY, Juan exhibited a habitual impulse to follow his brother Emiliano. Besides, he needed to ensure an income before making the leap and asking for Ramona's hand. He worked at the docks for a while, but although he was used to heavy work, being a stevedore was more extraneous than he expected.

Emiliano's enlistment made the American army seem an ideal employer, though Emiliano himself remained unsure of why he had signed up. On the surface, the reason stemmed from having lost a bet made while out drinking with his friends. They would have forgotten by the next day, and only in jest anyone recalling would have pressed for payment, but Emiliano took the bet seriously.

"Jesus," he said to his wife, Rosamaria, the next day while still suffering from a headache, "I have to join the army."

"Don't joke like that," she responded.

"I'm not kidding," he said, "I have to enlist."

He went down to the recruiting office in San Geronimo and signed up.

On returning home, he had to deal with Rosamaria.

"What will I do without you?" Rosamaria asked between sobs and tears absent since their wedding day.

"The training camp is close to San Geronimo, and I'm sure I'll get weekend passes to see you. Move in with my parents while I'm gone."

Emiliano's action imbued the American army with a mysterious attraction for Juan, who often imitated his brother.

"So it's a good idea, this going into the army?" Juan asked Emiliano, anticipating a positive answer.

"As good as it gets," Emiliano said in jest, already doubting the wisdom of what he had done.

"You must be right," Juan said.

"Sure, you get a rifle and a bayonet and best of all a good pair of boots. How much better can you do?"

"Good boots are hard to get," Juan concurred. The next day he went to the recruiting station.

Two sons in the military drove Julia beyond distraction. Indeed, when Emiliano announced his decision, the possibly ill consequences of having a son in the army in time of war escaped her, Emiliano always seeming immune from danger. She had no doubt that he would survive. Juan, on the other hand, in everyday life lacked the traits of a fighter. In a war, he would be much worse off. In town, the Americans displayed posters depicting German ferocity, and going in the other direction seemed even worse. She knew some people with German names, and they looked no different from anyone else, but she had never laid eyes on an Asian, and the boys might end up fighting the Japanese in the Pacific.

"How could you do this?" she screamed at Juan. "Don't you have any sense?"

"You haven't said anything to Emiliano," he answered sheepishly.

"Emiliano is a man," she uttered, her voice still in high volume.

He kept quiet fearing to arouse her more than necessary.

"Your father will have to go down to the recruitment office and get them to tear up your papers."

"They won't do that," he said, but he feared the possibility of ending up embarrassed and humiliated, unable to stroll in the town square without being the target of ridicule.

"We shall see what we shall see," she said, fearing that her husband would again behave contrary to her expectations. Verging on revealing to herself the true nature of Federico's character and confronting his incidental management of the family's welfare, she began an immediate retreat from her automatic expectations. The limiting of demands on Federico became increasingly necessary in order to keep disappointment and the contradictions of her unconditional love for him from becoming unbearable burdens. The suspicion that he would have no objection to Juan's following Emiliano made her distance herself from her son rather than from her husband. Indeed, Federico showed no reluctance to support the action of both boys, proud to be the father of soldiers, even in an American army, although he and his sons had no sense of being Americans. On hearing the news of their enlistment, he congratulated them and took them out on a drinking spree to show them off as real men. If he saw the difference between his two sons, on this occasion, he ignored it.

Lying in the army cot, a cigarette to his lips, Juan thought about the time his father had made him go out in the dark.

"Juan, go out there and check that corral gate is shut," Federico had said, as Juan sat motionless on the bench, just a child afraid of the dark.

"I'll go check," Emiliano said.

"You stay right where you are," Don Federico said.

"I don't mind going," Emiliano said.

"Juan is going," Don Federico said. "If he's got balls, he's got to act like it."

In the dark, frightening images appeared. The fact that if anything had really been there, it would have been impossible to see it in the dark did not occur to Juan. He checked the gate, and it was locked. He had made the trip for nothing, and just before he walked through the door back into the house he wiped the tears from his eyes. The next day the corral door wide open, the horse was gone. Having no way to prove that he had checked the gate, fear gripped him.

"I'm going to get it now," he said to Emiliano.

"I suppose you are," Emiliano said.

He waited for his father, who returned from the corral smiling. Juan wondered how his father could enjoy the prospect of beating him. "It was locked last night. I'm sure," Juan said, hoping that his father would believe him when he perfectly knew that his word wasn't enough.

"You're a lucky fellow," Federico said.

"You'll spare me?"

"I followed you last night. I checked the gate myself."

"How do you suppose it flew open?"

"The devil knows," Federico said and laughed.

Yes, Federico laughed, and Juan looked at Emiliano who also laughed, happy that his brother had been spared. Only later did Juan, beginning to put things together, imagined Emiliano, after everyone had gone to sleep, sneaking to let the horse out, getting even with his father for having made Juan venture into the darkness.

Juan wondered whether his mother had been right about army life. Not quite what he had expected, the weeks of physical adjustment, running and marching were more strenuous than work in the tobacco fields had ever been. He ate better, but he had to develop previously unnoticed muscles.

"All right, everyone up," the sergeant shouted into the tent before reveille.

"I don't hear the bugle," Juan said, believing that his hearing had been damaged by the physical strain endured since he had arrived at camp. He doubted hearing the sergeant's voice, or rather, he heard the voice, but he questioned its reality assuming that he was having a nightmare.

The sergeant bent over Juan's head and shouted in his

ear, "There's no bugle necessary today. Do you hear me, Private Idiot?" Juan's spine became rigid and the upper part of his body popped up like a jack-in-the-box.

"Yes sir, Captain," he automatically said, neither seriously nor humorously intending to promote the sergeant. An inner demon, bent on pushing him into difficult situations for the amusement of others, caused the phrase to emerge automatically.

The sergeant interpreted Juan's reaction as a rib. "You promoted me," the sergeant hissed gritting his teeth, "but you, I'm going to demote, if you, being already at the bottom, can imagine that, and I'm not going to tell you right now what you're going to have to do. I'm going to let you wonder about it while you do the morning drill."

The interchange between Juan and the sergeant happened before Emiliano was sufficiently awake. Normally, he would have kept his mouth shut and approached the sergeant later, in private, to reasonably explain his brother's quirks, but being yet drowsy, he blurted in Juan's defense. "He didn't mean to insult you, sergeant, really. Sometimes he's too nervous to say the right thing."

"Maybe that quirk runs in the family," the sergeant retorted, "and to cure the two of you, you'll share the penalty. You both report back to me after the morning drill. Okay, now everyone out, your packs empty," the sergeant said to the whole group.

Morning exercises with empty packs an unexpected bonus, many of the men failed to suppress a smile. The good feelings soon banished on arriving at a mound of rocks to fill their backpacks. Moaning emerged from the group but the sergeant ordered them to be silent, to imagine the enemy close by and for safety try to avoid attracting attention. Once they had the backpacks filled and on their backs, they fell into a steady trot, the sergeant along with them, but of course, he carried no backpack. The first two miles of the silence required an extreme effort on the part of the men, but after that, the situation became the reverse, and to utter a sound became an extra burden, the men glad to forgo it. The sergeant, on the other hand, had a different idea. Having noticed the men now glad to be silent, he ordered them to sing.

"This is too much for me," Juan said.

"You're all right," Emiliano assured him. "You'll make it all right, don't worry."

"My muscles and my bones don't want to stay together."

"I'll carry you if I have to," Emiliano assured him, praying that his words would keep his brother going. Fear of becoming a physical burden to Emiliano kept Juan on his feet. He survived the morning exercise with the full pack of rocks as well the cleaning detail to which the sergeant assigned them later in the day in payback for the morning confusion.

Sometimes the sergeant was less unpleasant.

"All right, Private Ortega, let's see you do what you're supposed to," the sergeant shouted. He was in a good mood that day.

Juan ran the bayonet into dummy, but instead of dust spilling through the ripped cloth, he saw blood flowing from the straw.

"All right, Ortega, so you didn't get enough sleep last night, but now you're on the field so wake up. The dummy isn't going to move, not going to hurt you, but on the battlefield it won't be a dummy waiting for you. It'll be a Kraut or a Jap ready to kill you. You get that? You have to get him first, before he gets you. It's that simple, Ortega. You get what I mean? It's either you or him. So now let's see you do it right."

Juan retreated to the starting point, and again charged.

"It's a goddammed Kraut," the sergeant shouted as Juan ran, but the image of a man persisted. "You'd be dead by now, Ortega. Is that what you want? Now, you keep doing this till you get it right."

The sergeant moved on to the next man, and Juan tried to figure out how to get angry at the dummy instead of seeing it as a helpless man. Maybe putting the sergeant's face on it would do it. He tried, but he couldn't bring himself to hate even the sergeant, not that much anyway. He did better on the firing range.

"There you go," Emiliano said to him. "You have a talent."

Praise from his brother was boost enough for Juan. He wanted to be as dashing as Emiliano, and if the army made Emiliano happy, Juan expected it to do the same for him. Indeed, Emiliano seemed happy wherever he went and with whatever he did; being a soldier no exception. He easily adapted to the hardships of training. Though as tired as everyone else at the end of the day, he remained upbeat, and the slightest incentive swung him back into activity. A source of cheerfulness, whenever in need of a boost of spirit, the group turned to him. He never nursed a grudge, not even against the sergeant. The terror of battle still unforeseen, he nevertheless understood the necessity of every act. He took life as it came without blaming himself for consequences beyond his control. He took chances willingly, because he was certain that the ultimate result would be the same regardless of the risk. The style came to him naturally without consideration or regret. Being a trickster, an irrepressible impulse with no intended malice, he never resented being the target of someone else's humor.

"Jesus, man, you're not going to play tricks on the sergeant, are you?" asked his friend, Trinito, who vividly imagined the consequences.

Emiliano's face broke into a grin.

"You'll live to regret it."

"I can't miss an opportunity to make you laugh," he said winking at his companion who was torn between the expectation of humor and the fear of the consequences.

"Will you be laughing in the stockade?"

"All of life is a chance," Emiliano retorted. "Laughter is the way to bear it." The words rolled off his tongue without much thought. "I'll tell you what, my friend," Emiliano said. "What if I make it worth your while? When I get away with it, you buy me a bottle of Palo Viejo, and if I don't, of course, you'll be the one to receive the consolation."

"You'll be the one who needs it."

"Perhaps, but in the stockade there'll be a restriction," he asserted with a laugh.

Playing a trick on the sergeant required some luck as well as talent. A stunt away from base would be simpler, but getting leave at the same time as the sergeant would be almost impossible, and besides, playing a joke on him without a military audience would be meaningless.

"You know," said Trinito, "the sergeant goes to the latrine after dark every night about the same time."

"The question is whether anyone goes there right after him."

"Probably not, at least for a while."

"Well, there's a situation worth considering," said Emiliano.

"What? Going in after him?"

"Not for a while," said Emiliano.

"Keep him in there?"

"I haven't said a word," Emiliano responded.

Secretly obtaining a beam from the wood shop to bar the door was simple enough. While some stood on lookout, other members of the platoon transported the beam from the wood shop to a spot near the latrine. At the expected time, the sergeant made his usual trip. Once the sergeant entered the latrine, Emiliano and his accomplices rested one end of the beam against the door and secured the other end on the ground.

The sergeant's activity in the outhouse took longer than expected.

"*Que jodienda*," Emiliano said, "he takes a long time in there."

"I wonder what he's doing," Trinito said.

"He's playing with himself. He can't do it in his own barrack; everyone else would hear him."

"You think that would upset the lieutenant?"

"Who knows? I heard he's a defrocked priest."

The sergeant began to bang on the latrine door, thinking it merely stuck fast. Shortly, he realized his predicament. His anger dredged up the predictable verbiage, and the men then had the task of muffling the sound of their laughter. Luckily for the pranksters, no one who would come to the sergeant's rescue heard his initial outbreak. His eruption subsided while he thought out the matter. If he continued shouting, he would arouse many people, increasing his humiliation. Only one or two persons might be responsible for the prank, and their claim to having achieved it might be considered dubious if no one else saw it.

On the other hand, his tormentors might have arrived at that conclusion themselves and at the moment might be fetching an audience to ensure their notoriety. The difficulty overwhelmed his reason, and he again burst into a rage producing a string of loud curses and threats directed at anyone within hearing. In fact, the audience for his outbursts had grown; some men, having come out to the latrines for natural reasons, had returned to their bunks to spread the word. The sergeant's carrying on brought a quicker resolution to his crisis, as the increase in commotion brought out another sergeant causing everyone to scatter and ensuring the release of the captive.

Sergeant Bonilla, the victim, would have kept the matter out of the hands of anyone in higher command, finding and punishing the culprits himself, but on hearing about the incident Lieutenant Rodriguez suspended all leave passes for companies on Sergeant Bonilla's side of the camp. Emiliano turned himself in to spare his companions the loss of their passes.

"Who else was involved?" Lieutenant Rodriguez asked. He was a man much interested in ascending the ranks and going down in history as one of the first Puerto Ricans to acquire a significant command in the American army; a very small number of Puerto Ricans at the time ranked above sergeant. He recognized having some common traits with Emiliano, and though unwilling to show it, he appreciated the humor of the situation.

"Just me, sir. I was alone."

"That log was too heavy for one man to carry."

"I dragged it all the way, sir."

"Your brother must have helped you."

"No sir, my brother slept through the whole thing. You can ask anybody."

Indeed, Juan had slept through the whole incident. Having missed the chance to participate in the undertaking, on hearing the story the next day, he became sullen.

"Well, anyone who knows he wasn't there must have been there himself," the lieutenant reasoned out loud.

"No sir, they didn't leave the tent all night."

"So you're willing to take the whole punishment by yourself."

"Yes sir, I did it all."

"I'll double it then," the lieutenant said and left it at that.

Juan went home on leave while Emiliano was in the stockade.

"You brought candy for me?" Rosamaria exclaimed despite the lump that formed in her throat the minute she saw Juan by himself.

Juan had bought three boxes of chocolate candy—one for his mother, one for Ramona, and one for Rosamaria. "It was Emiliano's idea," Juan said handing a box to his mother and another to Rosamaria. Julia retreated to the kitchen where she placed the box in a cabinet where it would become a forgotten object.

Juan, looking Rosamaria straight in the eyes attempted to reinforce his lie. "He gave me the money and told me to be sure to get something you like."

"I love chocolate," Rosamaria said.

"It won't taste as good to you as Emiliano, but it's a close second."

They both laughed, and Juan noticed something different about her. Afraid to overstep his bounds, the question came to his face but failed to transform into words. His lips failing to move produced only a vague expression. No one else in the family would have hesitated to question Rosamaria, but the question only displayed itself on his face.

"Why are you looking at me like that?" she asked, her smile persisting.

He had no answer readily available, and her constant cheerfulness puzzled him.

"Don't be shy," she said. "I do have a secret."

"Ah, well I need not pull it out of you."

"It's not much work to do so," she said. "It wants to jump out on its own."

"There's a whole house of people to tell," he said, sensing that to know something kept from everyone else would be a burden. He might be able to keep a secret from his brothers and sisters but not from his mother. His father also was entitled, by custom, to know everything about the women who lived in his house, though legally Julia owned the house, having obtained it with the proceeds of selling the one inherited from Arturo Ortega.

"I can't tell them," she said, "before I tell Emiliano. He's got to be first."

"Well, then you have to wait a month. That's not too long."

"I don't mind telling you," she said, "as long as you keep it to yourself."

"Better to wait for Emiliano. Sometimes my mouth moves without my wanting it to," he honestly said wanting to avoid any responsibility for adding difficulty to any of her problems. For what else could it be but a problem, if she had first to confer with Emiliano?

"I'm going to have a baby," she said.

"Someday, after the war, we'll all become parents," he said, following a line of thought he had explored with Ramona.

"I'm pregnant now," she said. The words had a more apparent effect on her than they did on him, for she sobbed and tears suddenly sprouted.

Surprised by her words, Juan took her tears to be the result of a misinterpretation of his reaction. "No, don't cry. It's great to be a mother. I didn't mean anything else."

"Emiliano is going off to the war. What if he doesn't come back?"

"Ah, don't cry," he said, "We'll never get to the front. The rumor is that we're going to Panama to guard the canal. We'll never see an enemy. That's why we volunteered. We'll be gone for a little while, and we'll be back soon enough. You have nothing to worry about."

With the back of her hands she wiped her eyes. "Everything will be all right," she echoed.

"Listen," Juan continued, "you don't have to wait a month to tell him what's happening. I'm going back to camp tomorrow, and you can come with me to see Emiliano. He can't leave the base, but you can see him. Many women come to the camp to talk to their husbands through the fence. He's anxious to see you, and he'll be happy to hear about the baby."

Knowing his brother to be unpredictable and lacking the habit of considering the consequences of his actions, Juan had no idea what Emiliano's reaction to the news would be. Juan's habit of examining things more closely made him wonder how Emiliano, in a world full of contradictions, managed to dispose of worry, if not by abandoning responsibility. Ruminating on those matters, Juan arrived at Ramona's house in a somber mood, the flowers failing to elicit the joyous spontaneity they had conveyed earlier in the day. In the years of courtship, Ramona had grown accustomed to his meditative moods, but this time he shared his concern without being coaxed.

"Emiliano will be happy," Ramona assured him, "Why would he marry if he didn't want to have children? He loves her."

"It seems to me that she isn't sure," he said.

Only women idealized love. Men endured it, the same as they did some virus with no remedy. Love would pass; it would die, just as sooner or later a virus did, but with no way to assure tolerable results, the consequences of the illness persisted. Had his feelings for Ramona fallen under scrutiny in the context of this argument, he would have been forced to push himself down further in the realm of his self-esteem. He considered his difference from other men in his family mostly a detriment, but in this case he took it as an advantage. His love for Ramona something other than what his brothers expressed for their own women. He had won her over after many years, and now he had to find a way to keep her happy forever.

"He married her," Ramona said. "Give him credit for that."

"I promised to take her to break the news to him."

"To give him the good tidings, you mean."

"Yes, that's what I mean," he said.

That weekend, he spent as much time as possible with Ramona knowing that he would have to be back in camp before reveille Monday morning.

Yes, he remembered having a good time that weekend before going back to the base, but he would always remember more vividly the day after.

"It's hot," Trinito had said looking up at the sun and pointing his rifle up into the air. "Bang!" he said and laughed. The heat of the day extreme, the sun made an extra effort as if competing for a prize. The camp tents, erected on wooden platforms, had their sides rolled up to let the breeze flow through and keep them from becoming ovens.

"Yeah, you're always good at what you do," said Emiliano.

"Make believe is always good," Trinito said.

"You're right," Juan said. "I feel cooler already."

"Do I hear thank you?" Trinito said.

"You're both crazy," Emiliano said. He had cleaned every part of his weapon and was now reassembling it.

"No kidding, I feel cooler already," Juan said.

"Good," his brother answered, "be cool."

"You sound cool enough," Juan said.

"He's like ice," Trinito said.

"I'm all right," Emiliano said. "I'm going to be a father."

"And that takes away heat?" Trinito asked.

"A cool guy is a cool guy," Juan said to join in ribbing his brother.

"You guys can laugh all you want," Emiliano said, "I'm on top of the world."

"Geography is not your strong point," Trinito said.

"Whatever you say," Emiliano retorted, pointing his weapon at the floor as he looked down to check the alignment of the barrel.

Emiliano's exuberance at hearing the news of his wife's condition relieved Juan, who had feared a negative reaction from his brother, but able to restrain the need to know the reasons for his own feelings, he postponed seeking an answer.

"You guys done with your guns?" Emiliano asked.

"Clean as a whistle," Trinito said. "I use spit on mine."

"You're going to have to take it home with you, then, when you're discharged."

"That'll be a prize," Trinito said. "What are you taking home?"

"Just the bayonet," Emiliano said. "That's all I need."

"So you're a knife man," Trinito said.

"He's always been a nice man," Juan said.

"Yeah, that's what I meant," Trinito said. He and Juan laughed.

"You guys are too much for me," Emiliano said.

"It's the heat," Juan said. "We don't take it as well as you do."

"There nothing anybody takes to as well as I do," Emiliano said.

"Well, that may be true," Trinito said. "We'll see how your son takes to you."

"A son will take to him well," Juan said.

"What about a daughter?"

"Well then, that's a different matter."

"That's for sure."

"Well, we shall see what we shall see, won't we," Emiliano said.

"We'll see Panama first," Trinito said.

"That's true. We'll be gone for a while. The baby will be born while we're away."

"Well, right now I'm away to the outhouse," Juan said, placing his weapon in the rack in the middle of the tent.

"Do well on your mission," Trinito said, his weapon still in his hands.

"Check out your work before the sergeant comes by to inspect," Emiliano said.

"I'm all right," Juan said as he walked out to the latrine.

"I meant Trinito," Emiliano said.

"I'm all right too," Trinito said.

"Sure you are," Emiliano said.

On reaching the door of the latrine, Juan heard the shot. He laughed, imagining Trinito humorously trying to deny the fear of a weapon going off so close to him away from the firing range. His hand on the door of the outhouse, Juan heard Trinito scream for help. "My God," Juan, alone by the latrine, said to no one in particular, "he shot off his toes, what an idiot!"

"I didn't mean to do it," Trinito screamed. "Don't let him die."

Juan ran back to the tent, arriving just in time to see his brother's final spasm.

Emiliano's death made life in the service unbearable, and given the option of an immediate and honorable discharge, Juan gladly accepted. For Ramona, resistance to Juan's amorous advances for years had been a clear necessity, just as her change of course, when it came, seemed to her a natural event. He and Ramona had agreed that they would marry at the end of his enlistment, and the time arrived before they expected.

"We don't need a feast," he said.

"Yes, that's true," she said.

But he saw that she would be unhappy to marry without including everyone in the celebration.

"We'll have to wait, then, until I have a job that pays enough," he said.

The prospect of that seemed far off. When would he work to earn that much money? What would he do? She knew that there must be a hidden answer to those questions, and the waiting continued, but Don Pedro's and his sons' objections at the beginning of the courtship transformed into a positive push.

"The courtship has lasted a long time," Don Pedro said to her.

"Time is not the same for everyone," she answered.

The meaning of her words escaped him as he looked down at the cracks between the floorboards hoping a clue would emerge to rescue him. The wait futile, he decided to honor his daughter and wait for an explanation she would provide sooner or later. How much later was the question. Her brothers too became restless, but she could not talk about money with them, a subject that made them squirm and upset her father.

"There was once money to be had," Romiro said.

"We should ask for it now to pay for Ramona's wedding," said his brother.

"When your mother and I walked off that land we gave up any rights to it," said Don Pedro. "Do not talk of it anymore."

The two sons had no desire to torture their father, yet they would never understand his reasoning on the matter of their mother's inheritance, which they were never to see.

"In any case," said Don Pedro, attempting to ease himself of guilt in denying his children any possible relief from the consequences, "divided between all your aunts and uncles it would come to very little, not worth the trouble. Your mother and I gave up any rights to that land when we walked away."

"Did you walk away?" Romiro asked gazing at his father, who turned his head to look at the blankness of the wall.

"I gave up what I had," Don Pedro said having turned again to face his sons. "And besides, to go after it now would be an insult to your mother's memory. We must make it on our own."

"And will Ramona not have a wedding?"

"Time will tell," said Don Pedro, for whom waiting was reasonable enough. He had no answer to the problem. "Something will come up," he said to his sons. In this matter, they saw no option but to follow their father.

Chapter 18

Altamiro Ramirez, in a rag tunic donned once a year for the occasion, descended the steps. The tincture of his face naturally black, only people close to him noticed the smeared charcoal. Those participating in the procession, as well as many there only to observe, had gathered in front of his house, the yearly event having become a neighborhood custom. Many considered Altamiro's relationship with the next world something to admire. Others merely saw an interesting figure providing a day of entertainment. He welcomed everyone to take part whether or not they shared his beliefs. Though by tradition a Catholic, the performance of his yearly ritual evoked something else. Some who lined the streets to watch him thought him comical, but the ritual fulfilled a need of many inhabitants of Vista Alegre.

All those who participated in Altamiro's yearly procession gathered in front of his house already wearing costumes. Most people supplied their own while still complying with the requirements set by Altamiro, but he provided costumes and props for those who needed them. No one attempted to deny him his position as the prime mover of the event he had initiated as a yearly performance, and though everyone who participated had a personal need to do so, Altamiro's role as the central character remained essential to the occasion. Almost everyone else who took part in the procession represented some figure who had suffered martyrdom, except for those dressed as angels to represent the ultimate achievement.

Altamiro walked to the middle of the street, and after

performing the sign of the cross, accompanied by all the other participants as well as some of the onlookers, he knelt to begin the journey from his house to the cemetery. Less than halfway to his destination, his knees would begin to bleed. But he uttered no expression of pain, the recitation of the prayers the only sound that emanated from his mouth.

Unable to watch Altamiro suffer, on seeing him fall to his knees, Ramona turned her head and retreated into the house. In the kitchen, she filled a bottle with water and buttered a loaf of *pan sobao*, which she would take to the cemetery to await Altamiro's arrival. He would be thirsty then, and hungry too, having fasted since the day before. He would only take a sip of the water and a bite of the bread, but he always looked at her with gratitude.

"What do you get out of this?" her brother, Romiro, asked her as she put the bread and the water bottle into the straw bag to carry to the cemetery. Even after years of having watched her take that small part in the ritual, her brothers, though they had grown accustomed to it, did not understand why she persisted. "You throw away a loaf of bread."

"I bought it with my own money," she said.

"What do you get in return?"

The overwhelming absurdity she saw in Romiro's mocking dissolved as she realized that were she in his place she might construe her action to be as ridiculous as he thought. "I cannot explain," she answered. She followed her own impulses without qualm, and she left her father and her brothers to wrestle with their own emotions about Altamiro's ritual.

After the procession to his wife's grave and having performed the prayers that concluded the religious part of the event, Altamiro rose to his feet to make his trip home, but the custom had become to carry him home rather than to let him walk. So, some of the men who took part in the procession had Altamiro, still dressed in rags and his knees bleeding, sit upon a litter, and raising its bars to their shoulders, transported him home like an ancient Roman noble. Back at his house the atmosphere of the day had a change in tone; what had been an exhibit of pain became one of joy; food and drink had been prepared to celebrate the return of the procession.

After she had presented Altamiro with the bread and the water, and he smiled at her with the usual gratitude, she had retreated to her own place of personal interest in the cemetery, the grave of Juana Soto Rincon. She wondered what her mother was presently doing in the place where they would some day meet again. Juan Ortega's voice startled her, the sound of his approach having been muffled by her intense thoughts.

"You didn't tell me you would be here," she said.

"I had forgotten what day this is," he answered. Indeed, that day he had walked to the cemetery for a different reason than everyone else's.

"You forgot Altamiro?" she asked without implying a wrongdoing. She knew well enough that the Ortega family had yet to absorb the customs of Vista Alegre.

"I came to visit my brother's grave," he said.

"I know," she answered.

"I failed him," he said. "I always come to ask his forgiveness, but I get no answer."

"He has no answer, Juan, since the question makes no sense. His death was beyond your control, and he knows that. He cannot understand why you have taken on such a burden. He always thought you too intelligent to do so. If anything, what you're doing will make him uncomfortable, since he will feel responsible for your suffering although he isn't, and there is nothing he can do about it."

"It may be that you're right, but what am I to do?"

"You must live your life."

Ramona urged Juan to accompany her back to Altamiro's, and Juan reluctantly agreed, feeling somewhat guilty that he had forgotten about the event. As the couple stood in the living room, Altamiro came up behind them and put his arms around their shoulders, the glee in his face difficult to explain given the condition of his knees. People who had never seen Altamiro's festive mood after the procession wondered how it was possible, but the people of Vista Alegre had gotten used to it. Though they could not explain it to strangers any more than they had been able to explain it to themselves when they had first observed it, now they considered it natural.

"So the two of you will soon be joined," he said.

"It all depends on what we mean by 'soon,'" Juan said, trying to be in humorous about his own predicament. "We have no money for the wedding."

Altamiro looked at Ramona, her gaze fixed on a knot in one of the planks of the floor. "Ah, now you're looking in the wrong direction. You have to look straight ahead to see the good coming your way."

"You're right," she said needing little encouragement to enjoy whatever chance brought her way. In an unpredictable life, constantly adjusting for the unforeseen became the path to happiness. She had suffered when her mother died. Having inherited all the domestic chores at the age of fourteen, she had fought off the despair. The work and responsibility of the household were not what made her unhappy. That had been a consolation. She adopted routines she had observed in her mother's life, as if on the floor of the house and in the paths and sidewalks of the neighborhood, she saw her mother's indelible footprints.

Chapter 19

SOME WEEKS HAD elapsed after Altamiro's yearly event when he, having recovered from the soreness of his knees, happened by chance to run into Ramona on her way home from the cigar factory.

"Ah," he exclaimed on seeing her, "I've been thinking about the problem of financing that important event that will usher in the rest of your marvelous life."

The smile on her face faded, leaving an expression of concern for having brought her problem to his attention. "Please, I beg you, do not worry about me. Juan and I will save enough money for the wedding. It will be simple, but everyone will be invited," at those last words the smile came back to her face as she imagined the pleasure of those attending the event.

"Worry? Nothing I do comes from worry," he exclaimed. "When challenges are gone from life, that's the day to worry. It is possible to get money for a holy event from God or from the saints. I just want to know whether, if it came from such a source, you would accept it."

The sudden appearance of money for her wedding would be difficult to believe, but she could not tell Don Altamiro to refrain from fabricating an absurd tale, so she supplied him with the positive answer he wished to hear.

"Well, then, talk to Juan and to your family to arrange for the event. I already know that the cost will be covered."

The mystery of the financing of her wedding would be no greater than the mystery of the financing of the yearly procession to the cemetery, and she wondered whether this new mystery would be as acceptable as the one already imbedded in the traditions of the neighborhood. When Ramona brought home Don Altamiro's words, her father and her brothers were just as puzzled.

"Well, he has money and he's willing to spend it on you," Ramiro said.

"If he has money, why is he willing to live in this part of town?" Incienso asked.

"Who knows? He's not all here," Ramiro answered, pointing his index finger to his own temple,

"That may be the case, but the question is whether to accept his offer," said Don Pedro. "It's not a simple matter."

"Accepting money is never simple in this family," said Ramiro who continually resented having lost his mother's possible inheritance.

"Perhaps he is telling the truth," said Ramona, "and the money is a miracle. Who is to say? A gift from God shouldn't be refused."

"That's true," said Don Pedro, wishing good fortune on his daughter, whose difficulties since her mother's death had added to the burdens on his conscience. "I will not stand in the way of whatever you and Juan decide," he said to her, as if a silver platter full of water had been brought to him, and he had chosen to wash his hands.

Breaking the news to Juan became Ramona's next task. She feared that Altamiro's generosity might be a more complex matter for Juan than it had been for her father, so his immediate acceptance of the offer surprised her. He did not express any reluctance whatsoever, as if he had been told about it before she spoke to him, and he had already resolved his doubts.

"So you have no reservations at all?" she asked again to assure herself of the accuracy of her perception. She didn't want reality distorted by her own desires.

"Well, of course I want to marry you," he said. "Haven't I courted you all these years?" Indeed, the five-year length of the courtship might have determined his positive response to Don Altamiro's unexpected liberality.

"I didn't mean that," she said. "What about Don Altamiro?"

"He's your father's friend, isn't he?" Juan said, perplexed by her continued questioning. He wanted to marry her and willingly suppressed any objection. He failed to see as a shortcoming the habit of letting his everyday feelings run their course behind a façade of equanimity.

Ramona saw the futility of continuing to question him. His failure to understand the nuances became part of the miracle, and any attempt to clarify them went contrary to the necessity of the moment. If she persisted, she would be guilty of attempting to thwart the will of fate.

"I'm glad then that you understand," she said.

"I understand that I love you," he answered, trying to ease the anxiety he saw in her.

Everyone in Vista Alegre was to remember the wedding for a long time, though eventually the two central participants' recall of it would differ, just as the evaluation of all the years they spend together would gradually diverge. Altamiro, never reluctant to entertain, offered his home as the place for the festivity. His house stood in a unique corner of Vista Alegre, where a number of houses enclosed an area they shared as a *batey*, an uncommon practice in towns, but necessity sometimes made it impossible to suppress. The space may be considered a yard or perhaps a square, but neither one of those words is an equivalent. Indeed, a batey may be said to be a mixture of the two, always connected to a private home but functioning as place for social gatherings, a custom derived from the Tainos, who populated the island before the arrival of the Spanish.

Altamiro kept coming up with surprises. He brought a wedding dress to Ramona's house, a dress beyond what she had ever expected to wear, a dress that only a wealthy woman could afford to have made. She could wear if she liked it, Altamiro told her. She suppressed asking where and how Altamiro had come by such a dress, though the questions banged on the door of her consciousness to be let out and allowed to express reservations. A different side of Ramona came up with an answer, but after having expressed it, she wished she had remained silent, for his response left her more perplexed than before.

"This was your wife's dress," she asserted rather than questioned, wishing the answer to be simple.

"Oh, no," he said, "In those days we couldn't afford such a dress."

"Whose dress is it, then?"

"I can't tell you," he said, "but you can wear it, if you wish." Seeing the concern on her face, he added, "Your wearing this dress was a fate destined since it was made."

"It was not my mother's dress," she said thinking the possibility of being wrong the only meaningful interpretation of his words.

"It was not," he agreed.

"What do you advise me to do?"

"Wear it," he said.

She added the dress to the items of divine intervention, just like the appearance of money to pay for the festivities. Only joy to be had from the occurrence of such events, she accepted the axiom that knowledge was not always a necessary condition for happiness. Eventually she would discover the source of the money and of the dress, and she would, at first, be disappointed that not God but a human being was concerned with her fate, the disappointment only momentary, as she realized that the intention of God often has no obvious magic associated with its performance but is hidden behind ordinary human action.

Romiro also became involved in the production of the event. He had been, at the beginning of Juan's courtship of Ramona, opposed to his sister's attention to someone at first glance unsuited for her, but he gradually became convinced of his error. Though his connection to the Ortegas' would never become intimate, his feelings for his sister would grow even with her taking on that name. For the wedding, he made it his task to hire the musicians, though he had no money of his own to fully perform the responsibility. Altamiro instructed him not to worry about the cost but hire the best he could find.

For the rest of her life Ramona would remember the day of her wedding as if it happened only the day before. On that day all the tribulations became meaningless, and she, the center of attention, dressed like royalty that had lost its way to Vista Alegre. Father Alfonso performed the ceremony at Santa Isabela, the church at which Ramona had been a primary member of the chorus, though having more work at home after her mother's death, that role had been reduced. Father Alfonso understood her predicament and did not pressure her to continue singing in the choir. Seeing her in the dress of mysterious origin amazed him; he too found its quality difficult to explain.

After Altamiro had brought her the dress, Ramona, still having some misgiving about its origin, had gone to Father Alfonso to ask his opinion. She did not take the dress for him to see but described it to him and explained her reservations. Father Alfonso, knowing from experience that the mind exaggerates the value of many things connected to emotional events, assumed that Ramona's concern about the dress had more to do with her feelings than with the actual value of the garment. He advised her to suppress her worries. When he saw her strolling up the central aisle of Santa Isabela, the possibility that he had been mistaken momentarily overwhelmed him. But he had perfected a technique of protecting himself from emotional upheavals at inopportune times, and with nothing to be done now about the origin of the dress, he expunged the whole matter from his mind never to consider it again.

Ramona's appearance moved many people who witnessed the event, though very few ascribed their emotions to the dress. They failed to attribute the turmoil that filled them to anything connected to Ramona. Each person, ignorant of what everyone else was feeling, considered the emotion a personal phenomenon to be ignored and eventually forgotten—all but Ramona, who lived the rest of her life aware of a day filled with miraculous happenings. After walking out of the church and proceeding to Altamiro's house, Ramona continued to experience the magnificence of the day. During the first dance when all the eyes of the guests focused on her and her husband, Juan danced naturally, an expert beyond the expectation of anyone in the room. Ramona wished that dance would last for the rest of her life.

Good Intentions

Chapter 20

Kneeling at a side altar in the church, having no control over what her mind and her mouth conspired to produce, the words suddenly came out of Ramona. "Please, God," she said, "let my first born be a son who will take care of me if ever the need arises." She had no image of what the need would be. Doubtlessly, Juan would take care of her till the very end, yet the words fell from her lips.

Her wish granted, her first child was a boy. Her second pregnancy resulted in a dead infant, and feeling responsible for the death, anguish overcame her. She believed the death to be the price for having requested, without considering the cost, a special attribute in the firstborn, and now she had to accept the responsibility of having incurred the debt. Her third attempt resulted in another boy, but unlike her previous two deliveries this one took place at home instead of at the hospital, where her second child had died at birth. This time she put her faith in a midwife. The third boy was big and strong. The first one, intended to be her protector in case of misfortune, seemed more fragile, but Ramona trusted God to know what He was doing.

Through the GI Bill Juan got a high school diploma and for a short while managed to attend business courses at the university, where he met Rafael Montenegro. The Montenegro family had bought land on the outskirts of the town. The area, still rustic and devoted to farming, had become easily accessible to townspeople by means of a road laid out by the army during the war. Dr. Aufemio Montenegro, Rafael's father, built a hospital on that land along the Military Road. Eventually the hospital would grow, becoming a major institution in the town as it became a city. The Montenegro land sprouted housing and byways indistinguishable from any other metropolitan area, but in 1948 that was yet many years away. At the beginning, dairy cows that provided milk for the clinic grazed in the pasture that surrounded the small hospital. Beyond the pasture, a small river, shielded by a copse of bamboo, served as a dumping ground for hospital waste.

Having to work to support his family, Juan's time in school became stressful. When not at the university, he worked at the docks as a stevedore, the work strenuous but for him necessary. Since boyhood, he had worked; tilled tobacco fields, harvested sugar cane, and now the cargo ships offered another opportunity to earn a living.

"God damn it, you're an intellectual," Rafael Montenegro said to him. "You'll kill yourself doing that kind of work."

"For now, I have no choice," Juan said. He was trying to get an education, but he didn't know how far he would get. He was learning to type, but he couldn't afford to buy a typewriter to practice on.

Rafael Montenegro devoted all his time to his studies, but the results were less than those achieved by Juan. Normally, that would have been another condition, besides their social standing, to keep them apart, but Rafael Montenegro refused to abide by those barriers. He admired the insights that easily came to Juan, and that urged him to befriend him.

"I can get you a job at the hospital more befitting your talents," Rafael said to Juan.

"I'm not a doctor," Juan retorted.

"A hospital needs more than doctors," Rafael said.

"I suppose they need janitors," Juan said.

"There's an empty office in the clinic. I'll ask my father to put you in it."

Rafael arranged an interview. The meeting took place at the Montenegro house, across the road from the hospital. Juan impressed Dr. Aufemio Montenegro as soon as they spoke.

Dr. Aufemio considered his life a series of fortunate occurrences, and the meeting of Juan Ortega a minor example of that kind of event, he added it to his list. In Juan, he saw a capable person willing to accept a moderate salary for a position at the hospital. Dr. Aufemio did not easily part with money. How his son, Rafael, developed a habit of overspending remained a mystery to him. The fact that the doctor's wife, Doña Izquierda, was just as thrifty as her husband, removed from the doctor's mind a genetic cause for Rafael's lack of frugality.

Despite his reluctance to part with money, Dr. Aufemio retained the ability to see other people's needs. He willingly offered help within the bounds of rational thrift. He had plenty of land on which the hospital would eventually develop, but for the present he was putting it to other uses. On the side of the pasture stood a house in some disrepair. It would have eventually fallen apart on its own, without his having to pay to have it removed. On hiring Juan, the house became for Dr. Aufemio a means to ease the qualms he had about the modest salary he offered.

Dr. Aufemio led Juan out to the balcony that faced south toward the pasture. "On the other side of that copse," he said, making a vague gesture toward the distance, "there's a house you can have rent free. It needs some fixing, but it's in fairly good condition. Go look at it and see what you think. It'll save you paying rent somewhere else, and the land around it you can use to plant anything for your own use."

"A sugar plantation out of the question?" Juan asked.

A few seconds elapsed while the doctor processed those words; then, he burst into laughter. "You're a humorous man," he said, "just what we need at the clinic."

Juan walked down the road and across the pasture to look at the house. The frogs croaked in the green expanse of *malangas* that grew on the south side of the building. The ground sloped down to create a basin for rainwater that made it an ideal place for the greenery planted either by some past resident or by an accident of nature. The house needed repair. On one side ran three bedrooms; and on the other, a large living room and a kitchen. Water pipes already attached to the sink in the kitchen. Electrical light fixtures, missing bulbs, hung from the beams that would have supported a ceiling had that been the style in such houses; instead, beyond the beams, the old galvanized tin roof remained exposed. No doubt it leaked, but he wouldn't know where until the rain came. He went out through the back door to the small latrine. It had been used to capacity and had to be replaced, all work he could do. The expense of paying rent would be removed and going to his job would be only a short walk. Surely, Ramona would be pleased to be always nearby.

Ramona saw the advantages of living in a house close to the hospital as clearly as Juan, though she also saw disadvantages that he had not considered. The isolated location provided no neighbors to relieve the monotony of the day. The doctor's house the closest but he had no daughters, and Ramona considered mingling with the mistress of that house out of the question. True that her own mother, Juana Rincon, would have felt perfectly at ease with such people, having come from a wealthy family, but to Ramona that had become a vague notion, the memory of her grandfather transformed into a childhood fancy. During the day, only the children would be with her in this new setting. They too would have no one their age with whom to play. She would have to take them with her when she went shopping. Alejandro, the younger one, did not yet walk; she would have to carry him along with the groceries.

"We can do most of the shopping on Saturday when I'm home," Juan said.

"You'll have Saturdays off?" she asked.

"Yes, of course, times have changed," he said smiling, "and they'll keep changing. We won't have to live here for long. I promise you. We'll get all the things people have. I've seen a lot of people have refrigerators. We'll have one right here in the kitchen."

"They're very expensive," she said, becoming alarmed. "We can't just spend what we don't have."

"We'll have plenty," he said.

Living with Juan, Ramona became aware of a personality more complicated than that of the young man she had once taken back to the dance floor. What she now saw confused her. Without consulting her, he went out to spend more money than he had. At first, she had no objection to the clothes he bought for himself. He needed suits to wear to work if he was to mix with doctors. She refrained from complaining that perhaps he spent more than necessary on clothes, but he spent erratically on other things too. Without consulting her, he ordered living room furniture, carved mahogany with fancy caning. Every beautiful object seemed out of place in the house they lived in.

"There are holes in the walls, and when it rains the roof leaks," she said to him. "This furniture is out of place here. Why do we need it? No one we know has anything like it."

"You haven't been to the Montenegro house," he said.

"How did you get the money?"

"It's on credit. I'll pay little by little."

She found the idea of going into debt unpleasant, but to him it seemed an ideal thing to do. "We're going to move from here," he said. "This furniture will be just right for our next house."

She calmed herself. He had a job. He was earning the money to pay the debts. In the hospital they saw his talents, and he had already gotten a raise. On the other hand, if you spend money before you have it, how do you know when to stop? One could buy on credit out of necessity, but food was the only necessity for which she considered credit acceptable. Juan on the other hand saw it as a convenient path to the kind of life he wanted, a life that would make him forget the days of his childhood when he had worked in the tobacco fields with only a piece of bread for lunch.

Chapter 21

A T THE MONTENEGRO CLINIC, Juan had his own office. He sat at a large desk from which a flap pulled out to hold a Royal typewriter. The courtyard of the hospital, a garden surrounded by stonework, at the center, a round structure overflowed with tropical plants visible through the window behind his desk. Several medical diagrams hung on walls, and on one corner of the room, suspended from a metal stand, a human skeleton. Juan's high school diploma, its importance at the time indicated by its large size, hung as a central exhibit on the wall to the left of his desk. Very few of the patients who came into the office noticed the level of education indicated by the diploma, many believing that a doctor sat behind the desk interviewing them for basic information.

On one occasion, as he walked by the emergency room, he noticed a young mother as she, in consternation, stood amazed that the doctor on duty did not immediately have a solution to her son's plight. "What is he waiting for? What is he waiting for?" she repeated watching from the hallway. "Please look in on what he's doing," she begged Juan, mistaking him for another doctor.

Dr. Rivera, the internist, waved for him to come in and see the problem.

"Jesus!" Juan exclaimed. "You want me to call Dr. Montenegro? He's got to be around here somewhere."

"He's been here already," Dr. Rivera said. "He passed the buck."

"All you'll have to do is yank," Juan said.

"Yes, I tried that already. This is really not a medical issue. It's clothing mechanics. Maybe a sports coach should be doing this. Give it try."

Taking the zipper handle between his thumb and index finger and with the other hand holding the boy's pants beneath the point where the zipper had caught his flesh, Juan yanked.

"Well, there we go," said Dr. Rivera. "I guess I'll have to do the rest of the treatment."

"I guess so," he said. "I don't get paid enough for that."

The boy's mother, still believing that Juan was a doctor, profusely thanked him. Smiling, Juan comforted her, and then shaking his head, he walked down the hallway to his office. He considered the hospital job as a precursor to what the rest of his life would bring.

On Saturday afternoon, Juan and Rafael Montenegro went out for a drink. Juan took his young son with him. He took the boy along whenever possible, as if it were a father's responsibility to start the sons crossing into manhood at the earliest possible time. Juan and Rafael sat the boy on the stool between them and ordered three beers.

"All right, drink up, drink up," they said to the boy who, grabbing the stein with both hands, brought the froth to his lips only to make a face and refuse to swallow.

"Are you going to finish the drink?"

"No," the boy said.

"Well, we can't let the beer go to waste. Who should drink it?" Rafael asked, winking at him.

"My daddy," Mario said.

"Well, this time I'll drink it for you," Juan said, putting his arm around his son.

After a few beers they got into Rafael's convertible, where, as they drove toward the edge of town, the boy in the back seat perused a Tarzan comic book. They arrived at the place and parked in front of a house from where the music and the sound of women's voices seeped through the curtains of the open window.

"I think he'll have to stay out here," Juan said.

"Nah, bring him in. He can just sit on the couch."

"I don't think they'll want him in there," Juan said.

"Why not? Women like children."

"Too risky," he said. "You wait here for me," he said to Mario, "just a little while. Read the comic book."

"All right," Mario said.

On their return home, Ramona spoke to the boy in an attempt to be included in every hour of his life.

"And where have you been today?" she asked the little one.

"To the bar," he said, as he wheeled the little iron fire truck across the table.

"A bar?"

"Yes," the boy said, "men go to bars."

"And what did you do there?"

"I sat there with Dad," he said.

"That's all?"

"I didn't like the beer," the boy said.

"Your father let you taste his beer?"

"He bought one for me," said the boy, "but I didn't like it, so he drank it."

In front of the boy, she suppressed her anger, but before going to bed it burst out of her, and after the altercation, she and Juan slept with their backs to each other. By morning, again she felt that she had overreacted. No doubt Juan played with the boy and would have let him only taste the beer. Men drank liquor and smoked tobacco. She had worked in a cigar factory to keep her family clothed and fed. To keep himself from starving, Juan had picked tobacco as a boy. Surely, Mario would drink and smoke when he grew up. She would have to let him grow to be a man.

"I'm sorry," she said in the morning. "I know you would let no harm come to him."

"I'm sorry too," Juan said. "Sometimes I don't think." Their embrace dissipated the tension of the night.

The next incident shook her up even more. On Juan and Mario's return from their Saturday excursion, the boy's new look shocked her. The boy that had left with Juan in the morning had been transformed. Ramona sat down on the wicker chair and let her tears flow freely in the hope that they contained some potion to alleviate her pain. The boy's long hair gone, he wore a pair of long pants held at his waist by a leather belt.

"I'm a man," said the boy, broadly smiling at his mother, who returning the smile through her tear-stained cheeks opened her arms for him to run up to her and be caught in an embrace she wished would last for the rest of her life.

Juan's taking the boy wherever he went had one advantage. Everyone observed a man responsible for a family, and though they saw only the boy, surely the boy had a mother. Still, Ramona's feeling of grief persisted.

She had good days too.

The man knocked on the balcony post to let her know that she had a visitor.

"I'm sorry," Ramona said, "I cannot have any male visitor right now; my husband is not home."

"Why marry a fool that stays away all day? You could have done much better."

"Really?" she said. "Aren't men all the same?"

"Some are better than others," he answered. "Here I am when he's not here."

"That's true," she said, "but still, I cannot let you in the house."

"It's pleasant enough out here," he answered. "In the light of day your beauty is unmistakable, though, no doubt, by moonlight none of it would be lost. Perhaps we can make a date to watch the stars on a moonlit night."

"At night my husband is always home."

"If he works all day, he might be too tired to notice your taking a short walk in the evening."

"You're a brazen man," she said. "What will your own wife say?"

"She doesn't bother to keep me under lock and key."

"Perhaps if she found out about your escapades, she would."

"And what would your husband do if he found out about yours?"

"I am an absolutely faithful wife," she answered.

"Is that why you have leaned over the rail to outline your rear?"

"Now you'll have to wash your mouth with soap."

"For that I'll have to go into the house."

"If you come into the house you might have to wash more than that."

They both laughed as he climbed the steps of the porch. He kissed her, and as she was being held tightly, she noticed Mario observing them from behind the door.

"Don't worry about him," Juan said, turning back to Ramona. "He's a man."

Her husband's words now disconcerted her more than having been observed by her son. Imagining the boy's journey into manhood filled her with fear.

Chapter 22

"I DON'T KNOW THAT I can sell you all three goats," Juan said.

"You plan to develop a whole herd?" Rafael Montenegro needled him.

"No, of course not," Juan answered. He had acquired the goat on a visit to Naranjito, his hometown. It was always a pleasant trip, the drive up the curving road, then the walk up the mountain trail to Aunt Suseña's house.

"Come, sell me the goats and come to the dinner also," Rafael Montenegro persisted.

"Alright, you can have the goats," Juan said, immediately regretting his words. His boy, Mario, considered the first goat a gift he had received on a trip to visit Aunt Suseña. That first goat eventually had two offspring, and the boy was attached to them also. Juan might have just sold the two kids, and the boy would have forgotten them, but he wouldn't forget all three. Juan had spoken too quickly but saw no way to retract the offer.

"It'll be interesting. Muñoz Marin and the governor will be there."

"I'm not into politics," Juan said.

"It's just a dinner," Rafael retorted.

"I've seen Muñoz twice," Juan said. "Once in fact the same day I got the goat."

On the trail down from Suseña's house, they had stopped at Don Alfredo's to chat. It was customary to stop at every house along the way.

"Muñoz Marin is up here for the day," Don Alfredo had said to Juan. "They tell me the man has good things to say."

"They all have good things to say," Juan retorted.

"They don't all say 'Bread, Land and Liberty' in that order," Don Alfredo declared.

"Well, then you already know what he has to say."

"There has to be more to it than three words," Don Alfredo insisted.

Ramona and the two children sat down in the kitchen with Doña Ana, Alfredo's wife, while the two men took the path up to a clearing.

The mountainous terrain providing a distant backdrop, a stout man, in a white short-sleeve shirt, sat in the shade of a guaco tree. The town major, in a suit and tie, stood close by. About twenty other men, most squatting in a semicircle, waited to hear what the politician had to say.

"There was a time when every man had a piece of land to grow enough to feed his family," the words came from Don Muñoz.

"Isn't it true that no one is supposed to own more than five hundred acres?" Andres Figueroa, a young man squatting in the inner circle, asked. His voice quavered slightly unsure that it was proper to ask a question of the man who had come to speak to them. "I heard that's the law, but down by Guanica the sugar mills have all the land."

"They have more than more," someone shouted from behind.

"All the land is planted with cane, but we can't afford to buy sugar for our coffee."

"I say every man deserves a plot of land," Don Marin interceded, his face expressing the sincerity of his words. "Every man," he repeated, "not every corporation."

"The American corporations want all the land."

"Corporations don't have nationality," Muñoz said, "No matter who owns them, they're giants eating up the land. They have a stranglehold on us, and we have to break it.

Land for every man is what we're working for, but even before, that there has to be bread on every table."

"That's right. Coffee without bread isn't enough," someone said.

"We have to work together, the government and the people and each man with the others. The government can set up banks, but we have to organize to ensure the best use of the land. We plan together or they'll run over us."

"That's for sure," came from the young man at the front.

Juan had listened wondering what those words had to do with his own life. His father, Federico, had land and grew cane, but Juan had given up the idea of working the land. A part of him would always be attached to that way of life, but the land had also been a burden. He remembered tilling the soil all day while feeling the hunger in his belly. That childhood memory would never go away, but he also remembered the undulating landscape of the mountains covered with green forests where the birds sang, where he merely picked the mangos that fell from the trees and gathered *quenepas* that grew along the path.

He was a townsman now, no longer a *jibaro*, someday he might be something even more. He tried to imagine life in New York, but he knew that enjoying the familiar images of the tall buildings gathered from photographs fell short of as being there in person. He wanted something else, not land to till, though he loved the land. He had to accept the fact that he was different. Muñoz had lived in New York and in Washington and yet, here in the mountains, he struggled to get these men to organize.

"Well, talking to him over dinner is not the same as seeing him at a rally," Rafael Montenegro said, "and you can watch him eat, which is also interesting."

"Is your mother doing the cooking?"

"She has a great recipe for goat stew," Rafael said, but

immediately realized he should refrain from alluding to the transaction. "And of course there's the American," he said changing the subject to get Juan's mind away from the goats.

Juan's face showed some puzzlement on hearing the word "American."

"The governor, Rexford Tugwell," Rafael said.

"Ah, well, I never met him," Juan said.

"You must have," Rafael said, "at the university."

A look of befuddlement overcame Juan's face as he tried to recall the governor at the school.

"He taught economics. He's one of those college professors who loves politics."

"I wasn't there long enough to meet every professor," Juan said.

"He's quite a character himself," Rafael said, attempting to move away from Juan's unpleasant memories.

"I suppose he likes goat meat," Juan said.

"I suppose he does," Rafael retorted somewhat disconcerted.

Getting to the reception at the Montenegros' was a short walk for Juan, even a shorter one if he cut across the pasture and approached through the dairy stall where the hospital cows were milked. To avoid the chance of stepping in cow dung, a mishap that would ruin his entrance if not cancel it altogether, he decided against that route. Halfway to the Montenegros', he saw two automobiles turn into the driveway to the right of the hospital, too far yet to discern who got out, perhaps the governor and his wife in one of them and the Muñozes in the other. Juan wondered whether to consider his arriving after the guests of honor a faux pas. Perhaps he should have arrived early enough to be in the greeting party and avoid the attention of walking in late. Fortunately, more people at the event than he had expected made his entrance inconspicuous.

The young woman who greeted him at the door looked familiar, perhaps a new employee at the hospital, a new nurse at the moment doubling as help for Doña Montenegro. Somewhat at a loss as to what to do next, Juan looked around the room hoping Rafael would soon come to the rescue and introduce him. However, Rafael nowhere to be seen, Doña Montenegro proceeded to Juan's aid. She had managed to retain a great deal of her youthful looks, but poised to cross into an acceptance of age, she had trouble being at ease. She sometimes flirted while trying to be motherly. "Ah, Señor Ortega," she said, relieving him of his uncertainty and letting him know that she knew who he was. Even though he worked at the hospital, just across the road from her house and he spent a great deal of time with her son, they had never been formerly introduced. "And your wife, is she here also?" Doña Montenegro asked, making Juan wonder why she asked, since surely, she was quite aware that even his being there was an aberration of social nuances.

"She's home with the boys," Juan said. "She doesn't like to leave them with anyone else. Looking after them has become her mission in life." Almost convinced of his own veracity, the words came to him as if he and Ramona had discussed the matter.

"Ah, yes," Doña Montenegro said, "and politics is a man's world in any case."

Unsure of how straightforward he should be, not being able to decipher with any certainty how she actually felt, Juan ambiguously nodded his head. "Come I'll introduce you," she said. "I'm sure there are many you haven't met."

He refrained from commenting on her understatement and merely followed her. "Statehood is a possibility of course," he heard someone say, though he could not see who in the group was speaking as they approached. Don Muñoz at the center of the group, the members waited to hear what he had to say on the matter. Most people assumed that secretly Don Muñoz harbored a desire for independence, but rather than being an agitator in the streets, he schemed behind close doors to attain his goal. When he campaigned for election, he avoided mentioning statehood, an issue far from the minds of those whose votes he sought, the common people, mainly concerned with getting enough to eat. Statehood appealed to the business elite who saw their interests attached to the Americans. Many in that group believed that Muñoz would eventually take their side since, after all was said and done, he too was one of them. A slight grin suffused the politician's face after having momentarily let a slight tremor almost unnoticeably slide under his features on hearing the word "statehood." "There are more ways to skin a cat," he said after the short pause.

Ears perked up to hear at least the list of the various ways if not a detailed description of each, but they waited in vain. For the time being Don Muñoz would let each person in the room draw his own conclusion. Doña Montenegro took the opportunity at the pause to introduce Juan. "This is Don Juan Ortega, an important member of the staff at the hospital," she said. Juan shook hands with each member of the group, and each seemed quite please to meet someone close to the Montenegros. "I'll leave you then to discuss politics," Doña Montenegro said.

She moved on to scout for other glitches that might need remedy to maintain the smooth running of the evening and ensure that her husband's image remained unimpaired. She had made that her aim in life on discovering that marriage was not what she had imagined. She did not remember when she had actually launched on her mission, except that it was not long after the ceremony. At first she had been under the impression that she had chosen whom to marry. Only later, after the initial euphoria of the honeymoon and the subsequent customary travail of adjustment had occurred, did she ask herself whether she had indeed had a choice. Certainly there were other men in the world, but she had never seriously considered any of them. She had been attached to her father, a relationship that became more puzzling and distant as she got older, as if on the day of her marriage he had departed on a long trip and subsequently their seeing each other resembled receiving a postcard from a foreign place. Her father had at first opposed the marriage, but seeing that nothing could be done to stop it, he viewed the ceremony as the signing of a treaty in recognition of the inevitable.

She never concluded that her father had been right in his view of Dr. Montenegro, even as she arrived at the acceptance of the fact that she had been wrong in her initial assessment. A marriage is a complex relationship. Certainly different from what she had expected, but on examining what she could discern of other marriages, she found nothing that fit the ideal expectations she had youthfully cherished.

For her, divorce was out of the question, though she had to admit that at several dire moments the possibility, even if fleetingly, had forced itself to be considered. At one of their darkest moments, she realized that he too was capable of contemplating a serious separation, as if their original union had been a temporary scheme to accommodate his youth. When the storm receded leaving them still together, she realized that she might be more valuable to him than she had imagined, and he more than willing to pay a price. She had suffered, but she had discovered that, as long as she kept her endeavors from threatening his manhood, she had power to exert in getting what she wanted.

Looking around the room Juan spotted Governor Tugwell at one end of the room speaking to several of the young men in his cabinet, the sort Juan and young Montenegro ran into when making the tavern round on a Saturday night. The governor's reputation as a man of radical ideas moved Juan to wonder whether the man's appearance reflected his opinions. As far as Juan could tell, the governor looked like just another American; giving rise to the question of whether his thinking differed. His idea of nationalizing the sugar industry to reduce the exploitation of the island led other Americans, along with those Puerto Ricans who did not support the Populist Party, to call him a communist. From his appearance one would never conclude that he would be concerned with the well-being of a *jibaro*. Stately, he carried himself with an air of superiority, and perhaps he had reason. He and Muñoz Marin agreed on many things, but this American would never mingle easily with the people in the street the way Muñoz did.

Juan recalled the second time he had seen Muñoz Marin in public, in town rather than in the mountains. All morning, cars with loud speakers had crisscrossed the neighborhoods announcing that Muñoz would soon arrive at the town square. Everyone was invited to attend, enjoy the music and speak to the man who, if elected, would improve everyone's life. Blaring music, the bus arrived at the square, and in his typical shirtsleeve persona, Muñoz disembarked. No platform had been erected for him to mount and speak. Rather, he walked from group to group in the square introducing himself: *"Buenos días, soy Luis Muñoz Marin, a su servicio."* Then he would wait for people to tell him their troubles.

"No matter what politicians say, we end up with the same problems," someone said straight to his face. "Why should we trust you?"

"Right here and now you don't know that I'm different, but all I'm asking you is to give me a chance. I'll put on my *pava* and if in four years nothing has changed you can vote me out. You need jobs. Factories are coming. You need land.

Land will be redistributed. Americans who have taken so much from us will have to give back. Someday we'll be a free country. We'll get there one step at a time."

"Yes, one step at a time," Juan thought as he observed Governor Tugwell, "and is this one of the Americans who will give things back?"

Chapter 23

"A H, JUAN NEVER bothers to hang his suit when he changes," she said out loud, with no one about interested in hearing her complaint. Norberto crawling on the floor surely did not yet understand her words, and Mario sitting under the kitchen table busy with paper and crayons had no interest in her words, another irksome development, the boy growing away from her, every day closer to his father.

A scent emanated from the jacket. Before arranging the suit on a hanger, she went through the pockets. Sometimes Juan forgot to take his desk keys and had to make the extra trip to fetch them. This time there were no keys left behind, only, in the inside pocket of the jacket, a folded piece of paper. She brought the paper up to her nose to verify that it was the source of the scent. Only a woman could have given him a note on a piece of paper that reeked of perfume, a totally innocent incident, a thank-you note from a grateful patient, or a request sent to him from a doctor who had borrowed a piece of paper from one of the women, nothing at all to be concerned about. Clearing her doubts would be to everyone's benefit, otherwise they would plague her and push her into unreasonableness. Surely, that would be less fair to him than unfolding the piece of paper to reassure herself. A moan followed her silence. In the crib, Norberto turned in his sleep, and Mario dropped his crayon and approached the door of the bedroom to stare at his mother. "What's the matter?" the boy asked.

The impulse to run to the hospital to confront her husband surged through her. She had to find the woman who had written the note, pull the hair out of her head so that she might be recognized in public as a harlot. The children could not be left alone in the house, but if she took them with her they would be part of a scene that would stain their lives when only their father and the loose woman deserved that. Her role as mother had in a few minutes increased in magnitude providing a means of dealing with the horror of the moment. They now had only her to depend on. Mario approached close enough for his mother to extend her arms and embrace him, reassuring him while comforting herself.

Surprised by the extent of Ramona's disturbance when he got home, Juan admitted the authenticity of the note as an appeal from the nurse, but he claimed that was all, that he did not return the feelings. He had paid little attention to it, otherwise why would he have treated the piece of paper so carelessly? The letter meant nothing to him, so he had forgotten it in his pocket.

"In the hospital, I let the doctors do the operating," he said. "How can you doubt me after all the years of my loving you."

She had considered those points before he got home, and though the argument made sense, she had failed to convince herself. The words coming from him at the moment sounded believable. They relieved her of a burden about to become intolerable, and relieved, she willingly accepted his explanation.

One day, he arrived holding something behind his back, his face glowing as he approached her, the excitement disturbing, his kiss failed to ease her.

"All right, stand up against the window where there's enough light," he said.

"Enough light for what?"

"Just go by the window," he said.

She moved, anxious to see what he was holding behind his back. Once she was bathed in sunlight he revealed the camera. Looking down into the viewfinder, he saw panic overwhelm her face.

"How much did that cost?" she asked, the anxiety in her voice taking the guise of anger.

"It didn't cost much," he said trying to keep falsity from altering the tone of his voice. "We need to take pictures of the children," he continued spurred by a need to convince her that he had done nothing wrong. "They'll grow quick enough, and we'll forget what they looked like when they were babies. Then what will we have to comfort us in our old age?"

She didn't understand why he threw fear so far into the future. How about next week or next month or next year, for the children, their food, their clothes, or being extravagant, their toys? The children had to be taken care of now rather than looking into one's own future that might not arrive. The image of her mother lying in the bed under the crucifix now distressed her, and looking into Juan's face, whose glee at owning a camera had been transformed into guilt, brought Ramona back to her supposed role as the understanding wife. "I'm sorry," she said, "I'm sorry, and you're right. We'll take pictures of the children." She forced herself to believe that they needed to be photographed, that someday the children would look at the images and recognize the world of their childhood. After all, the world would change. It changed all the time, already very different from what it had been in her childhood, electricity everywhere one went, even in the mountains, where she had known only kerosene lamps. On his way to a better life, Juan yet lacked extra money, but he had a good job. The money would come just like he said.

She still picked up the ice from the ice truck that stopped by the hospital, and she kept the ice in the small barrel in the kitchen to keep the milk for the children from spoiling, but someday she would have the refrigerator, as he had promised, and all the food for the children would be kept fresh, although it was not a big deal to do things the way they had been done for hundreds of years. Water was piped into the house now, though in her youth, and still in the mountains, it was carried in gourds from the well. Every day life changed from what it had been, so was it fair to blame him for eagerly trying the new ways? She had to control herself. She loved him, and she had to show him that she would love him forever.

The pasture extended from the hospital toward the Ortega house. The hospital road divided the field, cutting it in two and leading on to a cattle ranch beyond the hill. Across the road the green field pushed all the way to the river where a bamboo grove extended the greenery into the sky. In the middle of the field a guava tree stood isolated in the expanse of grass. The clouds constantly traversing above, to no avail searching for a place to rest, reminded Ramona of her own troubles which kept her always from being still, though unlike the white gauze in the sky, her form remained constant.

"Let's go pick up the ice," she said to little Mario, who, to everyone else's surprise, rarely gave Ramona anything to worry about. Ramona took his careful and observant nature as proof that her request had been granted, and she accepted him without wonder but kept the explanation to herself. The boy spent a great deal of time by himself playing with toys he had received as gifts to the firstborn or shaping figures from the clay ground that surrounded the house. Ramona took for granted his ability to make things with his hands, a wonder to many. Had he sprouted wings and flown about the house she would have thought it natural. She picked up the second child who did not yet walk, and carried him while Mario pushed the little red wheelbarrow. Cutting across the pasture shortened the distance, but they had to avoid stepping in the cow dung. They laughed if either one of them failed, though that added for Ramona the task of cleaning the shoes.

The ice truck stopped by the hospital, and Ramona handed the iceman the five cents for the block of ice. The iceman chiseled a block to the right size and with the giant ice clips he swung it into the little red wheelbarrow.

"Taking ice home is a man's job," the iceman said, smiling at Mario.

"Well, it's my job," the boy responded seriously, while his mother stood next to him proud of what she had been granted, a secret between her and God.

"Let's go see Papi," the boy said as he pushed the wheelbarrow along the side of the road by the hospital.

"We'll waste the ice," she said, "unless we take it home right away." She would have avoided going into the clinic even had the ice promised to remain intact. The office, a perfect fit for Juan, for Ramona existed in a world she didn't belong even as a visitor. As she walked down the road, one child against her hip and now and then running her fingers through the other's hair as he pushed the red wheelbarrow along, she tried to suppress her fears of losing Juan forever to that world. She could do nothing at the moment about this problem that she had not anticipated before her marriage. No other Ortega had shown any possibility of rising into that other world, different from the one they knew.

Even when Federico Atorey, the father of the Ortegas, though they did not carry his name, had acquired more land after the death of his oldest son, no barrier emerged between her and that family. She had come from people of the land. Though she had never enjoyed the material advantages of having descended from the Rincons, she knew that Federico Atorey would never be like Eduardo Rincon. She was a descendant of the Rincons, but that had become meaningless to her. The Rincons had been like the hospital's Montenegros, a different kind of people, and though she could see Juan assimilate, she could not see herself fitting in along with him, even though her mother had been a Rincon.

The little boy beside her pushing the wheelbarrow along the road comforted her, though sometimes now Juan seemed to be trying to take him away from her. She fought that feeling too. After all, Mario was a boy, the firstborn son, special for his father as well. Juan's interference took place in her imagination, she told herself, and in any case, she did not have to worry. God had given her the boy for a purpose, and no one on earth could take that away from her.

After putting the ice in the barrel and arranging all the items that needed to be kept cool, Ramona remembered that Juan's shirts needed to be ironed. Every day he wore a white shirt to the office. As a little girl, she had learned to iron with a coal iron, but now electric irons had come into use. That had made the process of ironing clothes much easier, no need to put glowing coals in the iron and then constantly check that they keep smoldering. The electric iron stayed hot as long as it was plugged in and the switch was on. In some respects life got simpler. Before going out to get the ice, she had sprinkled the shirts, each rolled into a ball and piled to await ironing. She put Norberto in his crib for his daily nap and Mario went out to play. Occasionally she looked out the window and saw him digging in the clay ground by the side of the house. She set up the ironing board and began the task. Each shirt, having been soaked in starch water, once ironed had a stiff quality whose comfort she doubted, but Juan had become accustomed to it. Just as she began to iron the final shirt she heard Norberto cry. The boy had stood up and, wanting to be taken out, held on to the railing of the crib. She checked his diaper. It needed to be changed. Having done that and deciding to take him to the kitchen for a snack, she lifted him. At that moment, she smelled something burning.

"Oh, God, what have I done?" she exclaimed, placing Norberto back in the crib. She ran to the ironing board. On lifting the iron, she saw the burn mark on the shirt. "Oh, Jesus, what will I do?" Her lamentation continued, and tears streaked down her face, "What will I do?" She sat on the bed and again held up the shirt to verify the damage. For the moment, Norberto crying in the other room became inaudible to her.

"Mario," she called from the window, "Mario! Go get your father," she said without specifying the message to be delivered.

The boy ran all the way to the hospital. "Come home, come home, Mama is crying!"

Alarmed and imagining a catastrophe, Juan rushed back to the house. On walking in, a glimpse into the room where Norberto stood in the crib allayed his first concern. Ramona sitting on the bed was still crying. The fact that the hospital was close by kept Juan's anxiety in check. Whatever the illness, aid was close enough. He put his hands around her shoulders. "What hurts you?" he begged.

Slowly she raised the shirt and braced herself for his anger. He needed but a few seconds to arrange the pieces of the puzzle. Laughter overwhelmed him, and he held her in his arms until her tears subsided.

Yes, he was a sweet man who loved her, but there were some things too difficult for her to understand.

"Let's take a walk up to Vista de las Flores. Just you and me," he suggested one Saturday morning.

The town, still small enough to walk easily from one end to another, had a new housing development on the north side, Vista de las Flores, a short distance from the main street that ran all the way to the central square. If only to look at places where he dreamed of someday buying a house, Ramona was glad to take a walk with her husband, up the road past the hospital, then along Military Road, until they got to Comerio Street. Before they got to the church, they turned to walk along the street that led to the new housing development. On the south side, a row of houses had been built, and beyond those houses, a sport field. The north side of the development proceeded downhill, and just where the street made a turn to descend, Juan stopped in front of a new house.

"So what do you think?" he asked Ramona.

"The wood hasn't rotted yet," she mirthfully said.

"Let's look inside," he urged.

"You know the owners?"

He nodded as he gently pressed her to enter. In the empty house, the kitchen was already set up with an electric refrigerator and a new model gas stove. No indoor bathroom, but through the kitchen window she could see a new outhouse, behind which the hill descended, at the bottom, a dairy barn surrounded by grassland.

"I guess they'll be moving in soon," Ramona said.

"As soon as you like," he answered.

"What has it to do with me?" she asked thinking his humor out of place.

Repressing a smile, he kept silent, and wondering at his lack of response, she turned to stare at his face where she read the answer to her question.

"Do you like the place?" he asked, as if her opinion still made a difference.

"It's the house we always wanted," she said trying to repress the fear that emerged whenever the question of money overwhelmed her.

But why doubt his judgment? He was a smart man. How could she, a woman who had dropped out of elementary school, sit in judgment of a man progressing in the world? She had to be happy about a new house with fancy appliances, no leaky roof, the location convenient, closer to the church. And Mario would be attending the school soon, a shorter trip to pick him up or to take a fruit drink to him at recess time. The fancy furniture they already had would fit very well in this house. She forced herself to appreciate the blessing.

Chapter 24

TIME KEPT ITS inexorable pace. Two more children came, a girl and a boy, before the girl, a miscarriage, then another after. Economically, life wasn't getting any easier. She dreamt one night that little children dressed in rags surrounded her. They silently asked for comfort. Looking at them, she despaired. Those standing close to her began to die. She looked up to see a pitiless image of God. She woke up thirsty. Juan fetched water for her, while she tried to erase the crowd of little beggars she had seen in her nightmare.

"I cannot do it," she said, when he returned with the water.

"We have no future," he said, "if we do nothing."

"We can abstain," she said.

He looked at the floor silently, and she reluctantly accepted the absurdity of her own words. To ask Juan to comply was unfair.

"It's a sin to prevent having children," she said.

"And to have so many that they must suffer in poverty, is that not a greater sin?"

"We must abstain," she said again, knowing the absurdity of her words.

Shortly after turning off the light and climbing back into bed Juan fell asleep, but Ramona was unable to close her eyes. In the morning, she automatically performed the routine of preparing breakfast for Juan and the children, pausing occasionally to examine Juan's face as he sat at the table. After their talk, he had slept the night through and now looked relaxed. The fact that he always seemed to have no worries amazed her. What did he do with his anxiety? He would not have suggested the procedure had he no worries about the future, but his fears were hidden and emerged only as logical conclusions. For her, the day had lost its luster, though she saw that the sun was out and the green fields beyond the dairy barn at the bottom of the hill reflected the usual brilliance.

She could think of no rational solution to the problem. She needed an indication from above. Surely God would not intend so many children to have a life of misery. She thought back to her own mother who must have faced the same question. If she had done anything about it, Ramona was unaware of it. Juana had given birth to seven children before she died still young enough to have more. Ramona would never know how many children her mother would have had had she lived longer. Death had been her solution, but surely it had not been her choice, a drastic way out, an unreasonable one assumed by nature, but wasn't nature an expression of God over which He had complete control? Could He not, being all-powerful over all aspects of the universe, have offered a more reasonable answer, a less painful one? Had we inherited, from the sin of our original parents, the guilt that required having to expiate time and again the crime of having eaten the apple? Who was to say that the now simple medical procedure, a long-awaited solution to a problem, was not provided by God? Men did not always recognize the messages He sent. Wasn't it God's custom to disguise His messages, always testing our ability to decipher them? Wasn't that the meaning of the story where the angel obstructing the path was visible only to the donkey?

"All right," she said to Juan when he got home from work that evening, "arrange at the hospital for me to have the operation."

Surprised at the sudden shift, he was quiet for a minute.

Foreseeing the unbearable result of having to put up with guilt, he had decided to avoid attachment to the decision. "Are you sure?" he asked. "There's no turning back after it's done."

"I'm certain," she answered, knowing full well that he was dropping responsibility for the consequences, but even had he failed to announce his exit, she would have let him go. Everyone in the world is responsible for every action of his or her life no matter what influences others exert. That condition made the idea of sin viable—the reason why the apple tree had been place in the Garden, why Adam was just as guilty as Eve. Every action in one's life is one's own responsibility.

Having concluded before the surgery that she had sufficient reason to proceed, the problem of guilt became for the moment a vague notion. The intensity of the resulting depression surprised her, though the doctor had advised her that emotional recuperation after any surgery took time.

"What shall I do?" she begged Juan.

He had no answer, but he knew enough to avoid reminding her of his warning. "What's done is done," he said, plagued by the memory of having originally made the suggestion. "We must go on to provide a good life for the children we already have."

His words brought up the specter of another danger. God's anger directed at her was a manageable fear compared to the one that now overtook her. Her innocent children might, through no fault of their own, have to bear the unpleasant consequences of her guilt, a worse punishment than anything she had previously imagined. "They're innocent, Lord. They're innocent," escaped from her lips whenever the fear overtook her.

When she went to confession, Father Alfonso's reaction surprised her. She had expected his disapproval and his expression of disgust, but through the mesh of the confessional, she heard something else in his voice.

"What's done is done," he said. "God is infinitely forgiving."

"He will never forgive me," she said.

"Have you no faith?"

"I need a sign of forgiveness."

"God has forgiven you; now you must forgive yourself."

"I need a sign," she said.

"Then pray for one, and you will get it," he assured her.

"Are you certain?"

"You try my patience," he said. "Only one thing I must ask you to do: keep silent about what you have done, else the practice will be encouraged."

Despite her faith, Ramona found Father Alfonso's words difficult to accept.

Exile

Chapter 25

IN THE MIDDLE of July, a post office notice announcing
the arrival of a package aroused Maria's expectations, a
surprise such a long time yet before Christmas. Except when
shopping from the Sears Roebuck catalogue, the necessity
to pick up a package at the post office rarely came up. In the
Ortega family, only Juan had a Sears catalogue, his window
to a world with an infinite number of objects to dream about.
The notice, however, was addressed to Maria.

On Saturday morning, after having checked at the post
office, she went to Juan's house to tell him about the arrival
of the package.

"It's too large for me to carry," she said.

"I will go with you."

"It's too large for you also," she said.

"We'll take a wheelbarrow. Justicio will lend us his, I'm
sure."

They walked to Justicio's house, where a wheelbarrow
idly awaited in the backyard.

"Of course, take it," Justicio said, "but I want to be there
when you open the package. From New York is it?"

"Yes from New York," Maria said.

The word spread that a package had arrived from New
York, and by the time Juan and Maria returned from the
post office everyone who had the slightest hope of receiving
something had arrived at Maria's door. Even some who
did not expect to get anything showed up to share in the
excitement of seeing the abundance of America come out of
a cardboard box.

Juan carried the box into the house, and placed it on the table. Everyone had gathered in Maria's kitchen. Maria cut the twine, slit the gum tape with a paring knife, and delved into the box as if at an archeological dig; the first layer, crumpled newspaper, unceremoniously removed. Maria then paused to gaze down at the first object, and slowly held up for everyone to see a pair of jeans.

"These must be for you, Juan. I think they will fit you," Maria said.

"Cowboy pants," Juan said.

He held the pants to his waist, not something he could wear to work at the hospital, but no one paid attention to the pants anymore. Maria had gone on to the next object, a shirt too big to fit anybody there, but no problem, she would find someone to give it to. Then she pulled out a white wool sweater with buttons down the front, a marginally useful object in a tropical climate with only one or two slightly cool nights a year. Many women, however, wore sweaters to church on Christmas Eve for reasons unconnected to the weather. Similarly, natives of the island insisted on a winter season, and no one went to the beach in the winter, though the tourists, who didn't know any better, flocked to them. A sweater was good, though the one that came out of the box looked a little too plain and not the right color. North Americans had no sense of color, but one could forgive them that. The faults of the rich only made them quaint. Maria handed off the sweater to the nearest person, Alejandra Tañon, more than happy to take it.

Though gratified to be the agent of generosity, Maria waited for the box to yield something suitable for her. The delay about to be remedied, she spied a garment apparently covered with green sequins. Reverently, she pulled it out of the box and held it up. A profusion of exclamations escaped the lips of the awed onlookers as Maria held up a party dress, the kind one saw only in the movies. Of course in North America everyone had a dress like that, and now Maria had one too. She continued digging out items and finding the appropriate receiver until everything was out of the box.

On their way home, after the unpacking of the box from New York, Juan said to Ramona: "She wants to go to America."

"What for?" Ramona asked. Leaving home was an uncomfortable idea for her. Life wasn't easy anywhere. Why would it be any easier in a strange place with cold weather and a different language? Not knowing what they were getting into, people got sucked in by the glitter, but life was more than glitter. You can't cook dinner in a sequin dress. Going to America wasn't for Ramona.

"Well, Tomas is going. He's leaving soon and taking his whole family. His sister, Inez, is already there. She ran off to New York with Alberto. You remember him? Once upon a time you used to dance with him a great deal."

She ignored the reference to Inez, whom she had never much liked and for whom she had considered Alberto just the right partner, at least on the dance floor. "All the more reason why she shouldn't go," Ramona said. "I love Maria. God knows she's my best friend, but I can't condone her behavior with Tomas. It's not for me to judge, God forgive me, but most of all God forgive her."

"I suppose she knows what she's doing," Juan said. He had very clear ideas of right and wrong in his mind, but in his heart they became murky. He knew that very well, but actions came from the heart not from the head. That too, he knew very well. All around, he saw everyone pay lip service to propriety, then proceed to self-interestedly act without compunction. He envied Ramona's ability to make both realms coincide. She seemed devoid of conflict, never tempted by evil thought.

"She's decided to go," he said. "I don't suppose there's anything anyone can do about it."

"No, I suppose not," Ramona agreed.

"I'm the last one left," he said. "I'll be alone."

"You have us," she responded, "me and the children."

"Yes," he said, but she could see that he was thinking about New York. "Do you suppose that it's true, what they say about America, that one can get rich there?"

She had never considered being rich, wealth something that came to people through an accident of birth, like being tall or short or beautiful. God bestowed wealth in some manner incomprehensible to her, so that at a glance it seemed random and arbitrary, an appearance brought about by the limitations of human understanding.

"We don't need to be rich," she said. "Don't we have everything we need?"

"We can have everything we need in New York and more."

"You have a job here," Ramona argued. "Why do you want to go somewhere else?"

"In New York I can make more money," he said.

"I will never speak English," she said.

"You will," he insisted. "You'll want to when you get there."

Had he looked into her eyes at that moment he would have seen the closing of the door through which the new language would have entered. He would have seen the latch bolted, the lock snapped, and the key thrown into a wilderness. The language would be denied an entrance, as her anger was denied an exit, an even exchange.

Chapter 26

"GO TALK TO HIM," Maria urged Juan. "Maybe he'll listen to you."

"I don't work the land anymore," Juan answered. "Why would he listen to me?"

"Mama doesn't want to sell the land," Maria said.

"If she can't stop him, who can?"

"You have to try," she said. "There's no one else here now."

From the city, he took a public car out to the countryside. At Mucarabones, he got off, walked down the road along the track, pass the loading zone to where, on oxcarts, the cane from the neighboring fields was brought to be loaded. Beyond the loading platforms he saw two large mounds of earth; from the top of each a column of smoke rose toward the sky, charcoal being made for local use.

He veered onto a dirt path wide enough for an oxcart, but approaching the gully, it narrowed. From the top, he saw the river winding into the distance in opposite directions. The trail led down hill to a wooden bridge. Tall grass grew on either side of the river, and beyond the bridge the path ascended on the side of the hill. Again the sugar cane, the road traversed through the fields of tall growth on either side, occasionally, by an undulation of the terrain, he caught a glimpse of the distant mountains. Finally, he came to an opening in the cane fields, and he turned left over the clay *batey* in front of his father's house. Cane surrounded the house; and beyond, extended the forest where the coffee grew in the shade.

All his brothers had left. Even before the war, Roberto had gone out to sea. All that time, Julia worried, especially after Emiliano was killed, kept her eyes away from the newspaper headlines, afraid to hear about the merchant ships sunk by German submarines. After the war, Roberto had settled in New York, urging his brothers to join him, and now Juan was the only one still home. Even so, no one wanted to get rid of the land. They had left the island thinking that they would return some day, back to the land that had come down through their mother, Ortega land rather than Atorey, and they carried the name, if not the blood; the name attached them to the land.

He had not grown up in this house. Still, the old life he had known as a child persisted with slight differences, almost unnoticeable to outsiders, but some signs of change, the kitchen stove no longer the sand table he remembered in the old house. Now kerosene, rather than wood, fed the flames. Water was still fetched from the well. In town, he had running water and electricity too, whereas up here in the country still the kerosene lamps. But life was changing, and electricity would come to this house soon enough and running water too, but ownership of the land had to be preserved, although he lived in town—a contradiction perhaps, but life was full of contradiction.

He walked through the front door without knocking. For a moment, he observed his mother as she sat at the table peeling green peas into an iron pot. She was alone in the kitchen and her face at that instant more relaxed than he ever remembered. He observed for the first time the child she had once been, before the burdens had etched her face creating a stern mask necessary against the world, hiding her true self even from her children. She sat there as if time had rolled back, and her body had transformed to what it had once been, before she had been swallowed by life beyond childhood.

Startled, he realized for the first time that the image he had cherished from as far back as he could remember might have been an illusion, that she was not, like a Greek goddess, a bigger-than-life personage in control of destiny. *"Como esta, Mama?"* he said, and she, awakened from her reverie, smiled before her mask returned to protect what was left of her. She got up from her seat to embrace him, and again he felt they had changed places, and he, entering an unfamiliar terrain, was expected to have more influence, she a damsel just arrived on a donkey and leading a steed on which hung a suit of armor for him to don a quest against the unknown.

"You came alone?" she asked.

He wondered whether she was letting him know of his insufficiency, that she needed consolation from another woman, even if from only a daughter-in-law whom she had kept at a distance. Perhaps she was preparing to succumb to Federico's will, as she had always done, something within driving her, pulling her, and she ultimately unable to resist.

"I came to talk to Papa about the land," he said.

She sat down again and resumed peeling the peas as if the task were soothing. "Yes," she said, "of course, but what can you do? He will not change his mind."

"Have you told him what you want?" he asked, knowing that her need would have no influence on Federico.

The answer obvious and his having asked merely a gesture to hide the rising sense of futility, Julia continued to peel the peas without answering her son's question.

"Where is he now?" Juan asked.

"Down by the coffee grove," she said.

"I'll go find him," Juan said.

Julia kept silent for a moment, certain that Juan's efforts would be useless. She would just wait for the inevitable. "Selling the land in Naranjito was all right," she said before her son reached the door. The floating image of Pepina had followed from Naranjito, refusing to stay behind. Federico never mentioned Pepina anymore, but Julia knew that Pepina haunted Federico also, worked her wiles on him, always trying to get him back. She sometimes saw on Federico's face the stress of resisting, other times the glee of having overcome, but always some sign that Pepina had not given up, that she lurked in the shadows, awaiting her chance to pounce and repossess him.

The image of Pepina still in Naranjito regretting her loss plagued Julia. Pepina could hardly walk, some people said, rarely got out bed. The thought of Pepina's death ending the suffering for both of them invaded Julia making her shudder, but realizing the absurdity of thinking herself that powerful eased her conscience. Still, the problem persisted.

Julia remembered many years back, soon after having moved from the place, trekking back to Naranjito and up the mountain trail to see her sister Ervina. In their conversation the subject of Pepina inevitably came up.

"I hear she's is not well," Julia said.

"She's not well at all," Ervina responded. "I go down to see her once a week."

"You feel compelled to visit her?"

"She's still one of us," Ervina said.

"How is that?"

"I don't know. I just feel it."

"You feel sorry for her, because I took her husband?"

"I didn't say that," Ervina responded. And indeed she didn't see her sister as having schemed, never having been told of the plan to produce a son before Arturo's departure.

"She's not well enough to take care of the child," Ervina said. "I've offered to let him live here with us."

"And have they accepted?"

"The boy wants to be with his father."

"You're suggesting that I take him?"

"I'm not suggesting anything," Ervina said. "I'm only telling you what's going on. Federico does owe the boy something."

"The boy is willing to leave his mother?"

"She's bedridden most of the time. He needs to be in a regular place."

"And his grandparents, they're not willing to take him?"

"He's not attached to them, or perhaps they're not attached to him. Possibly he reminds them too much of his father."

"And who wants to be reminded of such a man?"

"Forgive me if I offend you," Ervina said. "But I have to say what I see."

"Of course," Julia said. "I should see Pepina and offer to take the child."

"Oughtn't you first consult Federico?"

"He has no choice. He's the boy's father. In any case, he's indifferent about such matters. My speaking to her might be very awkward, but I know that Federico will not do it himself."

"I can go in your place," Ervina offered.

"No," Julia continued, "I need to face Pepina and assure her that I'm willing to take care of her son, if she's willing to let him go. But you can accompany me down to see her. It will be easier for her if you're there."

The main street in Naranjito looked the same as when Julia had walked by the town square under the gaze of the townspeople to whom she represented a conflict between Federico and Don Ivan. On her way to see Pepina this time no one noticed, as if no one recognized her or everyone had forgotten her and had moved on to monger new gossip. The apparent invisibility relieved Julia, but she wondered whether the development had an opposite effect on Pepina, whether the town's current indifference to Federico's

178 / MIGUEL ANTONIO ORTIZ

treatment of her intensified her pain. She had to endure the town's acceptance of Federico's attitude of indifference. He had created for himself a two-sided image, the desirable side making convenient the ignoring of the other. Julia understood the dilemma, saw that the town's attitude resembled her own, willing to hang on to the one side of Federico that fulfilled her fantasy of the perfect man.

But no, that was not it at all, she told herself. She had no fantasy of perfection. She saw his shortcomings, the part of him that led into darkness but made no difference to the allure he cast on her. She saw him as he was, and yet she could not keep herself from loving him. She had no other word for what she felt. Some would attribute her action merely to physical desire, but she knew better, certain that she could ignore the needs of her body. She feared saying that he had captured her soul, but what else could she say if she ruled out the body? She sometimes wondered whether a difference existed between the two, whether a boundary marked the end of one and the beginning of the other, or whether there was no boundary at all, each flowing into the other, the difference between the physical and spiritual only an illusion.

Julia and Ervina turned from the main street of Naranjito to walk up a hillside and traverse through the alleyways that wound through the neighborhood of shacks on that side of town. Already feeling sorry for Pepina, walking through that part of town increased Julia's discomfort and her feeling of guilt.

"Her life had come to this," Julia said to her sister who walked beside her.

"We're all but a step away," Ervina noted.

"I suppose you're right. Every day I worry whether Federico will buy land before all the money is gone."

"Pepina is beyond that," Ervina said. "Here we are."
She pointed to a shack.

"Why does she put up with this? Why doesn't she go live
with her parents?"

"She thinks Federico will never return if she does that."

"Federico will never go back to her even if he were to
leave me."

They stood by the door of Pepina's place, and Ervina,
having ascended the few steps, leaned into the opening and
called to Pepina.

Pepina, like a specter, approached the front door where
the two sisters stood, Julia transfixed by Pepina's gaunt
appearance.

"How are you?" Julia asked, the only words that came
to her mouth as she simultaneously realized the absurdity of
the question, the obvious answer before her.

"God only knows," Pepina responded in a tone that
negated the usual meaning of the phrase. "And you, how
are you?"

"I'm all right," Julia said as she wondered whether
Pepina recognized her. She had the urge to introduce herself
to ensure that Pepina knew who spoke to her, but she resisted
doing anything that might further complicate the moment.
She turned to her sister with an expression of dismay hoping
that Ervina would provide some reassurance. But Ervina
did not rush to her sister's aid, but merely waited. Julia
attempted to absorb the moment.

Pepina's image emerging from the semidarkness
brought with it a sense of timelessness. Julia wished that
she could go back to the moment when she had refused to
dance with Federico. She had believed in that refusal while
simultaneously knowing the impossibility of maintaining it.
Every day she made decisions that provided the illusion that
the outcome of her life depended on her will, yet she well

knew that she could not have acted other than she did. She did not foresee Pepina's demise, but even had she seen the outcome, she could not have prevented the suffering that she now saw before her.

"Pepina, you must take care of yourself."

"My illness is incurable," Pepina said with full conviction.

"You're imagining that."

"Am I?"

"Of course you are."

"Father Alfonso says prayer will cure me."

"He's right. You have to try."

That visit had been long ago, but Pepina's image still plagued Julia. It lurked in the background, no way to get rid of her for certain, buried away for a while, barriers erected to hinder it from returning but nothing permanent or insurmountable.

"You understand, don't you, that we had to leave Naranjito," she said looking up at her son and wondering why she was telling him this. Why imply that a burden came with the name, and if there had been a debt, wasn't it already paid off? Wasn't that what Emiliano had done, paid the price of having come into this world as a ruse? More than was due, the boy dead and she plagued with guilt at having put him on the altar, a sacrificial lamb with no choice. But perhaps that was the key to everything, since she had believed for a while, as she planned and carried out her scheme, the action her decision, her choice to carry out or not, but she soon found herself in the predicament of being propelled beyond her will; and then, the question arose: had she had at any time the power to withdraw?

"I'll go find him," Juan said. He knew that his feet would lead him to the spot, as if they had a mind of their own, and the rest of the body had no choice.

"Can anyone find him?" she asked knowing full well that her son was trying to convince himself of something he doubted, something that disturbed him, having caught a glimpse of a frightening reality he didn't at the moment want to face. Being practical, he put off the confrontation and waited for a more appropriate moment when the odds might be in his favor, as if he saw the possibility of overcoming an unknown force.

"There has to be something," he said, "that keeps him going."

"What keeps all of us going?" she asked not expecting an answer.

He looked at her, trying to decipher who she really was and what her words meant. There was more there than what he saw, and he wondered whether she was trying to tell him something in some mysterious language that he had yet to learn, another of his shortcomings rising to plague him. He should have prepared for the confrontation, but he had failed to do so, had neglected his duty. But really, how was he to have known, not having sprouted full grown from the head of his maker? He suddenly realized that there was nowhere else to go, knowledge that resembled a break in a sky full of dark clouds through which the sun suddenly made an appearance. Clarity available for an instant, but perhaps that was all he needed, all he was going to get at the moment. It provided hope, and he was ready to proceed as soon as he determined the direction.

"One step at a time," Julia said, reading his face, his eyes spouting the questions that had no answers, and she, having looked into them for so many years, knew precisely what he wanted.

"I don't know," he said and stopped, stood there thinking, perhaps trying to remember what it was that he didn't know; or rather, trying to decide whether to reveal the scope of his ignorance. The dimness of his eyes and the tight expression on his face masked some pain at an indefinite locality in his body, or perhaps not even in his body but in some other nameless part of him that he didn't want to reveal.

"Go talk to him," she said, having nothing else to suggest, feeling that words made no difference and silence might relieve her of the burden, one she didn't deserve, had not intended to take on, one that had overwhelmed her without her consent.

"That's why I came," he said, "to talk to him."

She heard the doubt in his voice, and yet she persisted in playing her role, for the moment ignoring the futility of the endeavor. He was shaken, a minute later, realizing that she might not be aware of it at all.

"Yes," she said, "you're the only one left."

Juan wondered whether he heard disappointment in her voice, whether she believed that some other of her siblings might confront Federico with more authority, one of those more bound to the land even though further away, or perhaps for that very reason, the land having become something else in the memories of those who had left, something which every day grew more attached and eventually indistinguishable from any other part of them. He wondered whether that was possible, whether he too would feel a more urgent need for the land if he were away, something to look back to, to imagine from a foreign place without the comfort of familiarity.

The woman sitting at the table and shelling the peas wanted to hold on to the land, to remember something else that the land was attached to, something from the past, impossible to forget even if never mentioned. Juan wondered whether someday he too would have something unmentionable to remember, though he could not at the moment imagine what that could be. There would be something. He was sure, if certainty could be ascribed to a premonition, seeing into the future beyond the physically possible but just as real.

"I'll go find him," Juan said.

She watched her son descend the steps into the backyard. The chickens and the ducks scurried about oblivious of everything other than the immediate task of pecking the ground and keeping others from beating them to each speck of grain, gobbling it once there first, but either way, forgetting that instant and going on to the next.

Juan walked down to the stream and followed the gully until he spied his father in the coffee grove. Showing no sign of welcome or of regret, Federico turned on hearing his son's footsteps, and Juan in turn vacillated uncertain whether already the outcome of his visit was determined. He saw his father for a moment among the trees as just another man whom he need not fear nor restrain from confronting. If life were only that simple, reason dominant, controlling the entrance to that other realm from where chimeras constantly threaten to emerge, and sometimes surely did, to overwhelm everyday reality. That phenomenon too had to be considered reality, just as important as anything else, or even more so, history a narrative of human madness, behavior with no rational explanation, all a sign of how at its inception life was designed to survive.

Juan gazed at the red berries that hung on the green trees, the beans to be roasted and ground to make the drink that spurred you in the morning, woke you from sleep that often provided a window into another world where the primitive persisted. For a moment, he saw his father as a figure from that other world, but he suppressed his fear and gazed at the old man whose fingers caressed the leaves of a coffee tree.

"There you are," Federico said.

"Yes, here I am," Juan retorted.

"Your mother sent for you?"

"No, I came on my own."

"Good then," Federico said.

"So you know why I'm here?"

Federico's vaguely smiled but said nothing. He waited to hear what had brought his son out to the coffee grove instead of waiting in the house. His mother's company was surely not too much for a son who seemed so different from the others. Whether that was good or bad he had yet to determine, his interest in such matters merely a curiosity, nothing else. He saw no connection between his own actions and that of his sons. Perhaps they would follow his footsteps but perhaps not. Only the devil knew such things, and of what use was it anyway?

"I don't suppose you've come to talk about women, have you?"

"That, I don't need to talk about," Juan said.

"I suppose not," his father chuckled. "Did you bring her along?"

"Bring who?"

"Ramona, of course, I don't think you'd bring the others to see your mother."

"There aren't any others."

"All right," Federico said. "There's time yet." He laughed and let go of the coffee branch. "When will you follow your brothers?"

"I never will," Juan said. "One woman is all I need."

"I meant going North."

"To the states, you mean?"

"Yes, to New York in particular."

"I haven't thought about it," Juan said.

"Haven't you?"

Why did the old man bring that up? Surely a distraction from the matter at hand, but Juan refused to be distracted. He came to talk about the land and saw the old man standing in the coffee grove, touching the berries, caressing them almost. Perhaps Julia had misunderstood his intentions. The land produced something that he could touch lovingly, a touch that had been denied to his own children.

"The time will come when I can't work the land anymore," Federico said.

Juan looked away from his father. He heard the gurgling of the stream at the edge of the grove. "That time isn't here yet," he said.

"It's time for me to move back to town," Federico said.

"And the land?"

"Do you want to work it?"

Federico picked a few berries from the coffee tree and rolled them in one hand. He turned to walk down the slope and across the stream onto the path leading back to the house. Juan silently followed.

Chapter 27

A N AUTOMOBILE DROVE up the dirt road and into the *batey* of the Ortega place. The noise of the engine startled Julia in the kitchen preparing lunch for her husband and son about to return from the field by the stream. Rarely did an automobile come this far up the road through the Atorey cane fields. Through the kitchen window Julia saw the stranger get out of the auto and walk toward the house. The man in a suit made Julia think of Sunday, a more likely day to see a man in such attire.

On hearing the knock on the front door, she went out to the porch to see what the stranger wanted, probably directions, having strayed, through some careless error, from the main road that ran pass the railroad loading dock. The stranger in the suit stood by the door, his hat in his hand. A bushy moustache cut across his face over his thick lips.

"Good day, I'm looking for Don Federico Atorey."

Processing those words took Julia longer than usual, not having at the moment expected to see a man in a suit searching for Federico.

"He's down by the coffee grove at the moment, but he'll be in for lunch soon enough," she said. "Come in an sit down, Mr...."

"Ramon Constable," the man said.

"A friend of my husband?"

"I'm here on business."

"Ah, for sure, what exactly?"

"I heard this place is for sale."

Ramon Constable worked for Agua Punto Sugar, a

company that bought parcel after parcel of land planted with cane as if the five-hundred-acre law did not exist.

Julia's facial muscles tightened, and she remained silent.

"Oh, I'm sorry," he said. "I don't like to break such news."

"I don't suppose you do," she said, "but you're probably used to it."

"Some things one never gets used to. I'll wait for your husband before I say anything else," he said, at the moment honestly concerned with Julia's feelings.

"Would you like some coffee?" she automatically asked and didn't wait for an answer. "Please sit down," she continued extending her hand toward the bench by the table as she retreated to the kitchen.

She thought of placing rat poison in the coffee, but that wouldn't solve the problem. Someone else would come along to buy the land. She had lived in town, and that had been pleasant enough, but now an uncomfortable urge to resist a return to that life overwhelmed her.

As she stood in the kitchen waiting for the water to boil, Arturo's image floated through the window. His glance inquired where he might find his son, and the revelation came to her that the next world didn't reveal secrets. Or perhaps Arturo had not reached the other world yet, still roamed the land he thought as his, even though everyone else thought of it as Federico's.

She heard the hens and geese squawk, and through the window she saw them scatter as Federico and Juan across the backyard approached the kitchen door. Federico preceded his son into the room to be met by Julia's stare. "The man from Aguapunto is here," she said.

"Ah," he uttered and walked into the next room where the man waited.

Juan looked at his mother, but no words came. He felt

dryness in his mouth. He thought of asking for a glass of water, but he refrained.

"He will sell the land," she said.

Juan drove the pickup truck he had borrowed from Montenegro Hospital up to Nuca Rabones to help his mother and father move down to San Geronimo. Julio Caraño and Ernesto Peron who had tilled the land and cut the cane at harvest time helped Federico and Juan load the truck. When everything was loaded, Julia walked through the empty house one last time. Starting at the front, she walked from room to room working her way to the kitchen all the way in the back. The room now empty of objects still contained the odor of country food that had seeped into the walls. The new house would not have that smell and perhaps would never acquire it, because it was made of concrete that would not absorb the smoke from cooking the way the wooden walls did. The new place was nice. Certainly, she would get used to it. The house was not really what she would miss, but everything else that surrounded it. She walked out through the back door and stood in the backyard where every morning she had strewn corn to feed the chickens and the ducks that scurried to pick up what she dispensed. She looked down the path that led through the copse, then pass the cane field and down the slope to the coffee grove

Out front the men doubled checked the truck to make sure everything was properly fastened.

"We're ready," Juan said.

"Go fetch your mother," Federico said.

Juan hesitated, stood silently wondering whether to insist that his father go offer some appeasement, but realizing the futility of standing up to Federico, he walked through the house to look for his mother. From the kitchen door, for a few minutes, he observed her in the backyard. She stood there erect, refusing to succumb to the moment.

Juan walked down the back steps to stand beside her. "Everything will turn out all right. You've left a place before."

"It's different this time," she said.

He knew what she meant, but he refused to dwell on it. "We never know," he said.

"I know," she said.

"We should go now," he continued. "Leaving won't get any easier."

"You're right," she said.

In the truck, heading toward San Geronimo Julia sat between the two men. She stared through the windshield at the road in front of her. The lump in her throat kept her silent.

Chapter 28

"THERE'S PLENTY OF ROOM in that house," Juan said, "and besides, it'll be only for a short time."

"Even a day will be too long for me," Ramona said.

"I'm sorry," Juan said. "I'll send for you as soon as I can."

Already caretaker of all the odds and ends, Julia voiced no objection to having more of the family under her roof. She had become a grandmother who played the role of mother to several of her grandchildren. Her oldest son, Emiliano, had fathered one child before the bullet found him. That child grew up in the Atorey house, Julia having insisted on keeping the child as Rosamaria tried to recover and restart her own life. Vincente, the same age as Mario, also lived with his grandparents. Vincente's father, Juan's younger brother, had moved to New York after his wife had been interned in an asylum. The Atorey household also accommodated Manuel, Pepina's son who found Julia's concern for him, along with being in sight of his father, a relief from his own mother's constant melancholy.

"I'll take anyone in," was Julia's mantra, "but everyone has to toe the mark without exception."

"Toeing the mark" became a debatable phrase, the "mark" constantly changing. At first glance, Federico followed no rules at all, the cause of Julia's depressions and outbursts of anger. Sometimes Federico failed to come home, and Julia pretended that he had gone out of town on business. No one dared to ask why he had failed to tell her he would be away, but if someone unfamiliar with the circumstances happened to ask, Julia would answer, "Of course I knew he would be away today," to most people a signal that more questions would be unwelcomed. Occasionally an insensitive person followed up by asking her why, in that case, had she set his place at the table and served his portion of the dinner before everyone else's. Sometimes her outburst response made the questioner sorry that he or she had asked. At other times, she remained calm and quietly explained the ritual of serving the man of the house first whether or not he was there for his meal.

Ramona and her four children moved into the Atorey house. Two upstairs rooms to use as she pleased foreshadowed how much space she would have in New York. She and her little girl shared a bed, and in that same room she put the baby crib for her youngest son. The older two boys shared a bed in the adjoining room. Everyday Julia Ortega got up at the same time. In the kitchen she picked up a pistil and a frying pan, and going from room to room with the pistil she banged on the frying pan. The daily reveille excluded Ramona's rooms, but the morning noises sufficed to wake her and the children. By the time they descended to the kitchen for breakfast everyone else had almost finished eating, Julia making sure everyone progressed. Almost always, Manuel would be missing, and Julia, taking the pan and the pistil to his room, held the instruments over his head and banged. All the young ones watched the comic effect of arousing Manuel from his deep sleep that resisted the first call of the day. "When you join the army, they'll have to blow the bugle over your head every morning," Julia said to him time and again as he opened his eyes in bewilderment at the sudden summons from his deep sleep. After a few days in the house, the older two of Ramona's children, Mario and Norberto, would in the morning stand by the door of Manuel's bedroom awaiting their grandmother's appearance with pistil and pan.

Ramona then prepared Mario for school and walked him to the gate of the courtyard that surrounded the church and the school. At recess time Ramona returned with a fruit drink. During the school day, the front gate of the church grounds closed, Ramona and other parents handed their children snacks through the iron bars of the back fence.

"If you want him to have a drink at recess, let him take it with him," Doña Julia one day said to her daughter-in-law.

"He's just a little boy," Ramona responded. "Why should I be away from him for so many hours?"

"Agh," Doña Julia uttered from the bottom of her throat. Boys would grow up to be men. They could be kept under control only while they were boys. But what did Ramona know about that?

"He's just a little boy," Ramona repeated.

Doña Julia saw the man he would eventually become, and that vision elicited the harshness, which Ramona took as disapproval of her, rather than of the man emerging within the boy. Had Julia been consistent, the misunderstanding might have been avoided, but consistency often impossible, the only way to avoid erroneous conclusions is to remove it from the scheme of judgment. Ramona believed that her children received less affection from Julia than did the other children in the house. Ramona took that as enmity directed at her. She searched for an explanation of Julia's antagonism. She might have simply asked Julia to explain herself, but the obvious simplicity of an action is often judged to be a weakness and prevents its execution. Doña Julia's hostility bewildered Ramona, willing to console her mother-in-law during her marital suffering that included Federico's infidelities as well as his lack of forethought in financial matters. Why he had sold the land remained a mystery, something which could have been kept in the family as opposed to the money that only he had access to and that eventually disappeared without an explanation even to Julia.

The children who roamed the Atorey house became victims of Julia's mood fluctuations, increasingly unpleasant, as Don Federico, desperately reacting to the assault of age, became less circumspect in his amorous sallies. More often now, at supper time the family experienced Julia's attempt to have everything go her way in order to compensate for her inability to deal with her predicament. Everyone at the table became nervous on noticing her dark mood, and even the boys inclined to be raucous tried to be quiet.

Chapter 29

"WHAT HAVE YOU done with your husband's books?" Father Alfonso inquired.

"They're under the house, stored in boxes," Ramona said. "I don't know what to do with them. It would cost too much to ship them to New York; besides, there's no room for them where he lives. I'll have to give them away."

"Have you checked them against the list of forbidden books?"

"No," said Ramona, "I never look at the books. I only read the missal and sometimes verses from the Bible."

"It wouldn't be a good idea to give away books that are on the forbidden list," he said, his voice deepening to indicate the emergence of matters from his repository of concerns.

"Juan wouldn't collect evil books," Ramona exclaimed, fearing the misinterpretation of her husband's intellectualism as a vice. She considered collecting books an unusual but harmless habit. She knew no one else who did such a thing, but there were much worse ways of spending time and money. His library was easier to tolerate than if, like his brothers, he kept a mistress.

"I'm sure he wouldn't do it on purpose," said the priest trying to calm her, "but he might not have been aware of which are forbidden."

Ramona agreed to let Father Alfonso inspect the books to make sure, before she gave them away, that none were on the forbidden list; that would prevent the possibility of an unsuspecting person being exposed to temptation; to what temptation, she didn't ask nor tried to imagine. Although the Ortegas all considered themselves Catholics, inviting a priest to the house would be looked upon unfavorably. Don Federico's attitude would probably be one of mirth rather than annoyance, but that brought up the possibility of having Father Alfonso feel insulted.

When Ramona informed Julia of Father Alfonso's desire to inspect Juan's collection of books, she was surprised by Julia's immediate assent.

"Don't tell Federico," Doña Julia went on to say. "He's hardly ever home. The priest can drop by when he's away."

Father Alfonso arranged to pay a visit right away. Suspecting that many of the books would be objectionable. Getting rid of them an achievement, he looked forward to delving through them. Spurred by the possibility of increasing the importance of the afternoon, he arrived at the house eager to search through the boxes, a task that would be the blessing of the day if not the whole week, depending on which books he found.

Doña Julia offered him the customary cup of coffee as soon as he arrived, and had he perceived the offer as mere politeness, he would have declined and would have proceeded to the task that had brought him to the house, but, knowing full well that she was not a churchgoer and that Ramona had been doubtful, at the outset, that his visit would be welcomed, he interpreted Doña Julia's attitude as more than civility. Suspecting an opportunity to do more than one task, he sat down to have the cup of coffee before dealing with the books, which, at the moment imprisoned, would remain so while he drank the coffee. He looked forward to the possibility that the mistress of the house wanted to undergo confession. If Ramona got up and left, he would know that they had arranged the encounter, and he would proceed with his duty. He slowly drank the coffee and waited in vain for that to happen. Doña Julia exhibited much charm, but the revealing of her sins failed to materialize. Slightly crestfallen, he reverted to considering the books the only purpose of his visit. Nevertheless, a man of spiritual optimism, he concluded that some attraction to the Church lurked in Doña Julia and would eventually emerge.

"Shall we look at the books?" he said, recovering from the disappointment of having failed to entice Julia's confession.

The women ready to lead him to the book storage, he followed them through the kitchen door and down the side to where the space between the ground and the first floor widened enough to allow entry with the least effort. Father Alfonso took his lack of height, in this instance, as a sign of good fortune. It provided him with ease denied to the others, and he went about the business with the least amount of physical discomfort. The two ladies, though of moderate height themselves, still had to stoop as they moved to where the boxes of books awaited judgment.

"It's a lot of boxes to go through," Ramona said, feeling sorry for the short man about to tackle the task of examining every one of them.

"What has to be done, has to be done," said the priest, like the optimistic child about to dig through the pile of dung in search of the pony. To him, finding books that required flames equaled physical ecstasy.

"I'll help you move the boxes," Ramona continued, feeling sorry for the man ostensibly working in her behalf.

Bent over to avoid the ceiling, Doña Julia came to her senses, and seeing no need to help, she excused herself and returned to the kitchen.

Finding the first objectionable book, *Madame Bovary*, surprised Ramona. She had expected to find none. Certain the book had gotten by without Juan's notice, she reasoned that everyone makes mistakes. It looked just like any other book, and the title contained no clue that it might contain the work of the devil. On finding the second and the third book, she became concerned. By the end of the search consternation prevailed. Clearly, Juan lacked compunction in choosing books for his library. Luckily the children, too young yet to read, had not been exposed, the objectionable books caught in time.

"What are we to do with these books?" she anxiously asked.

"We must burn them," Father Alfonso said very seriously. "That will keep them from falling into the wrong hands."

"I must get Juan's permission," she said, "They're his books."

"It's your duty to protect him from evil," the priest said. "There's no point in waiting to do what must be done. Besides, you said the books are staying behind when you leave for New York. We must keep them from being a danger to other people."

"What about the rest of the books?"

"I'll see that they find good homes," Father Alfonso said.

For a moment Ramona imagined that Father Alfonso had a library of his own, but that seemed too odd to be true. More likely, he would give the books away, perhaps to those members of the Gentlemen of the Holy Name who liked to read, if there were any. Surely there had to be some. Juan had been a member before he left for America. There had to be others like him who liked to read, though she could think of no one in particular.

Father Alfonso arranged for the books to be picked up. He decided to make the burning a public event. He would have preferred to conduct it in the churchyard, but to avoid damage to the lawn, where the schoolchildren had recess, he searched for another place. The housing development baseball field had been rented once to a traveling circus and another time to a traveling amusement park. The real estate promoters saw no problem in letting Father Alfonso use it for a book burning.

He arranged for the guilty books to be piled at a spot to which, from the church, he would lead a procession, a great event, with parishioners carrying banners and singing religious songs as they marched, candle in hand, to where the books would be set ablaze. To make sure that they remained in place awaiting their execution, he had the piled books guarded by two young men, but when the procession arrived at the burning site, Father Alfonso had the distinct impression that the pile of books had diminished. The two young guards swore that nothing had changed since they had arrived at their post. Having failed to list the books that had been condemned, Father Alfonso had no way to prove them wrong; and even if he had a list, he could not at the moment, with the parishioners looking on, delay the burning to check for missing books. The remaining ones produced a roaring fire, and he had to be content with that.

Doña Julia's complicity in arranging Father Alfonso's visit and her uncharacteristic sociability with him made Ramona reconsider how the relationship with her mother-in-law might proceed, at least while they both lived under the same roof. Doña Julia's ordeal, love for a husband who saw no need to relent his chasing after other women, aroused Ramona's charitable feelings. Julia resisted discussing with anyone the cause of her suffering, but as her character hardened, everyone saw the reason. Her short encounter with Father Alfonso revealed a possibility of reaching her before suffering mangled her beyond the possibility of repair.

"You know," said Ramona to Doña Julia one day as they worked in the kitchen, "all your sons and daughters love you."

"And you wonder whether I love them?"

"No, not at all," Ramona answered, determined to make

herself clear. "You have done the best you can. Father Alfonso always says we're only responsible for what's possible."

"I have failed at what I thought was possible," said Doña Julia.

Ramona refrained from asking why Doña Julia had ever thought that she could change Federico's ways.

"You don't know what I'm talking about, do you?"

"A man is what he is," Ramona said.

"I don't expect to change the man. I'm paying for betraying my first husband. What I didn't expect was for my children and grandchildren to bear the mark, the shame of having the wrong name."

"Is that all?" Ramona asked. The issue seemed meaningless to her. "The name is insignificant. None of them is ashamed to carry it."

"No one but me," Doña Julia retorted.

"The name doesn't matter," Ramona continued, "but I'm bothered by one thing: you're nice to all the children except mine. You ignore them. They too carry your name."

"I love them as much as the rest," Doña Julia retorted. "How can I not? They carry my blood and my name just like the others, as you say, but your children have you and Juan, while the others have no one but me."

That explanation failed to convince Ramona, but she dropped the matter. Doña Julia had enough problems, and Ramona would rather avoid becoming another thorn on her side. Soon enough Ramona would leave to begin a new phase of her life, while Julia would remain behind mired in a relationship that had little chance of improving. Though Julia had not uttered the words "for better or for worse" in front of the altar, the fact that she had so long lived with Federico and had borne his children amounted to the same thing.

Ramona saw little point in now making a fuss. Soon she

and her children would be leaving. Juan had already written to say that he had an apartment ready for them. All he needed now was to save enough money for their fare to New York. Ramona didn't look forward to making the trip, and the waiting increased her anxiety. Why was it taking so long when money lined the streets of New York? She imagined kicking a can on the sidewalk and watching the coins roll into the gutter.

Chapter 30

RAMONA AND THE CHILDREN descended from the four-engine plane into a world of subdued autumn light. Juan's embrace failed to dissipate the chill in her body. "The cold weather is not his fault," she told herself. "Humans do not control the climate." At least they were together again. She let the grief of having been separated rise to the surface. She had followed her husband to New York without embracing the fantasy that the move would improve her life. She had left everything behind to arrive at a place that would be forever foreign, where another language was spoken, one she would never learn. Yes, she would hold on to her language like a drowning person holds on to a buoy. She would not trade in her native tongue even though her children would grow up speaking the foreign one she would never understand, another price to pay.

"Don't cry," Juan begged. "You'll get used to the place. Give it a chance."

"I'm so glad to see you," she said. She would look only at him and the children from then on, and the dimness of the northern sunlight would become meaningless.

"Everybody loves it here," said Grego, who had driven his brother to the airport to pick up the family. "You'll love it too. Just wait and see." Grego had perfected a style derived from his father by adding a seductive honesty. Seeing Grego caught in the trap just like all the other Ortegas, except Juan, Ramona accepted the contradiction. She viewed Juan's escape as a fair exchange for the absence of tropical light. Moreover, she had to expiate what she believed to be her great sin, and she equated living in New York to suffering in purgatory; her arrival had at least that positive purpose.

"Now you'll get a ride home in the greatest car in the world," Grego said, "I washed it and shined it up this morning just so you'd have a grand entrance into the Bronx."

Indeed, the black Chevrolet had been waxed and would have sparkled, but Ramona knew it was meant to shine for some other woman. In the back, Ramona and the children now rode from the airport into the city. She had never before seen a building taller than two stories, so she now experienced the sensation of being swallowed by a beast that lacked compassion.

"Look at those tall buildings," Grego urged. "What do you think? Amazing, right? You're going to love it here. There's one wonder after another."

Grego interpreted the slight sound she emitted as a sign of awe. But Juan knew the lack of words was a negative signal, and seeing her in distress pained him. She would feel better tomorrow, or the day after, when she got used to the new setting. Yes, she would feel better, he insisted, trying to keep the malignity from overcoming him. Like Balaam's donkey and not its rider, he recognized the obstacle, but at the moment, just so that he might have an excuse for an excuse, he wished for the blindness of the master rather than the sight of the beast.

"It's a long walk up the stairs," she said when they got to Rogers Place, the apartment five flights up.

"You soon get used to the climb," Juan said.

Ramona settled down into a new life. She had to get used to living in a five-story building, from where keeping an eye on the children out on the street all day was impossible. This enormous difference between indoor and out had not existed at home and required a different way of looking at life. But she had other problems besides readjusting herself to provide just what the children needed. She had lived in poverty before but not in constraint. Yes, that's what it meant to live in a three-room apartment on the fifth floor of a building, a small space with no easy access to the freedom of the outside. Soon enough she had to consider another factor: the difference in climate that she had heard so much about unexpectedly startled her. Imagination had failed to provide her with the details of what cold weather meant. She observed through the window the white flakes descend from the sky to hide the blackness of the street under a white cover.

Coming from the tropics had failed to prepare her for that first winter, and Juan, denying the problem even to himself, had said very little. Even without boots she made her way to the church through the white powder. She accepted the pain of frigid feet as another means of expiation. She trekked to the church to do the Stations of the Cross, the cold on her feet nothing in comparison to the pain she saw depicted on the wall. She knew of nothing more arduous than the ordeal a Man had endured for the sins of the world, so she hoped that her own suffering had a purpose.

Sometimes she stood by the window and tried to figure out the meaning of what now confronted her. She would never get used to this world, the details of which she had failed to envision before she arrived. Doubtlessly, it was part of her punishment, and she had to bear it. Perhaps she would get used to it. She had experienced many transitions that required changing her view of the world, a normal progression in life, but she had not expected to be overwhelmed by a natural phenomenon like snow falling; or more persistently, having to constantly decipher a language that her mind and her soul resisted. True, she now lived next door to Juan's brother, Grego, whose partner, Rosario, friendly enough, did her best to assist Ramona in getting used to the new place.

"You can save money on the electricity," Rosario said to Ramona.

"I keep the lights out as much as possible," Ramona responded. "There's nothing else I can do. What else is there but the refrigerator, and that has to be kept on."

"Don't be silly," said Rosario. "I keep the lights on all the time. Why torture yourself to save money? You can stop the meter from running. It's simple. I'll show you how to do it. Come with me."

Both meters were side by side in the hallway between their apartments. Rosario dragged a chair out to the hallway and climbing on it pulled a metal strip she had previously placed behind the meter to keep it from functioning.

"You do that all the time?" Ramona asked trying to hide her anguish at witnessing a crime.

"Everybody does it," Rosario answered. "It's nothing. We have to survive."

Chapter 31

ROSARIO HAD HER own worries. Her relationship with Grego was her second try at living with a man, her first husband having deserted her, leaving her with a child, now a teenage boy. Rosario and Grego had a child of their own, but Rosario did not take that as a guarantee of Grego's attachment. She had gradually discovered the Ortega syndrome, and, convinced that she had been too lax with her first husband, she saw no remedy but to keep a sharp lookout. She believed that if she had kept a closer eye on her husband, she might have prevented his straying. She wouldn't make the same mistake with Grego, so she prepared for whatever action might be required. Any impartial observer would have concluded that she was building a house on a geological fault, counting on the violent inclinations of nature to remain dormant and hoping that her fears would never materialize.

She became alarmed when she noticed a change in his routine. He began to arrive later at night. At first he claimed to have changed his work hours, but he kept leaving at the same time in the morning. When she pointed that out, he slightly changed his story, saying that he worked two shifts to safeguard the spot for a friend who had been hospitalized.

"You can come to work with me," he said, "and ask everyone there whether I'm telling you the truth."

"You know you'll be in trouble if I do that," she said, though she knew full well that his colleagues would cover for him. At the same time, she wanted his words to be true. How could this be happening again?

"I don't know if he's telling the truth," she said to

Ramona. "When he tells me, he doesn't have the lying look on his face. It's almost impossible to lie without a hint."

"That's true," Ramona said, though she knew that the Ortegas were born actors who chose what to present to their audience, all but Juan, who lacked that talent.

"I can tell when he's lying," Rosario said, trying to convince herself, but at the same time wondering whether Ramona had reached the same conclusion.

"If he wanted to leave you, he would tell you," Ramona said.

"He wouldn't tell me anything," Rosario responded. "He knows I'll kill him if he cheats on me."

"You'd rather lose him altogether?"

"I don't share a man," Rosario said. "I'm not like his sister."

"Ortegas are Ortegas," Ramona said.

"What about Juan? You let him cheat on you?"

"Only his name is Ortega. He's not like the rest of them."

"So you think. Sooner or later you'll find out."

She recalled the note from a nurse at the hospital she had once found in Juan's pocket. The memory lurked about, sometimes completely out of sight, like a beast that slept for a whole season or a flower that bloomed only when the weather promised sufficient sunlight. Ramona would rather have immediately uprooted the plant, have let it die, have fed it to the animals, but it had resisted all her attempts to destroy it. Now she counted on Juan's fidelity to keep a shadow on it, ensuring its eventual death.

"I should hire someone to follow him. Then I would know for sure," Rosario said.

"You don't want to know," Ramona said.

"Wouldn't you?"

"If Juan were cheating, I'd rather not know," she said, but she immediately felt guilty for lying.

"Well, I have to know," Rosario continued. "I'll have to get someone to follow him when he leaves work. Then I'll know where he goes."

"And if he just spends time at a bar with his friends?"

"If he just hangs out with other guys, that's all right with me," she said.

"Ah," Ramona murmured, as if that were the one thing that would disturb her.

"If Juan were out drinking, it would bother you, but if he was with another woman you'd overlook it. You've become an Ortega," Rosario said.

Ramona let that phrase sink in, deceiving oneself something much worse than being deceived by someone else. "Don't you also want to be an Ortega?" Ramona asked, overwhelmed with sympathy for Rosario who had been too trusting of an Ortega, but so had she, and she saw herself coping with her fear just as irrationally as everyone else.

"I can't let him abandon me and Lydia," Rosario answered, anger quickly swallowing her fear.

"You must do what you must," Ramona conceded.

Early on Saturday morning a few weeks later, noise from the street awakened Juan and Ramona.

"Oh, my God, it's Rosario," Juan said, as Ramona followed him to the window to see what was going on.

In the street, with a large wrench borrowed from the super, Rosario methodically pummeled Grego's black Chevrolet, smashing window after window as she walked around the vehicle. She was just about to smash the engine lid when Grego ran to stand between her and the beast she was trying to destroy.

"Get out of my way unless you want to get hit," she shouted.

He believed her and for a second dealt with the quandary of choosing to protect himself or the car, but on seeing the police arrive and knowing that one more blow to the car would make little difference, he retreated.

The two policemen, trying to maintain serious expressions, stepped out of their car, and on seeing the two persons involved, immediately arrived at an accurate assessment of the scene.

"Put down the wrench, ma'm," the first officer said. Each of the patrolmen had now put both his thumbs within his belt, near the buckle.

Rosario looked at them intently trying to determine who they were and why they were talking to her about something that was her business and no one else's.

"Is this your wife, sir?" one of the officers asked Grego, attempting to verify their assumptions. "It's my car," Grego said, his mind thoroughly absorbed in the condition of the auto, the policeman's words just as clouded to him as to Rosario.

"Okay, it's your car. Is it your wrench too?"

"Wrench?"

"Put down the wrench, ma'm," the other patrolman said. "Let's make it easy on everyone."

Rosario put down the wrench.

After having her move a few paces back, the first policeman picked up the tool. "We'll have to take this in as evidence," he said.

"What about the car?" Grego asked in consternation. Physically losing the car would cause him more pain.

"If you're going to sue her for damages, just take pictures of it," the policeman advised him, "but she's your wife, so I don't see that suing is the way to go. You want us to take her in?"

"In the house?" Grego asked.

This time the policeman, unable to retain his demeanor, laughed and turned to his partner saying, "Maybe she hit'm on the head, too."

"Down to the station," the other said, trying to remain composed.

"You're not taking me anywhere," Rosario said coming out of her stupor.

"Be calm," the first policeman said. "Do yourself a favor. You wrecked his car; that's punishment enough for whatever he did."

"So you say. What about my heart? A car is nothing compared to that, and what about his daughter? Is he thinking about her?"

"We're not the family court," the cop said. "You go there and work out your problems. Right now we'll just take the wrench." Turning to Grego he added, "You come down to the precinct and pick it up in a few days."

"It's not my wrench," Grego said.

"We'll just take it then," the policeman said, passing it over to his partner. "It's a useful device."

"Don't take it home; your wife might use it," one officer said to the other as they got back into their car.

"That'll be the day."

People had come out into the street and both Rosario and Grego, subdued, made their way past the group and up the steps of the building.

Chapter 32

IN THE AFTERNOON, having been up since six in the morning, Ramona was alone in the apartment. From the time she had prepared breakfast and seen the children off to school, she had worked almost without stop. Her body signaled a break in the day. She had finished her morning chores and she had now to reorganize her energy to tackle the afternoon. Tired, but not the dead tired she knew she would be by the time she would kneel to say her evening prayers, the exhaustion that seeped into her bones had yet to become unpleasant. It made her aware of her body, and it made her long for a hot bath. But she had no time for indulgences. Instead, she sat down in an armchair for a few minutes just to give herself a breather.

Her hand came to rest on a worn spot in the upholstery, and she looked around to the other pieces of furniture to confirm what she already knew, they were all in poor condition. They had not been in the best of shape when purchased, secondhand, on credit. Her eyes moved to a discolored spot on the linoleum floor. Children are hard on an apartment, she thought, but you can't keep them from playing. They're only children, and it's better that they play inside than in the street. They spend too much time in the street anyway. She stopped short. The children had nothing to do with it. The furniture was worn. It had not been new to begin with, and furniture got worn in normal use. She had to stop blaming the children. Accusing them was wrong, but sometimes she couldn't help it, one of her many failings, and she asked God in his infinite mercy to forgive her.

Sinful pride made her resent the old furniture. She had to bear without resentment her lot in life. No one was to blame—not even her husband. He did the best he could, a good man. She had not worn a new dress in years, but that wasn't terrible. She hardly ever thought about that. Sometimes she looked in the mirror and saw age encroaching. She had not expected those signs so soon with still more to come. She chastised herself for her selfish thoughts. The children had greater needs. She suffered sending them to school in their worn clothes. She tried to ease their self-consciousness, and they tried to assure her they would manage.

She would have preferred a different life. Having to sit in such shabby furniture mortified her when she had visitors. She would have liked to put on a better appearance, and why not? She didn't want so much, only the possible, if her husband were only more sensible in managing money. She had of course to be thankful for his goodness. He didn't gamble. He didn't drink the money away, precious little to begin with. God knew that she had not expected an easy life when she married him, but certainly she had not expected constant debt, constant worry that he would spend the rent money on an electric can opener or some other gadget. Anxiety made her quarrelsome. No matter how often he promised to be careful about how he spent money, his resolve seemed to make no difference. Sometimes she thought his carelessness was intended just to pique her. The conflict ate away at her. She didn't want that. Her love for him was the great event of her life, and she could conceive no greater catastrophe than to be without him.

Sitting in the armchair, in a city far from her homeland, a smile flitted across her lips, ironies of life sometimes amusing—how great her love had grown from nothing! He had courted her for five years. For five years she had refused him, but he had persevered. How ugly he seemed when she had first met him—his face covered with acne and his thin frame awkward. How could she, such a beautiful girl, be seen in the streets with him? Everyone would laugh, she so gay, and he so somber. At festivities, she never stopped dancing but flitted from one partner to another. He sat watching her. She couldn't get rid of him. Sometimes when she saw him come in by the front door she slipped out by the back. He was undeterred. She grew to know him: his kindness, his tolerance, his soft voice that always spoke reasonably. Her father and brothers didn't like him, and she unconsciously welcomed the chance to strike back at them. When they saw matters getting serious they proposed to give him a good thrashing and send him on his way. The day they waited in ambush for him, she sneaked out of the house to warn him.

Eventually they got married. She recalled the wondrous wedding dress of mysterious origin, later discovered to be Aunt Gloria Rincon's secret gift in opposition to the Rincon resentment toward the Sotos. She remembered those early years nostalgically. She loved him! And she didn't foresee his compulsive accumulation of debt. Of course she welcomed the stove with an oven. Very few people she knew then had a stove with an oven. The refrigerator, a blessing, but when they had to worry about the payments, the ice barrel seemed good enough. She learned the lesson quickly, but for him there was no hope.

She got up from the armchair. She looked around the parlor again and thought: "This is my cross to bear, and I must bear it with a cheerful heart. I'm paying for my sin." With that she went to the window to check the weather. The air chilly, she wondered whether the temperature would be the same on the street. She disliked living so far up, so unnatural, and climbing the stairs a task added to all the others. She put on a sweater to go out for the day's shopping. Halfway down the stairs she tried to remember whether she locked the door. Fear of someone breaking in forced her climb back to check. She found the door locked, her climb for nothing. Back home no one locked doors in the daytime. Here the door had always to be locked, no way for human beings to live. Again, she descended the steps, glad to emerge into the street leaving behind the smell of stale urine that emanated from behind the stairs. Yellow leaves fallen from a maple tree covered the sidewalk, and Ramona felt a childish joy to hear them crackle under her feet. Down the street she saw her little boy, the youngest, playing with other children. When he spotted her, the chubby dark-haired boy ran to meet her.

"Where are you going? Can I go?"

"I'm going shopping. You stay here and play."

"Please, can I go?"

"I'm going to church first," she warned him.

"I don't mind. I like the church."

"Do you?" she teased him.

Ramona went to church as often as she could, every Sunday and Saturday and several times a week. During Lent she went every day. Her son took her hand, and they walked down to St. John's on the corner of Claremont and Webster. In the church, she knelt to pray at one of the side altars. The little boy knelt beside her, but he soon became restless and got up. He walked up and down the aisle scrutinizing the Stations of the Cross. The painful scenes fascinated him, but for him pain was not redeeming. He switched his attention to the stained-glass windows, his eyes jumping merrily from one color to another. Tired of playing games with the colors and shapes he skipped back to his mother just in time to hear her whisper: "Please God forgive me my great sin."

After they left the church, the day took a turn for the worse. One Hundred and Sixty-third Street replete with vegetable stands, every shop overflowed into the sidewalk.

Stopping at one of those places, Ramona carefully chose three potatoes and handed them to the shopkeeper who placed them on the scale hanging over the vegetable bin.

"Two-and-a-half pounds," he said.

"Two-and-a-quarter," she corrected him.

"Right," he said.

She handed him four onions, which he proceeded to weigh, and seeing that she kept her eye on the scale he called out the correct weight. She handed him a cabbage. As he placed it on the scale another customer reached forward distracting Ramona for an instant. The shopkeeper had taken the cabbage off the scale before she noted the exact weight.

"Please weigh it again," she said to the grocer.

"I know how much it weighs," he said.

"But I don't," she responded, her voice rising.

"If you don't want the cabbage, don't hand it to me," he said.

"I want to see it on the scale," she said louder than she intended, the stress of the moment having made her lose control. No matter what vegetable stand she patronized, sooner or later they tried to put something over on her. She kept a constant vigilance on every penny in her purse.

His mother's haggling with the shopkeepers, her loud voice drawing attention, embarrassed the boy. "Hush," he said to her. He had gotten used to her loud voice at home, but out in the street it embarrassed him.

"Don't you dare speak to me that way," she angrily scolded him.

He sulked all the way home, and she regretted her harsh words. She didn't want to make life for any of her children harder than it had to be. Watching him, she reproached herself. She watched him cast sidelong glances at the toys in the shop windows, and she wished that she might make everything up to him by buying him something. But she knew that would be an indulgence more for her than for him—the kind of thing her husband would do, the kind of thing that made life more difficult.

By the time they got home, the other children had returned from school. The volume of noise they generated seemed limitless, a trait derived more from her than from Juan. Tormented by her own reflection, she saw that as God's judgment.

Indoors the boys often became rambunctious.

"Stop quarrelling!" she admonished them.

"It isn't me," Norberto said. "It's Mario."

"That's a lie. He started it."

"I don't care who started it, just stop."

A little while later she had to scream: "Stop running. This isn't a racetrack. In a house you walk."

"We are walking!"

"Don't walk so hard," she shouted.

At that moment they heard tapping on the floor coming from the apartment below, occupied by two old women, who often applied a broomstick to the ceiling.

"There you are," said Ramona. "You want to drive those poor old ladies to their graves?"

"If they can't stand a little noise maybe they belong in the grave," Mario blurted.

"How dare you say that?" she screamed. "Only God decides who lives and who dies! Are you God? Tell me, are you God?" She went on in that vein for a while; nothing would appease her, as if she had a recording inside of her that once turned on had to be played through. The children pretended deafness as they waited for her to calm down. Any attempt to assuage her useless, they let the flare-up run its course.

As the afternoon proceeded, Ramona resolved, as she did every day, to cope with the small irritations without losing her temper. For long, she had been making that resolution without success. On getting home from work, her husband added to the turmoil. Then, Ramona had five children to deal with rather than four. She patiently listened to his criticism of the dinner, always too salty or not salty enough or it had too much oil or the rice soggy. Afterward he sat down to read or to play with the children and Ramona off to the kitchen again.

By the time she got through washing the dinner dishes, she was ready to collapse. Her whole body ached, from the bottom of her feet to her shoulders her muscles sore. The discomfort penetrated her bones. Her head throbbed. She anxiously put the dishes away, and then she retired to the bedroom to say her evening prayers.

The ringing of the doorbell startled her, and she became more flustered when, on opening, she saw the bill collector. Not his regular day, Ramona, a little embarrassed, silently stood by the door. She didn't know quite how to behave with bill collectors. The man stood in the semi-darkness of the hallway. His round flabby face hovered above a shabby trench coat. In the darkness, Ramona couldn't discern the color of his eyes, and she never recalled from one time to the next whether they were brown or blue. She remembered, however, his rather large, red nose—a sight that ordinarily she would have found humorous.

The door ajar, she seemed confused about what to do next. Usually, she went to the kitchen cupboard to fetch the payment book containing five dollars. She would hand the book and the money to the bill collector who would put the money in his pocket, write down the amount in the book and on his own record card and hand the book back to her. When Juan left no money, Ramona or one of the boys would say, "He didn't leave anything today." This time, Ramona said nothing but stood at the door, merely looking at him as if she had forgotten her lines, glad to retreat when Juan stepped up behind her.

She listened to the conversation between the two men, and picked up enough to conclude that payments on the furniture were in arrears. After the bill collector left, Juan tried to slink back to the living room without looking into Ramona's face.

"How far behind are we?" she asked.

"Only a few weeks," he said, trying to avoid a scene.

"A few weeks? How many exactly?"

"A few weeks, woman! What difference does it make?"

"What difference?" her voice quivered. "I see! It makes no difference to you! Of course not! What do you care? But I care. I'm ashamed to live this way."

"There's no need to carry on," he said.

She didn't want to argue with her husband. His good qualities flashed before her. The helpless expression on his face moved her to want to comfort him, hold him, assure him that everything was going to be all right, but no sooner had those thoughts come to her that some trick of the eye made his expression seem grotesque and repugnant. Disgusted by his weakness, in confusion, she transformed her fear into anger.

"No, of course not. You never see any need. You have no shame. It's me and the children who have to bear this."

"What do you have to bear? Are you hungry? Is there not enough food on the table? Is there not a roof over your head?"

"You never understand, never!"

"It's you who don't understand. What do you want me to do, manufacture money?"

"You know perfectly well what you have to do."

"I suppose you think I drink the money away."

She only wanted peace, but his seeming lack of concern

provoked her. She saw it in the lines of his face—his indifference, his thoughtlessness, mocking her. She saw that his bland and calm expression only masked his real and diabolical self. Amazed by how clearly she perceived him at that moment, she wondered why she often lacked that clarity.

"I don't think that, but drinking isn't the only vice in the world," she responded.

"Well then, what are my vices? Tell me!"

"Oh God, help me! Do I always have to see my children dressed in rags? Lilia has to go to school with holes in her shoes, but does that ever cross your mind? Does that ever worry you?"

He remained silent.

"I'm the one who has to worry. I'm the one who has to bear the shame. I'm the one who has to haggle over pennies in order to feed your children. That's something you always forget. They're your children too, and you should have some thought of them."

"Do you think I don't have feelings? Jesus! What am I to do?"

"You can start by explaining why you didn't make those payments."

"Why? Because there was no money, that's why."

"And your salary?"

He was perfectly aware of the futility of trying to explain. He retreated to his male prerogative. "I don't have to give account to you."

"No, you don't have to account to me, but someday you'll have to account to God for the suffering you inflict on these children and for the bad example you're setting them."

"You're trying to turn the children against me. I see that."

"I don't have to set them against you. You do that yourself."

"I don't have to take this from you."

"That's right, you don't."

Having opened the door, he looked back in desperation, and getting no reassurance from her, he slammed it as he left.

Offended, as well as overcome by a sense of guilt at having driven her husband away, she stood dumfounded. He would be back in a couple of hours after having a few beers, but this was not what she had wanted. A curse, her punishment—her mouth always faster than her reason, no control over her words, she always realized too late that she was making the moment worse. She proceeded to the bedroom. The children, trying to escape, didn't turn away from the television as she passed by them. Ramona sat on her bed for a long time, rosary in hand, before she began to pray.

"Oh great God," she pleaded, "I know that I deserve to be punished, but please, Lord, don't make it hard on my husband and the children."

Chapter 33

"VERY THOUGHTFUL TODAY," Sylvia said. She arrived at work every morning with a smile on her face and always ready to hear a joke; even the most lame ones got a chuckle out of her. She had a dash for dressing—a tight skirt and high heels, as if she were going out for the evening. "You've been sitting there without a word all morning," she continued.

"I want to buy a car," Juan said. At least, he could tell that to her if not to Ramona.

"Every man wants a car these days, when it's more trouble than it's worth. You want to take rides out to the country?"

"I just want a car," he repeated. "All my brothers have cars."

"So you've been left out. I know how that feels."

"You couldn't lend me a few bucks, could you? I'll pay you back with interest," he said.

She laughed. "I look like a bank, do I? Why don't you try Mr. Roland? He's got money up his you know what. Ask him for a raise."

He had already discarded the idea of asking for a raise. The company wasn't going to pay him more than the going rate. If only he had gotten his degree in accounting, he would be making a lot more money now, but going to school at night was too much after being at work all day. He had taken a course at Baruch, the City College business school, but getting a degree a few credits a term would take forever. He would have to work day and night for the next twelve years, no life at all. He sat at his desk looking over the ledger, two piles of receipts, on the left side, incoming payments, on the right side, outgoing ones.

He could borrow money from no one in the office. After work, he walked down to the used car lot two blocks away. He had seen a 1958 Dodge going for six hundred dollars. That was more than he wanted to spend, since he really had nothing to spend on a car. At any price, he would have to buy the card on credit, just like he bought everything else. Buying on credit made everything more expensive, but the alternative was buying nothing at all, a worthless life. He wanted the car. Owning it would make him happy, would make him forget all his troubles. If he waited, while he saved the money for the car, life would go by him. Life wasn't forever, and wasted years are irretrievable. He had to buy the car now, and enjoy having it as he paid off the debt. Of course, he had to think about Ramona. She would be angry at his acquiring another debt, but that would pass. Anyway, how much angrier could she get? He had not anticipated that side of her. It had emerged slowly over the years. Now, she willingly transformed happy moments into painful ones.

He saw nothing wrong with having a car. Anybody who was anybody had one. Still, Ramona wouldn't see it that way. She would want to know why he needed a car when the bus or the subway would take him wherever he wanted to go. She hardly ever went anywhere, always in the house or in the neighborhood, shopping, cooking, looking after the children. Of course, for that kind of routine there was no need of a car.

His three brothers had cars. He was the only Ortega without one. That wasn't quite right, the only one of them with some college education, the only one who worked in an office, and yet the only one without a car. Why couldn't Ramona see that as reason enough to get one? The subway unpleasant, away from the sunlight, away from any familiar sight, just the train and the strangers on top of you. She should be perfectly content to have a car. The whole family could go out for drives on Sundays, take the children out to the Bronx Zoo, or just go down to the Barrio to visit his family.

New York was different from back home where everyone could be trusted, where there were no strangers in town, doors never had to be locked. Here, violence in the street common enough, gangs of young people hung out at the corners. He had to worry about keeping his own boys from the heroin addicts down the block. A problem, and Ramona ready to blame him for that too. "Why have we brought our children to this God-forsaken place?" she asked. "We didn't have any of this at home." The car would help now. Keeping the family together on weekends would be easy with a car. A day at the beach simple, better than the crowded bus to Orchard Beach, the trip wasn't easy on the bus. He would make Ramona see the good of owning a car. The debt would increase, true, but only for a short while. In a few months everything would even out. He worked it all out on paper, and he could show Ramona the plan. She wouldn't be able to rebut that. She would have to accept the logic, and her anger would dissipate.

Perhaps coming to New York had been a mistake, if it had been a choice at all. He had to get away from the creditors back home, too many debts. He wasn't going to do the same thing again, and yet life would go by, and he might miss enjoying all the things that made it worthwhile. He remembered the days in the tobacco fields—from sunrise until sunset with only a piece of bread for lunch. When he got home he would eat the dry codfish and red rice with *gandules*, but the day was long, and after the midday sun had passed he could think only of getting home to that meal. He couldn't forget his days of little to eat. This time he didn't want to wait until the end of the day to get what he wanted.

He wanted the car, and he could buy it on credit. He had worked out a budget, and he believed that he could keep the debt under control. He didn't really have to convince Ramona. Of course, she would be angry, but he was getting used to her anger. Nothing he could do about it, except ignore it. She didn't understand that life had to be more than suffering from want of things everyone else had. "Save the money first," she said. "Then go buy what you need. You're giving money away on interest. If you save, it's the other way around. Why is that so hard to see?" But if time goes by without getting what you want, life becomes worthless. Just waiting was too much for him to bear. He had gone through that already as a boy. Why continue? This was America, the land of credit. Anyone who was anyone had debt, the American way. In some places only the rich borrowed money and had debt; in America everyone bought on credit.

He saw Ramona's anxiety transform into resentment. Why was she angry? He had done what he could. He was now a long way from that first New York job in the cafeteria. He had tried college again; at night after work he traveled down to Baruch. For a while, he thought that would put him back on track, on the path to achieving his aims, good job, good money. He got enough accounting to become a bookkeeper, no more washing dishes in a cafeteria, and yet he was always short of money, as if he had a hole in his pocket or his wallet served as a magician's box from where things disappeared, and he had yet to learn the incantation to make them reappear.

What made Ramona so angry? At the beginning she had been so even tempered. He remembered only her smiles, sometimes her embarrassment covered with a wide grin, when they played games, he walking by the house pretending to be a stranger interested in seducing her. Looking up at the stars, they would walk at night into the pasture to see meteors streak across a darkness fabulously speckled with dots of light revealing a universe replete with mystery and beauty. Now, much fewer stars visible, but surely they were still there. "The stars are gone," she one night said to him, as they observed the sky from the roof of the Bronx tenement, but he didn't remember whether he explained to her why they had become invisible. He must have, but the memory had been buried, perhaps under the pile of mental stones that hid so much else. He had forgotten the source of the stones just as he had forgotten what was under them. Perhaps they had the same origin as her anger, only she would not let her enmity become stones. Maybe she was angry about the haze that enveloped him, but he doubted that she saw it. For some reason he believed that a one-way obstacle obstructed his view of the world, nothing gone but only covered by a haze. He wondered whether everyone else also labored under the muted sunlight or whether only he had contracted this inexplicable illness.

He did not know what he was looking for, if looking for something, perhaps his youth. For years he put up with Ramona's bickering, her complaints about everything he did. Of course, in a way, she was right, putting up with a great deal, never enough money, coming to New York a mistake. The move didn't turn out as well as he hoped, but life would have been worse had they stayed.

Whenever he looked into Ramona's eyes he saw the smoldering blame. He had fallen into a pit and the struggle to scramble out was futile. He looked back trying to determine what he had misjudged—what had caused him to underestimate the obstacles that now confronted him, a mystery with no explanation other than blindness. He had imagined traveling to the good life, and his brothers had assured him that it wasn't a fantasy, that they were already experiencing benefits beyond expectation. They had arrived at the Promised Land, and it awaited him also. He had convinced himself that to ignore the call would be a mistake.

"Why did we come here?" Ramona once asked. "Did you just want to be with your brothers?"

"Do I hang out with my brothers?" he asked in return.

"I hope that's where you are when you're not here," she retorted.

The question revolved around more than the three-room fifth-floor walk-up and the debt at the grocery store across the street. His expectations had been different, he assured himself. He asked himself whether his brothers had lured him, whether they had given him false information, but he knew that he had ignored an obvious fact: he was different from his brothers, and the world they saw was never the same as the one he lived in.

He became aware of an obstacle, a wall that had to be penetrated, but he saw no door, which, even if locked on first encounter, would be an indication of something on the other side, an answer to the question of whether determining the outcome of one's life involved something beyond the mere appearance of choice. He wanted to better his life, and he had reached an impasse after a promising beginning. He had given up his life at Montenegro Hospital and everything that his job there implied, but looking back, the possibility of some other choice was doubtful. He couldn't honestly say that he could have consciously chosen to stay. He saw no indication that an unseen force made events inevitable, and yet he saw no other possible decision but the one he made. In examining the past, the semblance of choosing rather than following an inexorable path persisted.

On his way home, he heard a raspy voice behind him, "Ah, Mr. Ortega."

He recognized the voice, and he considered ignoring it, but turning, he saw a short thin man reminiscent of another time and place, Artie Zuckerman, the peddler—on his long face, as if designed by a cartoonist, a disproportionately large nose—body bent from carrying, always over his shoulder, the large bundle of wares to sell. Repulsion, as well as a feeling of superiority over a disfigured creature, overcame Juan.

"How are you, Mr. Ortega?" Zuckerman said trying to construct a smile to minimize the unavoidable signs of centuries, something that even he, when he looked in the mirror, wondered how or why he had inherited.

"Ah, Zuckerman," he said forcing a smile that bordered on being a smirk.

"Of course, I have plenty of things to show you," Zuckerman said, as if Juan had asked the question. "Plenty of things. Of course, there are other things to talk about, but we can get to that later."

"I know what you want to talk about, but today is Tuesday."

"Ah, yes, Tuesday," Zuckerman repeated, his face taking on the expression of being in deep thought trying to figure out the significance of that day of the week. He placed the bundle down to ease his arm. "Ah, yes, Tuesday of course not my usual day here, is it?"

"That's right," Juan said feeling that he had scored a point, and he had to emphasize the fact, to make sure that his advantage was understood.

Zuckerman picked up his bag and swung it over his shoulder to continue walking down the street. "Yes, of course, you understand I'm not yet trying to collect for this week," Zuckerman said. "This week's payment is due on Thursday, of course. Would I say otherwise? No, of course not. You're right, you're right about that. I would only collect this week's payment on Thursday."

With that admission Juan presumed that his point had been made, and he decided to cross the street to get rid of Zuckerman, but Zuckerman followed.

"Really, I don't want to buy anything today," Juan said.

"I understand, I understand," Zuckerman said. "Not every day is a buying day. I wish it was, you understand, but I know how it is. Still business is business."

"I thought we agreed about the day."

"Ah, we did of course we did, for this week's payment, of course we agreed."

"Then what?"

"Well, of course, I'm willing to accept last week's or the previous, and we can work out a deal on the late fee."

"Late fee? What late fee?"

"On credit there's always a late fee. With me, I would let it go. I understand it's a burden. I would let it go, but I'm instructed to do it."

"What do you mean, you're instructed?"

"I'm instructed," Zuckerman repeated.

"You mean you work for somebody else?" he asked, his voice becoming louder without his being aware of it.

"That, I didn't say," Zuckerman continued, realizing that the main issue was being obscured. "Pay me whatever you can. You have a little, give a little. I work for a living. I too have to eat."

"I can't give you what I don't have," Juan said.

"You look like you have. What can I say?" Zuckerman waved his hand up and down pointing out to an imaginary crowd the excellence of Juan's attire.

Juan became more incensed at what he took to be an insult, the falsity of appearance obviously being pointed out. The peddler was nobody, and Juan stepped right up to the bent figure.

"Let me go," Zuckerman begged. Juan had grabbed him by the collar trying to pull him up to his own height. Panic distorted Zuckerman's face, and Juan, disgusted, suddenly realized what he was doing. His hands on the man created a union more significant that he wanted to admit. Juan relaxed his hold, and Zuckerman bolted down the street.

Chapter 34

JUAN WAS ONLY going to visit his sister, Maria, that afternoon. He wasn't expecting to meet anyone else.

"This is my friend, Inez," Maria said.

Ah, yes, he remembered Inez doing the mambo with Alberto Montoyo at the Christopher Columbus Society dance so many years ago. Now, Inez just smiled without saying anything, like a teenage girl embarrassed at being introduced. His marriage not going well at the moment, something he had not foreseen, but those things are unpredictable. That's the way life is: many things happen just by chance. What other explanation was there? Was Inez a Siren, and he not tied to the mast? Well, it had to be something like that, because he had no other explanation for what happened. He tried to remember what attracted him, for sure not her looks. She wasn't beautiful like Ramona when he had first met her and followed her to the Christopher Columbus Social Club. There would never be for him another woman who looked like that, still beautiful when he saw through her anger.

"Come visit me," Inez said to him that day.

"Sure," he said, just trying to be polite. He swore he did not intend to see her again.

"Well, here," she said, tearing a piece from a brown paper bag lying on the kitchen table and writing her address and phone number on it.

He put it in his pocket intending to throw it away as soon as he was out in the street. Except that he didn't throw it away. He kept it all week. If Ramona had still been going through his pockets, she would have found the piece of paper, like she did so many years ago when the nurse at Montenegro Hospital had written him a love letter. Only, back then, that letter had been just that nurse's futile attempt, because then he had no interest in anyone but Ramona. And still, he swore, he loved no one else but Ramona. Anyway, he didn't throw away the piece of paper but kept it in his pocket until a week later when he pulled it out and called Inez.

"Sure, come on over," she said.

He intended merely to chat and drink a cup of coffee. He realized later, when he recalled, how silly that sounded. Dealing with a woman was never simple, and to attach himself to another woman was the last thing he wanted. Of course, men are often unfaithful, and the women are the ones who end up on the short end of the deal. His father, Federico, an example of just such a man, had abandoned his ailing wife, Pepina, for Julia, to whom he was just as unfaithful. Well, not quite the same; he always returned to Julia, a big difference, though Julia suffered anyway. Juan swore that he would never do to Ramona what his father had done to Julia.

He visited Inez just to pass the time. He told Ramona that he was going window-shopping up on Southern Boulevard. Maybe he would stop by Maria's place on Faile Street, just beyond the boulevard. "All right," she said. She had no inkling of where he was really going, and neither did he, he would swear. But when he got to Horseshoe Park, instead of turning east on 165th Street, he ascended the park steps toward Prospect Avenue. Inez lived on Tinton, just a short walk. He'd have a cup of coffee and talk to her for a little while, and that would be all. He'd be home before dinner time without Ramona having any idea of where he had been. Why should she? She would be very relaxed without him around. Just his presence made her think of the money problems. The linoleum in the living room all worn, not having enough money to replace it tortured her every time she looked at it.

He had promised to take care of it soon, but more pressing matters came up. The children would need new clothes for school in September. Ramona didn't want them to suffer the way she had as a child with no shoes to wear to school.

"I'll bet you can use a drink right now," Inez said once he was sitting on the couch in her living room.

"Yes," he said, "I'd love a cup of coffee."

She laughed as if he had told a joke, and he smiled back trying to cover up his confusion.

"I have a bottle of Palo Viejo in the kitchen," she said.

Then he understood why she laughed, but he didn't really think anything was funny. "Just a cup of coffee will do for me," he said.

"All right," she said. "But you can spike up the coffee if you want."

She brought him a cup of coffee, and she poured herself a glass of rum. Pretty soon she was telling him how her husband had abandoned her when the children were still young. Her daughter, the oldest one, pregnant had recently moved in with a guy. The son was sent away upstate to a youth camp for addicts. "Maybe it'll do him some good," she said. Then her tears came.

"Oh, why am I crying?" she said. "Let's forget our problems and have a good time."

She sat next to him on the couch and leaned her head on his shoulder. He put his arm around her just to comfort her.

Expiation

Chapter 35

H E DIDN'T REALLY want to deal with Inez, but each day Ramona grew more distant. Inez offered him some solace. Except that pretty soon she was saying that she loved him. At first, he didn't mind hearing that, but soon she was asking him whether he loved her.

"I'm here, aren't I?" he said.

"All right," she said. "Let's drink to that."

"Sure," he said as he watched her pour another drink.

At first, he didn't make anything of her always having a liquor bottle around. That was normal, he thought, but soon he began to notice the number of empty bottles in the kitchen. "You have a party last night?" he asked her one day.

"No," she said, "you're my only guest these days."

"Then you ought to stop drinking so much."

"I get bored when you're not here," she said.

"Drinking's not the answer."

"I suppose I won't be as bored when the baby comes."

"What baby?" The words came out of his mouth automatically, as if she had said something bizarre, and he had no idea what she was talking about.

"Women do get pregnant," she said, "or is that news to you?"

He did use a condom most of the time. Of course, sometimes putting it on got to be a hassle, and caution was overwhelmed by necessity. Inez didn't want to have an abortion, a sin to be avoided, as if everything else she was doing was all right. A child on the way, an unexpected snag, that was life, always an unanticipated complication. Disaster was inevitable. The arrival of that moment always surprised him, as if each time were the first. He asked himself why, as he walked down the street, and he concluded that there was no answer. Destiny unfolded without the assurance of controlling the outcome. What other conclusion could he reach when clearly he had not intended another child to arrive?

He had a problem, but of course he wasn't the first to be in this predicament. His brothers were all experts in dealing with this matter. He could ask them for advice, but why bother? He knew what they would say. "Don't worry. Have a drink. It's a woman's problem." But what about Ramona? He had never meant to hurt Ramona. She would find out sooner or later, then what? This getting involved with another woman had nothing to do with Ramona. Well maybe he resented her not understanding why the debts piled up. He was just trying to provide a good life for her too. She didn't see it that way. She blamed him for being reckless. If she only knew how hard he worked at making life bearable for her and the children.

He reached Maria's block without having decided to go there. He went up the steps of the building and found his sister home.

"You don't look well," Maria said.

"No," he said, "I don't. What can I do now? Inez is pregnant."

"And that was your doing?"

He looked at her askance, wondering whether she was making fun of him.

"Is that all you're worried about?" she continued. "That's the normal course of events. You have to think about it beforehand not afterwards."

"Ramona won't take it so calmly."

"Then stop fooling around and go home to her."

"What can I say?"

"Just come clean and tell her what you've done and apologize. That's all. She'll forgive you. If she's put up with you this long, she'll put up with you forever."

"I can't tell her. It'll be too much for her to bear."

"I think it'll be too much for you."

"And what about this child? I'll have another mouth to feed."

"There'll always be enough for one more."

"I don't think Ramona will see it that way after all that's happened."

As he walked out of his sister's place, he intended to go home and confess his transgression, but by the time he reached Rogers Place his resolve had ebbed. He figured he didn't need to add another complication to his life with Ramona. Dealing with one problem at a time seemed at the moment a more reasonable approach. The problem had swallowed him. He had never thought of Inez as a permanent addition to his life, not an addition at all, only a temporary distraction, that's all, but a child was something else.

He had resolved not to follow in his father's footsteps. He had watched his mother suffer and had determined that he would never do that to anyone, especially not to Ramona. He had convinced her to marry him even after she had pointed out all the reasons why their union would be unworkable. He persisted where others gave up, but now, failing to keep his resolve, he had botched the arrangement. He had taken a wrong step, something he had convinced himself he would never do. He was human and made mistakes, but this was the one mistake he had promised himself to avoid. He had not intended to hurt Ramona, but he saw no way of avoiding that except by keeping quiet. But that too was a transgression. There had to be a solution to the problem, but it refused to reveal itself.

He waited but only the child arrived, another innocent who had to bear the consequences of his actions. The added responsibility failed to keep Inez from drinking. Again Juan wondered why he had imagined that one problem would solve another, why the burden of looking after the newborn would keep Inez from the bottle. The stress of responding to the child's needs at all hours had the opposite effect. The possibility of the child being neglected became for Juan another fear. The first time in his life he had to worry about that. With Ramona that had never been a concern, just the opposite, taking care of the children the mainstay of her life. He suddenly had an understanding of what that meant. How much more he should have appreciated her dedication to the children.

From the hallway, as he approached Inez's place, he heard the baby crying. When he entered, he saw Inez sitting in the kitchen, as usual a bottle on the table, a glass in her hand.

"The child is crying, for heaven's sakes, why are you just sitting there?" he said.

"They do that," Inez said.

"Go see if she's all right," he snapped, but Inez remained still.

He proceeded to the bedroom to look in the crib. The infant needed to be changed, so he lowered the railing and started to do it himself. Right away, even before he removed the diaper, he saw a severe rash on both legs. He became more disturbed as he realized that the rash extended up her back. She must have been in need of a diaper change for a while. He rushed back to the kitchen ready to strangle Inez, but when he got there, suddenly, almost in a panic, the realization of his own stupidity overwhelmed him. Why did he ever get involved with this woman? There she sat, in a stupor, completely oblivious of the rest of the world. What was he to do about the child? He couldn't leave her there. The child would die of neglect. He had to take her with him, but where?

Chapter 36

THROUGH THE WINDOW, Ramona looked at an old mattress rotting in the empty lot that had become a dump yard. Across the street stood the grocery store and next to it, between the store and the grocer's house, a driveway leading to a row of garages in the back, rented to whomever wanted to keep his automobile from the vandals who roamed the streets. Always in debt to Don Justino, looking at his property unpleasant, she gazed over the houses to Horseshoe Park beyond which taller buildings lined the curved street. For some reason the image of Julia came up to keep her company. Ramona recalled the last time she saw her mother-in-law.

"It's nice to be here," Julia said. "It's been years since I've seen most of my sons. Only Manuel, Pepina's boy, remains back home. The one who's not my son drops by to see me every day. Who would have thought my own would abandon me?"

"They always think of you," Ramona assured her, "but men are men, and getting them to sit down and write a letter is another matter."

"Well, here I am, whether they like it not."

"You know they love you. They sent for you, didn't they?"

"I suppose they had to. I'm sure Federico urged them."

"Now you're here. Enjoy yourself."

"I have to see Grego. Of all my sons, he's the most pleasant. I know you're partial to Juan, and I love them all, but Grego is the only one who'll tell me a story to make me laugh. And where is he? I thought he too lived in New York."

"Well, he did all these years. But of course you heard about his troubles with Rosario, so he's left the city altogether, with another woman of course. What can I say?"

Julia saw in Ramona's eyes the question with no answer. She had asked herself that question in the old days, whenever Federico failed to come home, and she had wondered whether her turn had arrived to follow Pepina into oblivion. Ramona was the only one of her daughters-in-law that had yet to experience that waiting in vain for the husband to get home in the evening, and Julia could not assure her that the time would never come.

"Sons followed their father's footsteps," Julia said.

"Juan's different from the others," Ramona retorted.

"Perhaps," Julia responded. She could say nothing else as she tried, for the moment, to reassure Ramona. Better to prepare for the inevitable. "In any case, fidelity is not the staying away from others."

"What is it then?" Ramona asked.

"They search for it everywhere," Julia said. "Become the one that is irreplaceable, and he'll always come back."

"And the waiting, how does one bear that?"

"The world is imperfect."

"Is that all you can tell me?"

"There's nothing else," Julia said. "But right now Grego has to come down to see me. How far off has he gone?"

"Juan will drive you up to Grego's place in Connecticut."

Sitting in the front seat of the car, Julia had gazed at the landscape. In this part of the world different from what she was used to, she took it in like a child for the first time on a long trip, the road endless, hills in the distance overwhelmed by green forests. The scenery brought back memories of her own days in the mountains of Naranjito, the trail leading down to town and the people looking at her askance as she walked across the square. The Ortega woman, they *whispered as she went by, when indeed she was Federico Atorey's woman, no longer merely his mistress, but still not his wife as long as Pepina lived. She remembered turning her head to gaze up the hillside where Pepina in vain waited, hoping, praying that Federico would return. But he would never go back to that woman who had first claim on him. Despite his continuous infidelity, he always returned to Julia and to no one else.*

Some unknown force had driven her to him, kept her attached to him, but obviously, she saw clearly that the tether was knotted at both ends. How else could she explain his constant return? Time on her side, the years passed, and everyone forgot about Pepina, everyone but Julia who rued the fact that Pepina had a child named Atorey while all of hers were Ortegas. Eventually, she came to terms with that. Her need to satisfy her first man, the easing of his departure, providing him with a son to carry on his name, succeeded beyond expectation. All of her five sons carried the name Ortega, a fact she long rued, until one day as she looked in the mirror, she experienced a revelation. What at first had seemed a punishment became rather the blossoming of her scheme, the idea like a seed planted on a fertile hillside, the ordeal transforming into proof of her indomitable nature. How could she have expected anything she planted to have only one offshoot?

Yes, more than one, she had had five sons and two daughters. The first son killed during the war. She had been sure that he would be safe from enemy bullets no matter where he might be sent. She never imagined that anything would happen before shipping out. No, not Emiliano, her worries had been about Juan, but there was no way of foretelling such things, no rhyme or reason to life's ups and downs. She had worried about Juan but not about Emiliano, whom she believed to be magically protected. She no longer remembered how she had arrived at that conclusion, only that she had taken it for granted. She had intended Emiliano to be the one and only Ortega. Perhaps her expectations truly transformed him into an Ortega, and in that guise he had followed the Ortega path to an early end.

We pay for our sins. But why pay for something that's beyond our control? She could not see how she could have done anything else. True, that she believed, as she carried out her plan to satisfy Arturo, that she was in control, had made the decision to act, had planned the ruse to cheer Arturo as he made his exit from this world. While she schemed, she had no doubt of a choice and of responsibility for the outcome. But once beyond the first step, ensnared by a power beyond her control, one she had failed to foresee, the predicament overwhelmed her. She wondered what had blinded her, what had made her oblivious of the common danger faced by men and women now and in the past and surely forever in the future. Caught like a beast in a trap, she was still uncertain whether the bait had been worth the ordeal.

Of course, she could not imagine a life without Federico, not even after bodily pleasures had diminished. But her love for him was not about that, not about the flesh, as was commonly believed. Certainly people would say that the physical ecstasy experienced behind the waterfall carried her away, but that wasn't true. Federico was more than that to her, though she could not explain what else, other than the object of her love. She had not intended her feelings to develop into that. She had merely wanted that first son before Arturo's final hour. Yes, she had good intentions, and wasn't that all that mattered? Telling herself that for many years, she usually believed it, yet doubt inevitably crept in.

Suffering overcame her on nights that Federico failed to come home. Then she thought about Pepina, still alone and waiting for the father of her one child. To that house *he would never return, and at those moments fear gripped Julia, for what power did she possess that would ensure his return to her? Sometimes she asked herself whether she caused Pepina's pain. Wasn't she, like Pepina, just a woman who had no chance at all? Only his return at first relieved those moments of anguish. The question of what she had expected had no reasonable answer. When she had met him at Doña Urbana's, that first time after Arturo's death, deep inside she sensed fidelity absent from the deal. Darkness that swallowed all details enveloped her in his arms, transported her into another world, or she was merely absorbed by the one that surrounded her, the boundaries gone that usually separated her from everything else. What else could she say? Nothing, of course, to whom could she express such an absurdity? Did he not experience the same thing with her? Why else would he have left Pepina?*

Love was the dissolving of the self as it merged with another. Whether he could dissolve himself with any woman or only with her became the question. Certainly he was the only man with whom she would again allow that to happen, so she was bound to him forever despite his infidelity. Surely, though he kept trying, he was unable to do that with any other woman. He always returned.

She looked through the windshield of Juan's automobile at the green foliage that suddenly rushed at her. This too was an unexplainable puzzle, her son sitting next to her, an expression of horror on his face. She could only think of asking him for the last time, "Son, what have you done?"

"Life goes on," Ramona said to her husband. "You went through this before," she continued, trying to point the way for him by alluding to Emiliano.

Juan merely looked toward the window, his face expressionless. She assumed that he was merely pretending, putting on a façade behind which the turmoil took its course. She had gotten used the calm demeanor that automatically set in whenever he was threatened, something he had picked up from watching his mother deal with the man she loved, someone who now had to deal with her departure. Juan looked at Ramona as if questioning what she was saying, as if the death did not concern him.

"I know how you feel," Ramona said, but she wondered, for a moment, whether she really knew. He was showing nothing, and she wondered how that was possible, how he managed to keep everything hidden, something beyond her, her emotions always close to the surface, always ready to burst out whether she wanted them to or not. He was different of course; she had discovered that over the years. He often kept his feelings hidden until he could logically express them, but she failed to see the usefulness of that.

"Do you?" he rhetorically asked.

And now her turn to be silent as she wondered what he meant. Did he not remember that her mother had died? As a child, not yet having built a protective rampart, she had been overwhelmed.

"We all have to go through this," she said.

"I suppose so," he answered. "But it was my fault."

"Only Fate is to blame," Ramona said.

"Sometimes."

"There's doubt in your voice," she said.

"I'm only human."

"Indeed," she said, hoping that he understood. But how could she doubt him? Always she had thought of him as someone who could think, who read books replete with knowledge unavailable to her. She was less than familiar with all the ideas that illuminated the world. She sometimes wished that she too could study and observe the way he did. But at other times his failure to grasp the obvious puzzled

her. He failed to deal with emotions, to express them and put them in a proper and visible place so that life might proceed even when the price was high and the adjustment less than simple.

"She had a life," he said.

"A full life," Ramona concurred.

"It could have been better I suppose," he said, "if she didn't have to put up with my father."

"It was her destiny," Ramona said.

"What else could she have done?"

"We all do what we have to," she said gazing at her husband.

He wondered whether she saw through the surface he presented, the one behind which his true self wriggled trying to emerge and cease the deception, no longer remembering why he had to hide, but at the moment the fear still impossible to overcome.

"She put up with a great deal," Ramona continued, invaded by thoughts beyond what she wanted to express but unable to repress them.

"She did," he said. "She was upset when Father sold the land, and they moved into town. The land meant a great deal to her. He said it wasn't profitable. She didn't believe him, but what could she do? That's all in the past. What's the sense of talking about it now?"

"True," Ramona said. "Still, she cried over the land and other things too. And now he has to face life without her. We'll see what he does with that."

"I suppose it won't be easy," Juan said. "Whatever he did, he always went back to her. That was something."

"Yes, something," Ramona said.

Intent on the cityscape, she did not hear Juan enter the apartment. Only when he reached the kitchen, where she sat by the window, did she turn to see him standing there, his face transformed by fear of what she would say.

"I had to bring her," he said. "She'll die if I leave her with her mother."

Motionless in the chair, Ramona wondered what Juan's words meant, whether in his arms he held something he had salvaged from the empty lot that through the window she had just been contemplating. How uncharacteristic of him to retrieve a discarded object—contrary to his habit of acquiring new things whether or not they were necessities, usually something useless but glittery, something he would use once and then put away never to retrieve again. He held the object close to him like something valuable that might be wrested from him. He should have known better than to expect such action from her.

"Please say something," he continued.

She wondered why he thought her purposely silent when she was merely trying to decipher his look of fear. She had for some time been tolerating his excessive acquisition of the useless. She had given up trying to make him see the foolishness of acquiring things that only briefly caught his imagination. Nothing in the world was perfect, but sometimes a problem was impossible to see until it was too late. She had no way to prevent his spending more money than he earned on all kinds of unnecessary things. Indeed, he preferred acquiring the useless, imagining himself to be like the wealthy who had more the more they spent. Forced to find a way to guard against his excess, whenever she had a few extra cents she put the money away to use when his spending resulted in a crisis. But now she saw him holding something someone else had obviously discarded. "What have you got there?" she asked.

"I couldn't leave her behind."

That was reasonable enough, more than reasonable.

Ramona wondered why the word "reasonable" now reverberated within her.

"Say something," Juan begged.

"What have you there?" she again asked, still sitting in her chair, a puzzled look still dominating her face, as if every word from Juan's mouth only added confusion to the moment.

"It's a girl," he said as if the sex of the child was the crucial fact to be conveyed at the moment.

A strange sensation suddenly exploded within Ramona; the feeling rose through her body and got caught in her throat. The possibility of death by suffocation flitted before her, and she tried to breathe deeply to prevent it.

"I have to put her down," Juan said walking into the bedroom where he placed the bundle on the bed.

Ramona followed in a stupor, which began to subside as she stared into the dark eyes of the infant now lying on the bed. "Whose child is that?" she asked turning to face Juan.

"What does it matter?"

"I'll find out when she comes for the child."

"She won't," Juan said.

"No mother will give up a child," Ramona said overwhelmed by her own view of the world.

"You never see the world the way it really is," Juan said as if he were begging her for once to make an exception. "If you take the child, I'll never be away again."

"Away?"

"I've learned my lesson," he continued, "and I have this child to always remind me."

"Who's her mother?"

As if the answer to a riddle were coded on the fading linoleum pattern, Juan examined it with a fixed gaze hoping that success in this endeavor would provide a solution to all his problems. Silently, he again looked at Ramona begging to be excused from revealing anything else. As far as he was concerned, all the necessary pieces were in place, and the identity of the child's mother was irrelevant.

"You must tell me who her mother is," Ramona insisted.

No longer having control of the muscles of his mouth, Juan mumbled a name that even his own ears were unable to decipher. Ramona stared at him in disgust, causing him to make another attempt to utter the name. Hearing the name distorted Ramona's face.

"You see, it was better not to know," Juan managed to say, the words struggling to emerge from his dry throat.

Uncertain that her knees would much longer sustain her, Ramona sat on the bed. "How could you?" she mumbled.

"I don't know," he answered, and immediately regretted the implication that only Inez was responsible for what happened.

"I must see her," Ramona said.

"What good will that do?"

The word "good" reverberated through her searching for a place to lodge where it might have a chance to survive. At the moment, there wasn't any good in the world before her, not by looking through the window at the slowly decaying neighborhood, nor in her own kitchen confronting the man in whom she had placed her trust. There had to be something somewhere to restore her faith, to provide if only a hint of some universal scheme of reason. There was no way to arrive at that point by thinking; if that was the route, she was lost forever. If she accepted the absence of an ordered world, she faced an abyss into which she would have to leap with no hope of survival. Nothing she saw provided reason for her predicament, but perhaps she was Balaam and not his donkey. She had to let go and follow her impulses, though she did not know their origin. A puzzle without solution: the message from heaven or from hell, no way to distinguish the messenger, for had not Satan once been an angel?

"You must take me to her."

"I don't want to see her anymore."

"Just tell me where she lives."

"Why?"

"I don't know, but I must see her."

On the verge of feeling sorry for herself, Ramona tried to find the path intended for her. She had to give up the notion that she had power over the forces that controlled the world, that she could make the rest of humanity behave in accordance with her desires. She could think of no rational explanation of why she had to see a woman who was trying to destroy her life, yes her life, for she could think of no other way of describing what she felt. Still, she had to see Inez to understand what had happened, what power had lured Juan.

Chapter 37

SHE WALKED DOWN Rogers Place to Horseshoe Park and
up the park steps to 165th Street. She crossed Prospect
Avenue, her pace increasing as she got to Tinton, where Inez
lived, a street that looked like any other in the neighborhood
but would never again be the same for Ramona. She saw
the boys playing stickball just as they did on Rogers Place.
Surely, if she walked farther down the block she would find
a grocery store that sold on credit just like Don Justino's.
Yes, it was a common street, except that Inez lived there.

On the stoop, Ramona paused to ask herself what she
was doing, but she had no answer. Still, having lost control
of her feet, she did not retreat; they insisted on taking her to
Inez's door. She continued up the stairs to the third floor until
she arrived at the door behind which there had to be answers
to her questions. Perhaps Inez had answers, or perhaps she
was just as confused as everyone else; why else would she
have let Juan walk out with the child? No mother easily lets
a child go. Even if she were to lose Juan, Ramona still had
the children, including the one she had asked God to provide
in case she was ever in dire need, the one assurance that kept
her from despair, a consolation to which she tightly held.

"Inez?"

Gazing at the visitor, the person who had opened the
door stood motionless, as if trying to determine the identity
of Inez and where she might be found. After a long pause,
"Ramona," she said in a raspy voice.

The grating sound made Ramona suddenly realize that
she had failed to interpret the image before her, the dilemma

of the physical world—an unstable environment where nothing familiar was safe from unpredictable change.

"I'm glad you came," Inez said, the words incongruous to the signs on her face that revealed indifference to Ramona's presence.

"I had to see you," Ramona said.

In the kitchen, Inez automatically sat down at the table. Reaching for the half-empty glass next to the bottle of Palo Viejo, she hesitated. Her facial expression trying to convey something, she looked up at Ramona, but the message failed to emerge.

"Why?" Ramona asked. "Why?"

There had to be an explanation for all of this, perhaps a due payment for her sin. She could think of no other reason for such pain to descend on her after she had done all she could to prevent it. Where had all the promise of her youth gone? She had tried as hard as she could to prevent a mistake. She recalled that for a long time she had resisted Juan, but he had persisted. She had waited until she was sure that he was the man intended for her, until she saw the sign; surely, it had to have come from above, for where else would a sign have come? But what did that matter? Wherever it came from, she had to be attentive; she had to follow. What else could she do? The path always marked, she just had to recognize the signs and follow them to the intended destination.

Expiation required suffering. Her pain had to have a reason. She found that comforting, a positive way of looking at the circumstances. She would pay now for her transgression rather than wait till later when the punishment might be unbearable. She had assumed right away, right after she had the operation, that she would have to pay, but she had never imagined what her penance would be, never saw Juan's actions as the instrument of retribution. She contemplated the idea that he was being used to punish her, and perhaps he was suffering too, being punished also for his share of the sin.

No, there was no share of guilt. Everyone is responsible for his own action, and she had acted on her own. She had not been taken by force to the hospital, nor dragged against her will into the operating room. She had decided to do it, and she was responsible. And how was she to know for sure that she was being punished? Had not her mother, Juana, suffered the year of her death, and for what? Ramona could think of no sin her mother had committed. So why was Juana punished when it was her husband who had transgressed against her. There was no connection between misfortune and guilt.

Nothing made sense to Ramona at the moment. Memories of the past invaded her. She recalled that soon after he had returned from the army, Juan had gotten the job at the hospital. Ramona had never before known anyone who did that kind of work. Juan was not an ordinary person. He had been rising in the world. As a boy, along with his brothers, he had worked in the fields under the hot sun. In Ramona's family too, they had all worked on the land, machete in hand, cutting the sugar cane and driving the ox carts down to the mill. She had been working in the cigar factory when she had first met Juan, before he followed his brother, Emiliano, into the army.

Juan had loved her then. She was sure of that. He had pursued her for five years after he had run out of the Christopher Columbus Club embarrassed at having no step on the dance floor. She had run after him that night to comfort him and lead him back to the dance, because she had promised to look after him, something she would have done regardless of whether Maria had asked. Assisting anyone who needed help came naturally to her.

Before their marriage she had failed to notice that Juan

always spent more than he earned, and perhaps there had been no way to know. You have to live with a man to know him. And even had she noticed before the ceremony, the observation would have failed to make an impression strong enough to keep them apart. She would have assumed that he would change when necessary, that he would be practical, a reasonable enough expectation, and she had never met anyone more reasonable than Juan. She had been certain that she could always depend on him to do the right thing, never doubted his good intentions. Mistakes always possible, even necessary, but they happened once and the next time corrected. Yes, she believed that. She had to believe it, although all around she saw senseless repetitions. She relegated the unexplainable to obscurity, but now and again it insisted on reemerging. Sometimes she remembered her mother's agony on discovering Pedro's betrayal. The event had no reasonable explanation; there was no way to restrain evil. At the moment, overwhelmed by a desire to transpose her anger, Ramona saw a needy person in a filthy apartment, the sink full of dirty dishes, under the window, the garbage can overflowing and emitting a foul smell.

Inez blankly stared at Ramona.

"Do you know why I'm here?" Ramona asked.

Inez turned her head slightly to better view her inquisitor. Her lips fluttered trying to produce a smile, but something prevented its appearance. Her muscles having forgotten what to do, only a puzzled look remained.

"You're not even here," Ramona said.

"I wish that was true," Inez muttered.

Ramona pondered the meaning of those words, whether Inez wanted to sober up or whether she wished to leave this life altogether. Perhaps Inez wanted to escape this world, a useless endeavor. Whatever problems she had she would take with her to the next; Ramona was sure of that. The soul could be healed if one tried. What counted was the attempt, and the effort had to be made right here in this world. There was no way to escape. She had come to see Inez for some reason that now evaded her; perhaps to beg her to let Juan go, she had not trusted his words of contrition. Now she saw Inez powerless. How could she have lured Juan to do anything? There had to be some other explanation. Her resentment towards Inez transformed into pity. Until then, she had felt victimized by the heinous scheming of some evil person, but all she saw at the moment was another victim damaged beyond repair. Inez was the one in dire need. Advice useless right then, Ramona could do nothing for Inez. One had to be ready to hear it, and Inez seemed far from that point. Still, Ramona had to do something, even if the action proved futile and the result the same as if she had never found Inez.

"Inez, you have to wake up."

"Did you come to get the baby?"

The question startled Ramona, as she realized that Inez had again retreated into another world.

"I had a baby," Inez continued. "The last thing in the world I wanted."

"You have to pull yourself together for the child's sake."

"Are you from the Welfare Department?" Inez asked, and receiving no answer, she proceeded to arrive at her own conclusion. "I suppose not. They always dress up to make their visits." Inez paused for a moment trying to recall the subject of the conversation. "I didn't want another child," she said, "to have to put up with me."

"Do you know where the baby is?" Ramona asked.

"She's asleep," Inez said, "in the bedroom. I have to be a good mother; that's what I have to do."

Ramona got up from the chair and walked through the messy living room to the bedroom, just as disorderly, the bed unmade and the yellow curtain on the window having slipped from its hanger. In contrast to everything else the empty crib against the wall was new. She then walked back to the kitchen where Inez acted as if she were unaware of the bottle and the glass that now contained less rum. Inez having become a victim, Ramona tried to think of some way to help her, but nothing practical came to mind.

"Wait," Inez said, trying to reemerge from her stupor. "I will give you the baby. She will be better off with you than with me. Maybe that's why you came here today."

Strength drained out of Ramona's knees. She reached for the back of the chair to keep from falling, and slowly allowed herself to sit. She recognized what she had been waiting for and had almost given up hope of receiving— the great opportunity, at first disguised as a calamity. She would be saving the child from what would surely be a life of misery. The truth was an intense revelation—clearly a scheme in what previously had seemed a chaotic world. She might have easily missed it, may have been blind to what was intended. Inez showed a side that Ramona had not anticipated. Some would think the offer another expression of a weakness, Inez's avoidance of responsibility for her own transgression, but Ramona saw Inez's recognition that the child's salvation required that she give her up.

"Along with the baby," Inez said staring at the floor, "take Juan back. It wasn't me he wanted."

"I know," Ramona said. After a pause, she continued, "I'll raise the child, but she'll know you're her mother."

Inez's face again went blank, and Ramona, seeing that there was nothing else she could do, left the apartment, walked down the stairs and out to the street, where the bright light of the midday sun reminded her of home, of the mountains and the undulating hills, of the river that flowed under the wooden bridge that was sometimes washed away by the torrential rain.

She remembered the sound of the church bells that swung from the spire that overlooked the town square where in the evenings she had sat with Juan to watch children play tag and sometimes dance to imaginary music. Perhaps they heard the tune the way she heard it now and felt it flow down to their toes as it now seemed to invade her own. She remembered walking along the mountain trail searching for sweet *quenepas* or standing under the mango tree waiting for one of her brothers to toss down the fruit, her brothers who had gone to church only occasionally to hear her sing in the choir where she was honored as one of the chosen. All those memories, overshadowed and buried for a while, resurrected at the moment as she recognized the beginning of a new life.

www.ingramcontent.com/pod-product-compliance
Lightning Source LLC
Chambersburg PA
CBHW020205270626
47157CB00028B/1162